Femme Noir

Visit us at www.boldstrokesbooks.com

Femme Noir

by

Clara Nipper

2009

FEMME NOIR

ISBN 10: 1-60282-117-8
ISBN 13: 978-1-60282-117-0

This Trade Paperback Original Is Published By
Bold Strokes Books, Inc.
P.O. Box 249
Valley Falls, NY 12185

First Bold Strokes Printing: September 2009

Credits
Editors: Cindy Cresap and Stacia Seaman
Production Design: Stacia Seaman
Cover Design By Sheri (graphicartist2020@hotmail.com)

Acknowledgments

For Kristopher Kris, it's all for you and all because of you.

For Radclyffe, Publisher Extraordinaire—signing a contract with BSB was one of the best and most rewarding decisions I ever made. You have restored my faith.

And Cindy, Editor Deluxe—you got mad skills. I am lucky to work with someone so talented, precise, and logical. All of life should be so painless and easy.

For my new family at BSB: all of you are as wonderful as a sack of diamonds and as much fun as a basket of kittens. I am forever grateful and looking forward to being an asset to BSB for many years to come.

Dedication

For Kristopher Kris

Together we are the spark and the path forever

Prologue

I was thirty-five the year I started drinking gin. It's not a pretty story and I don't come off smelling like a rose, but it's time to tell it. With a story like this, gin is the only thing astringent enough to clean the dirt from my mouth. Gin is snappy and crisp and washes away my sins, at least for the night. I love everything about gin, but maybe that's because my love affair with it is new. The smell of it is a cold wintry tang in the nose; the look of it is hard and clear like liquid diamonds, and that's deceptive because the taste of it is smooth and sweet yet sharp too, like a beautiful woman with a knife. Gin slides down my throat like an ice snake. It's bitter and oily, wavering in the glass like a silver mirror, and when it is a mirror is when I drink most. I'll take it any way—neat, a shot, on the rocks, in a martini, in a Tom Collins or a fizz, with stupid fruit draped all over the glass, I don't care. But my favorite way to drink it is with tonic because it reminds me of Her. I got the idea that gin is a disinfectant like hydrogen peroxide and if I drink enough, it will boil out the infection, which is this story I must tell.

I found I'm a woman of excesses. I love cigarettes, I love gin, I love women, and I love winning, all to a fault. I was born for trouble without knowing it, and that is the worst kind. Suddenly, I've found that sometimes, a woman must drink alone.

So I was thirty-five the year I started drinking gin. It all started one day with a call from my ex.

Chapter One

The ringing was insistent, urgent. I let myself into my apartment as quickly as I could because nobody calls at four a.m. with good news. I flicked on a light and ran for the phone, a heavy, corded black dial phone that I loved for its old-fashioned rebelliousness.

"Yeah?" My voice was hoarse from lack of sleep. Karen's appetite was insatiable. I shrugged off the sweaty T-shirt and damp cotton shorts I wore to and from Karen's house. I never needed regular clothes there and felt it was too much bother to dress up just to go to her and come home. Underneath, I was nude.

"Nora?" The voice was crackly and scared and chillingly familiar. Michelle. My last and worst ex.

"What the hell do you want?" I demanded. After all, Michelle was with someone else and living in Tulsa, Oklahoma, and I was in Los Angeles, completely free and not obligated to lift a finger to save Michelle from her persistent destructive foolishness.

"I, I'm sorry to call so late…to call at all—" Static blocked her voice.

"Yeah, you have some nerve." I wanted a cigarette badly. I needed to suck one to ash in two seconds flat. I made it out of Karen's clutches without one, and now, I *had* to have that dry, hot taste to return me to myself. Sex took it out of me in a way that only cigarettes could restore. Plus, I needed to be soothed for this conversation. I spied a pack across the room. "Hold on!" I barked as I put the phone down and dove for the pack. I crumpled it and moaned. Empty. I smelled my hands with Karen's ripeness coating them. I licked my lips. I picked up my wadded shorts, now a wilted pile of color, and checked the pockets. Nothing. I needed a shot. A shot of something. Maybe tequila. I also needed a shower and some sleep. I needed a wife to come in and clean up this place and maybe do some laundry and ironing. I padded back to the phone wearily.

"—need you!" Michelle pleaded when I returned.

"I can't help you no matter what you need," I told her acidly. I found some wooden matches, my preferred method of lighting cigarettes, and flicked one after another with my thumbnail. I felt the tiny fire was comforting, as if I were about to have a cigarette. Like the promise of foreplay. The flaming match told me that there would be eventual satisfaction. Was it possible to get a sudden ulcer? Maybe I should go back to Karen's where there was beer to soothe this sudden craving, plenty of hot water, clean towels and sheets, all the cigarettes I could smoke, and of course, Karen. Karen's cool, cocoa arms around me all night.

Static. "—please!" Static. I angrily banged the receiver against the table, taking mean pleasure in possibly hurting Michelle's ears. I flicked more matches, savoring the smell.

"After these few months, don't you have someone else to call?" I asked.

"It has to be you. Only you can help. I need you to—" Static.

"What? What do you need?" I scraped one calf with my other big toe.

Crackling and hissing. "—trouble. Bad."

"What sort of trouble?" I was perversely enjoying this drama, so it never occurred to me to get Michelle to call back for a clearer connection. The more inconvenienced Michelle was, the better I felt.

"Sloane Weatherly." Static. "—hear me? *Sloane Weatherly.* Don't—"

My instincts made me write down the name. When I heard a noise in the hallway, I looked up, realizing I had left my front door open, and my upstairs neighbor stared in at me with frank appreciation. I suddenly saw myself through his eyes: a tall black woman sprinter-lean, my mahogany skull shaved clean. My ebony skin gleamed from sex sweat. My large nipples were chocolate satin on my flat chest and my belly was hard and cut into an eight-pack.

"Jack off on your own time, asshole," I shouted, kicking the door shut.

"What?" Suddenly, for that one word, Michelle's voice was clear and full in my ear, her breath hot with panic.

"Nothing. What kind of trouble are you in?" I scratched myself lazily at various points on my body where the Karen sweat had not yet dried. Little secret pockets of wet sex energy that itched when finally exposed to air as they evaporated. I now regretted having answered the phone. I flicked more matches.

Crackling, hissing, beeps. "—trying to tell you. Where were you? I've been trying to call you for hours. The phone has been ringing forever!"

"Out," I answered curtly. Except for tonight, *this call*, I always wanted to speak to whatever girl was calling at the moment she called.

"Please, please help. I need you! Please come to Tulsa to help me straighten everything out!"

"You're breaking up. I can't understand much of this. You want me to *come there*?"

"Help me, Nora! I'm coming over right now!"

"No you ain't, cracker! You stay right where you are." I admired my pile of burnt matches.

"*Oh, God, they're after me!* I'm headed to your place so you can—" The line went dead. I stood in shocked silence with only the growl of the dial tone to underscore my sudden quick fright.

If there had been an after-sex glow, it was certainly gone now. Leave it to Michelle to ruin a good thing, even two thousand miles away.

Abruptly, I felt naked. I jerked on my shorts and made sure all my doors and windows were locked. From the freezer, I removed a pack of Carltons some femme had left on an overnight that I kept around only for emergencies. I had undying loyalty for Marlboros and loved them when I could get them. In my endless attempts at quitting, I never bought cigarettes. It was a matter of principle. But these Carltons looked like cigarettes, were shaped like cigarettes, lit up and burned smoke like cigarettes, and they were here in my hand, available, and willing to surrender themselves to my mouth. Just like I was accustomed to in all things, and I loved that most of all.

How short and how long ago it seemed that I kicked Michelle out. Only three months before. It hadn't taken me long to get back in business. I remembered our last fight. Michelle might have been a lazy student-of-all-trades while we were together, but she possessed coiled strength in her limbs. It had gotten very physical. Michelle hadn't wanted to leave. She resisted and threw things, breaking a lot of stuff. Michelle accused me of cheating, which I had done. I skewered Michelle on her stealing, which she had done to a compulsively embarrassing degree. Michelle seemed utterly destroyed, crying in great sobbing whoops, hiccupping and coughing, and finally throwing up. It was the worst breakup in my experience. It went on and on, the longest weekend in history. When it was finally over, Michelle stood on the sidewalk in full fury, her arms full of things she had taken from our house, hers or not, and in the interest of brevity, I let her go with all of it. Michelle screamed that I would be sorry, that I would pay. Then, "I hate you, I hate you, I hate you forever." I just nodded wearily from the porch, wishing to see Michelle drive away. When at last she had, I cleaned up the house, packed the few remaining items, and moved into my current apartment with triple locks. Then I had opened my precious little black book that had been in storage for too long.

I heard from mutual acquaintances that Michelle had moved immediately to Oklahoma—How had she chosen there? I wondered incredulously—and that Michelle had found a girlfriend right away and they moved in together. Also, these friends told me breathlessly, Michelle was probably having a hot and heavy affair with someone else who was in a committed relationship. "Busy girl," I said dryly. And that was it.

I debated what, if anything, to do about this unsettling call from Michelle. She *better* not be coming over here. I tried call return but it didn't work. I tried to call the Tulsa number Michelle had given me weeks ago, but now it was disconnected with no new number. In a strange desperation I couldn't explain, I even called the Oakland phone number Michelle had told me was her parents'. But it turned out to be a Chinese restaurant's answering machine. I felt a foreboding and didn't know what else to do. Call the police? I could see them now, smirking and calling me "ma'am" sarcastically. "Oh, you say you got a weird phone call from your ex from whom you've had a messy break? Oh, yeah, we'll get right on that, *ma'am*. File a report? You want us to file a report? Why sure, we'll file a report for you. Here it is, if you'll just sign here." I imagined a cop holding nothing in his hands but pretending to hand me a piece of paper. And those were the male police. The women were even harsher.

So I sat by the window until dawn, watching the street, flicking matches to life with my hard, yellow thumbnail and smoking the sissy, pissant little cigarettes. Even the smoke was thin and weak, not deep and full of the flavor and nuance and subtle language that I craved. It was a tightass anorexic cigarette, just like the girl who left them. But my nicotine brain was grateful just the same. I tried not to sleep, but fell into an uneasy catnap in the chair by the window.

The phone didn't ring again.

CHAPTER TWO

A couple of hours later, I was awakened by the telephone. My back ached from my angle in the chair and cigarette butts were scattered on the floor. I stood and walked to the phone. My bones popped, complaining of no bed and too little sleep. I checked the time: six a.m.

"Hello?" I hefted the weight of the receiver.

"Hello, lover, how about breakfast?" It was Cherisse. Ah, Cherisse of the yielding body and big booty. I smiled and closed my eyes, feeling the small aches Karen had given me.

"Sure thing, be right over." I hung up and found some jeans that I slipped into without underwear. I tried calling all of Michelle's phone numbers again. No answer at any of them. I again debated calling the police and again rejected it. In the light of day on my way to meet Cherisse, the danger of Michelle's call seemed even more ridiculous. Then, as I sat heavily on my chair by the window pulling on boots, I realized I might be getting too old for this constant poon chasing. I glanced around my apartment: dead plants in one window (one woman's idea to liven up my place), dirty plates stacked in the kitchen, unmade bed, cigarette butts everywhere, lipstick-smeared glasses on every surface as if I had just had a cocktail party.

"Mama, have mercy." I shook my head ruefully. I needed to get myself in hand, take responsibility for my mess, and get my life in order. But all I cared about right now was basketball and women. This was no place to bring a woman, my conscience scolded me. Women liked lace curtains and flowers and scented candles and fresh sheets and clean kitchens and spotless bathrooms and plenty of toilet paper and bubble bath and secret hordes of cookies and chocolate. My place was simple and Spartan and dirty. I had a Corgi model Batmobile, from an ex who called me Batman, parked on an antique desk, my basketball trophies and some miscellaneous sports equipment such as golf clubs, tennis rackets, racquetball rackets and goggles, softball and glove, Frisbee, soccer ball, skis—my only belongings left from the breakup—and an ironing board, a bed and a chair that I bought a month ago, and my only indulgence, a state-of-the-art sound system with hundreds of CDs. Nothing else.

I felt aroused at the thought of Cherisse. At the thought of making my apartment suitable for some soft, lush woman.

"Or maybe letting that woman come in and fix me up," I murmured, amused.

I got off on the authoritative ring my boots made on the wood floor as I walked about, gathering keys, wallet, Day Runner, dental dams and gloves and lube, and fresh underwear. Maybe Cherisse would give me time to shower.

Four hours later, in the bright kitchen, Cherisse served me breakfast. As I crunched toast, I asked, "What do I know about Oklahoma?"

"More than I do, honey," Cherisse replied, pouring coffee. Something about the way she held the pot in her hand made me newly appreciate her delicate brown wrists, her rich, meaty thighs, and her tasty rump undulating under her satin nightgown. I ran my hand up Cherisse's leg, resting for a moment in her kinky pubic hair.

"Uh-uh, Nora, you got to quit all that now. You wore me out." Cherisse sat heavily and sipped coffee.

I grinned. "You're sweet." I was appreciative of the breakfast.

Of the generosity of all the wonderful women I knew. "You really are."

"I know," Cherisse said, grinning back. "Sounds to me like she wants you back." She frowned over her cup, her brows knitting together. "And you can't do that."

"No, no, it wasn't like that."

"Mmm-hmm." Cherisse, disbelieving, helped herself to eggs.

I ate silently, wondering what had happened to Michelle. My helplessness to know, to *force* answers, infuriated me.

To me, Oklahoma was a wasteland past the end of the world. There was obviously no phone service, and if it hadn't been for footage from the Oklahoma City bombing that showed the capital city to be similar looking to other towns, I would've thought Oklahoma was dirt roads, Native Americans in teepees, and fat white men driving Cadillac convertibles with long bulls' horns mounted on the hoods.

I surmised Oklahoma to be backward, redneck, religious, ultraconservative, dry, dusty, hot, and ugly.

"Do black people even live there?" I asked.

Cherisse nodded as she chewed. "Don't be ignorant. Sure they do. There's Langston University, and remember Greenwood? The black Wall Street that was destroyed in the twenties?"

"The race riot," I whispered fiercely in recognition. "Right, I do remember something about that. I thought that was in Kansas or Nebraska. What happened, some poor brother got accused of rape? And then the whole town went up in flames?"

"That rape thing was only the last straw," Cherisse said. "I've read up on it a little. Racism had been simmering nationwide for years. It didn't just happen in Oklahoma. A race riot happened in nearly every state. Tulsa's was the worst."

"Whatever," I said dismissively. My eyes were burning and I made up my mind to go meet this Tulsa.

CHAPTER THREE

When I returned home, I found the door open and my apartment destroyed. My stereo was demolished and most of my CDs were snapped in two. My dishes were broken and my clothes were strewn everywhere. Oddly, my basketball trophies and sports equipment were untouched. Nothing was missing. Why wouldn't thieves take everything instead of smashing it? That stereo was worth a mint. When I finally looked up and noticed the walls, I gasped. Spray-painted around the room was the message: *Where were you? Fuck you, asshole!* in a lurid red. Michelle had come by after all.

I felt like I had been kicked in the gut just when I was regaining some of my footing and recovering from that nightmare relationship. I collapsed on my bed and struggled to keep myself together.

"Damn that bitch. Goddamn that nasty white bitch for getting me mixed up in this. I should've killed her when I had the chance." I breathed deeply until I went from weak to strong. As my anger became manageable, I heard a knock on my still-open door.

"Yeah?" I called from the bed.

"It's me." Tonya cautiously entered, stepping over debris.

"Oh, Tonya, honey chile!" Glad for a sane, sympathetic face, I launched myself into Tonya's arms. We had known each other a few wild times in the past months.

"What's happened, Nora? You piss off some other butch? Or some other coach?" Tonya stroked my back.

"An ex" was all I said.

"An ex did this? What in the hell did you do to her? Wait a minute. Was it that crazy white piece of shit you were sprung on for three years?"

I shrugged. "What did I do to her? You know, the usual." Then I picked up the phone.

Tonya put a hand on top of mine. "Whatever you do, don't call the LAPD!"

Surprised, I laughed hard. "Listen, I've got to go away for a while, but I want you to know where I've gone so if something funny happens…"

"Sure, sure." Tonya nodded, smiling reassuringly. "I've got your back, N. You want me to call some brothers to take care of this cootchie for you?"

I smiled tiredly and caressed Tonya's face. "No, thanks, I'm gonna see what I can do myself."

"Hmph. Famous last words."

"Let's hope not."

"Where are you going and when?"

"Tulsa. In a couple of days."

"All this is about Tulsa? I would've thought Chicago or at least Detroit. Tulsa? Isn't that the middle of nowhere? Cowtown, USA."

"T, don't be a dumbass, you know it's in Oklahoma."

"Same thing, N. And you are not that cute," Tonya retorted. "Why don't you stay with me tonight?" she asked as she surveyed the wreckage.

"Just what I was thinking." At least my infernal craving for smoke and drink had subsided. For now. "Will you wait while I pack a little?"

"Of course." Tonya sat on the bed, crossing her molasses-colored legs in a breathtaking way.

I packed hastily, hardly caring what I took, not knowing where I was going or what I would find.

"Can I make some calls from your place? To let the college know and to make flight arrangements?" I sighed, relieved that it was summer and the basketball season was over and I didn't start training my team for a few weeks. Tonya nodded. Women were so lovely and accommodating. I never understood why men didn't get how gentle, enormously generous, and caretaking all women were if you respected the simple checks and balances. It may seem old-fashioned, but there were a few rules that I observed like a religion: open all the doors regardless of her protests, hold her hand, buy flowers and perfume, send romantic cards, always call the next day, notice all hair and dress, carry packages and sacks, kill the bugs, take out the trash, buy her tampons and chocolates, hold her when she cries, touch her face, listen without advising, compliment her house, change the empty toilet paper roll, give nonsexual massages, go shopping with her, light candles before sex, and above all, most important nonnegotiable, keep her happy in bed. A woman who is happy in bed is not going to be unhappy anywhere else. She's compliant, agreeable, and cooperative. I had gotten with femmes other butches had warned me against who had committed the ambiguous crime of being uppity bitches. I laughed in the faces of my friends who warned me. All those women needed was me. Me all night, sometimes all day, sometimes all week. I never left until my preliminary work was done. I left them cooing and sighing on mussed sheets, blinking drowsily. You just had to determine what each one needed and overwhelm her with it. With some it was hours of kissing, some it was role-playing games, others it was hard and fast penetration, sometimes it was S/M, others it was fisting, others it was vibrators, others it was nonstop cunnilingus, some it was spanking, still others it was rimming till dawn, and I wore all of them out with orgasms. Just one thing never worked all the time (except plenty of cuddling). You had to have *all* the tools on the belt to walk with me. And in return? Oh, God, if men would understand this, the female floodgates would open for those lousy, privileged selfish pricks. In return, women will do it all, given half a chance and kept happy in bed. Women will gladly do everything for the modest exchange of some quality attention. The better you give, the better you get. No woman was a bitch after a night with me. That is, no one but Michelle McKerr.

On a hunch, I called directory assistance for Tulsa and got several listings for McKerr. I called each one and no one told me anything until the last one. I had developed a thin ruse to explain my call. The woman who answered sounded like she had been crying.

"You want to speak to Michelle? Who are you? What do you want?"

"I'm a…friend. I have some money for her. Can you tell me where she is?"

"You're a friend and you don't know she's dead?" The woman began crying softly. "Killed. Shot in the head. Oh, Lord have mercy, my baby—"

I hung up without a word.

Tonya took me into her house and gently into her arms.

The next day, I played hoops for ten hours. If I wasn't joining pick-up games, I played by myself or sat under a tree staring into space. I played in the old outdoor lots with battered chain link fences and broken asphalt. I needed to be close to something urban and ugly. The squeaky-clean beautiful hardwood floors and pristine outdoor courts of my college were repellant to me now. I played until Tonya came for me on her way home from work. Tonya gently pried my numb hands off the ball and pushed me into the car. I passed out into sleep on the way home. Tonya woke me gently and boosted me into the house, tucking me into bed without dinner. I slept, not moving, until dawn when I reached for Tonya. I drowsily sucked Tonya's luscious black nipples into erect bullets. Tonya groaned sleepily and shifted her big hips up to meet my slow, firm stroke. With my eyes closed, I grinned as I felt Tonya's legs spread wide and smooth the sheets in an arc. I tenderly cupped Tonya's body close as she arched her back. Barely conscious, I nuzzled Tonya's throat and she curled her heavy body around me and relaxed into a long, deep orgasm. I loved the feel of Tonya's wide hips and belly roll. That's the way all women should be. Ample and voluptuous and able to fuck for hours. Tonya was still undulating with pleasure as I kissed her brow. When Tonya finally lay limp, I moved to her slippery cunt and took her swollen clit in my mouth. She gasped and her eyes flew open.

"Mornin', sunshine," I said to her glistening pussy. "We're just getting started."

Two hours later, Tonya's alarm clock woke us from a sleep-glutted sex haze. I realized how sore and exhausted I was. With the bright light of day, my catatonia returned and I went back and played basketball for another twelve hours. By the time Tonya came to get me, I felt a little clearer, somewhat steadier. Tonya tried to talk me out of leaving and going to Tulsa, tried to get me to stay with her longer and think things over, but I was resolute.

My face and attitude would've been recognized by my team as absolutely nonnegotiable. I had carefully and patiently built four dream teams over the last fifteen years and sent many a talented and ambitious player to a good career. I groomed my players for championships and they never disappointed me. My Panthers were a West Coast phenomenon and years ago, I had been famous as a powerhouse player myself. Some reporter started calling me the Pat Summitt of Los Angeles and it caught on. I was waiting for the day that Pat Summitt would be called the Nora Delaney of Tennessee.

I inherited my determination from my beloved grandmother, who passed it to my mother and then to me, just like the gold Ugandan coin on a chain I had inherited from them. That coin was as much a part of me as my fingerprints, and I had nearly been hospitalized when I lost it.

My grama, white-haired but still a tall, majestic queen, had told me the simple story of the coin when I was a child.

"You see, our ancestors were royalty. We used to wear brilliant robes and great crowns. We were the rulers of the cradle of civilization. You are a descendent of the Acholi Tribe in Uganda." Grama paused to let that sink in. I listened with all of my ten-year-old heart.

"And when a war came, a princess saw a hard future ahead and sewed gold coins into her dress so that she might sweeten her fate. Chaos and cruelty came to Uganda. What family was not slaughtered or burned were either lucky enough to run away or unlucky enough to be kidnapped and sold into slavery. The princess was unlucky. She lost her home, her family, her position, her wealth, all the life she had known. She was not much older than you. Two or three years, maybe."

I blinked, feeling great pride in the resourcefulness of children like myself.

"She used her coins one by one. At first trying to buy her freedom, but when that didn't work, she used them to bribe food from her captors and to persuade them not to rape her. When at last she arrived in the New World, she used her remaining money to buy a better station in life. She saved her last coin to remind herself of who she really was. She prayed with it in her hands at night, carried it in her bosom at day. It never left her. See how it is rubbed smooth?" My grama tilted her wrist so I could touch the warm coin and feel its silky surface. I nodded.

"That is how many prayers have been rubbed into this coin. That's how many women have carried the heritage and the memories. My great-grandmother got it off her mother's body after she died, before the slave owners could steal it. Then my grandmother carved a hole in it so she could wear it. Then my mother gave it to me, and I'll give it to your mama this year on her birthday. And someday, it will belong to you. You must treasure it always and never lose it. Remember who you are and the wishes for a better life that the princess has passed down to you."

"Okay, Grama."

My grandmother, Elsie Merica Madewell, saw the antebellum South in depressed shambles with picking cotton as a black person's only possible future, so she packed up her husband and nine children and moved, by horse and buggy, to Los Angeles where my grandfather, Amos Madewell, started a restaurant to feed local railroad workers and my grandmother took in sewing and started a little church.

My mother, Emily Anne, pitched in with the rest of her siblings, helping with the restaurant and working hard getting her education. During college at Mooreland University, Emily met Benjamin Delaney and they married. My father was one of a handful of black veterinarians serving the black farmers and black cowboys and rodeos of the entire Southwest region. When my father was killed by a horse trampling him, I was ten years old, and the hardest hit.

That was when I discovered basketball. I was a skinny, knock-kneed, googly-eyed, nappy-haired, broken-hearted girl alone on the court. Even though the boys called me names and tried to keep me out, my mama had power and influence in the community, so she was able to put me on a team even though I was the only girl.

I excelled and went to my parents' collegiate alma mater on an unheard-of basketball scholarship.

That night at Tonya's, after basketball all day, after dinner and sex, my shock broke like a fever and I felt alert and strong and ready to leave Los Angeles.

Through Tonya, I had gotten a referral for a hotel and a bar. Tonya knew someone who knew someone who knew someone who had been to Tulsa. "The Phillips Hotel and Jody's Bar and Grill," Tonya said, hanging up the phone. I frowned at the piece of paper with addresses on it. "The Phillips is downtown, and

Jody's is on south and east of that, whatever. And I checked my *Lesbian Connection.* There's a contact dyke in Tulsa, Darcy Tate, who might be helpful. Will you be okay?" Tonya handed me the scrap. I nodded. I needed to be alone for a while to think. I needed a plan. Tonya left me alone by the pool in the back until I had a game strategy and a game face. Then I wordlessly took Tonya to bed.

Chapter Four

The next day, my plane took off from LAX headed for Tulsa International Airport without a single empty seat. I was surprised to see so many people wanting to go to Oklahoma. I expected an empty plane where I could stretch out, perhaps be the only passenger. Who the hell else would go to Oklahoma and why? If it was going to be a crowded airplane, I expected barefoot hillbillies in overalls and live chickens under their arms. But these people were polished, well dressed, well groomed, polite and well spoken.

I was squeezed in between a large, red businessman and a young female student. My knees were wedged firmly against the seat in front of me. I had bouts of breathless claustrophobia so intense that I forgot to flirt with the flight attendant. I grabbed the beers out of the attendant's hands and gulped them. "Jesus, help me," I muttered in resentful surrender as the student gave me a vicious shove in the ribs and a brilliant smile. I gave up, hugging my chest and holding my beer under my nose like an aromatic sedative.

Tonya! I sat up straight suddenly and banged my cup of beer onto the tray table. I needed to call her. The businessman glared at me as I twisted around, removing my cell phone that I despised using, even as Dick Tracy as it was. I dialed and then heard Tonya's voice in sweet, safe LA.

"Hey, baby!" I shouted over the deafening vibration of the plane. "Just wanted to call and thank you for everything. I had such a great time over the weekend." I smiled my sunniest smile into the phone, wrapping it around Tonya.

"Me too. Where the hell are you?"

"In the plane."

"The plane? Girl, are you crazy? See you soon and take care of yourself."

"I'll be looking you up when I get back. I owe you big."

"I'll say. Take me out to dinner."

"You got it, baby. That and much more." I hung up and called Cherisse. Then Karen. When I finally replaced the phone in my pocket, the student was stifling giggles and fingering her WWJD bracelet. The businessman had abandoned his armrest, trying to hold himself as far away from me as possible.

"Jealousy," I spat as I placed Tonya's headphones on my head and rang for my fourth beer. "John Coltrane, take me away." I closed my eyes and spread my arms over both vacant armrests, smiling.

My second surprise was the "international" airport. I laughed. International? There was nothing international about it, and no city with a tiny toy airport could have any serious trouble for Michelle. It was probably a waste to have come. I carried my bag, wandering through the deserted building. The airport had escalators and elevators and security and snack bars and lots of ticket counters, and very shiny floors and airline gates and long concourses and cheesy souvenirs and insurance machines and flags from many nations bidding me welcome, just like any airport, but it was so clean and quiet. It was eerie. I stopped at baggage claim not to get a bag—I had only carry-on—but just to take a minute to absorb this strange atmosphere. And where better to stand, looking lost, than at baggage claim?

"Ma'am, are you lost?" a security guard asked.

I stared at him, speechless. Politeness, courtesy, concern for people—what in hell had I gotten myself into?

"Perdida?" the man asked gently. *"Perdue?"*

My mind was blank. The security guards spoke Spanish and French?

"I'm sorry. I don't know any African languages. Hmm, let's see…"

That snapped me out of my trance. "No, no, I'm all right. I'm from LA," I said, feeling stupid immediately.

"From LA," the guard repeated inscrutably. I thought he put something sinister into it too. "Well, you looked a little stunned, so I wanted to make sure you were all right."

I blinked. "Yes, yes, thanks."

"Welcome to Tulsa. Have a nice stay."

"Sure," I replied. The guard turned to leave when I said, "Car?"

"You need a ride?" he asked. "Out at the curb are taxis or hotel buses. Where are you staying?"

"The Phillips."

"Oh, nice. They don't have a bus, but you can take a cab or rent a car right over there." The guard pointed. I felt like an idiot for the second time in five minutes. Not a good sign. Just across the baggage claim conveyor were all the car counters in a row, brightly lit with the uniformed agents smiling perkily, not forty feet from where I stood. I glanced to my side out the wall of glass, which was the airport exit. A line of yellow taxis was right there. What do you know. I was struck again by the silence of the place. No yelling or running or harassed mobs. No travel tension at all. No rudeness or rushing or stress. The baggage belt began moving with a jerk. The people waiting for bags, murmuring quietly, all stopped talking and leaned forward expectantly.

"Thank you again," I said to the guard and stuck out my hand, knowing myself to be a dolt.

"Sure thing, anytime." The guard shook my hand briskly and walked away.

I looked around and sighed, finally getting my bearings. I was the only black person here. I was the only person of color at all. My gaze met that of an elderly Hispanic man pushing a broom and rolling a trash barrel on wheels. He nodded and I smiled, starting to relax. I decided to rent a car, drop off my luggage, and head for the local watering hole. My beer buzz was wearing off in this smothering silence. Approaching the car rental counter was strange because I was the only customer, and the agent smiled stiffly. The entire long walk from baggage claim to counter, neither my nor the agent's eyes dropped and neither of us said anything. The other passengers had collected their bags and headed home on the arms of loved ones. I heard my boots ring on the slick, polished floor. I rented what passed for a full-size, hoping for enough legroom.

The agent was chipper and helpful and drew a route on the cartoon map of how to get to the Phillips.

"It's an historic building, you know. From the early oil boom," the agent said.

"No, I didn't know."

"And they've completely renovated it. I haven't stayed there, but I've heard it's real nice. Let's keep our fingers crossed that the Plaza is next, right?"

"Right," I answered feebly. I couldn't picture Michelle living here when there was such infernal unsolicited friendliness.

"Where are you from?" The agent handed me the keys.

"Africa. Uganda." That should throw her, I thought. I was beginning to have a little fun. Hadn't the agent just seen my driver's license?

"Really? What part?" the agent asked smoothly.

I laughed. "Los Angeles."

"Oh." The agent frowned. "I thought that was in California."

"Well, thanks." I walked away.

"The lot is right outside. Have a great stay."

I waved. My boots were the only sound on the long, empty walk to the exit.

Once outside in the actual Oklahoma summer air, I couldn't

breathe. The air was thick and wet and so hot that I thought my skin might boil. I began sweating instantly and I struggled to pull air into my lungs. I felt like I was underwater. In the rental car, I turned the air conditioner on high. I couldn't touch the steering wheel; it burned my fingers. I leaned helplessly against the seat until the car was cooler.

CHAPTER FIVE

At my hotel, I was relieved there was no chatter. The clerk was formal and rather disapproving, as if he could look into my recent past and see my bite marks and nail scratches.

After I tested the bed, I opened the curtain and looked outside. Pretty town. Very pretty for a thermal aquarium. I showered, ate overpriced, mediocre room service, and called the name that Tonya had given me.

"Darcy, go!" the person answered abruptly.

"You always pick up the phone that way?"

"Who is this?"

"Nora Delaney. Just here from LA. An acquaintance of Tonya Mays gave me your name and I wanted to talk to you about Michelle—"

"Meet me at Jody's tonight at nine o'clock," Darcy whispered and hung up.

I checked myself in the mirror, smiled at what I saw, ran a hand over my bald, shaven head, and returned to the front desk.

"Can you tell me how to get to Jody's?"

"Never heard of it," the desk clerk answered.

"Well, it's—"

"No, I don't know how to get there," he said sternly.

"Then tell me how to get to this intersection," I ordered.

Eventually, I found my way and parked. The wet air

oppressed me like an iron fist on my chest. Even after dark there was no relief. I had a sweat mustache just opening the car door.

The bar could have been any dive in any town. The outside was nondescript. An awning over a door at the end of a strip mall. I opened the door and walked in. To my right sat an old jukebox and a couple of pool tables. To my left, a small dance floor. The air was as stale as the inside of a coffin and it reminded me of my cigarette jones. Suddenly, I was fiercely glad that I was in Oklahoma, where people still smoked in clubs and bars.

After being carded, I took a seat at the bar. The bartender gave me an approving nod. "What can I get you?"

I looked around. A nice-sized crowd. Everyone was drinking beer. I ordered that too.

A voluptuous woman who made my eyes close and my mouth fill with water walked slowly by. I remembered a quote from some sex book about the ideal female: "If a woman like this is seen from the front, the sight is ravishing, if from behind, fatal." I whispered, *"Es muy caliente, muy guapa."* I was in an ass-trance.

She stopped and tossed her hair. It swung around the clean curve of her jaw. She snapped, "*Touche pas. Fairmez la bouche.* This is not for you," then continued her switching saunter to the dance floor where she danced alone, eyes closed, in a sensual rhythm.

"Yes, it is for me." I slugged my beer and another appeared instantly. I never took my smoldering stare off her. The woman had long, flowing wavy hair that was deep, dark red. Raven red, I thought involuntarily. I had never seen anyone so white. Not a single freckle. I imagined a century and a half ago, on a plantation in South Carolina, she would've been my Young Miss. A flare of anger kindled and I approached her again. We walked toward the bar together and stopped in front of a bar stool.

"You're just a corn-fed butter-eater, aren't you?" I was in my adorable flirty stance. The woman's eyes flew open and she glared at me.

"And you're just a chitlin'-slurpin' pickaninny, aren't you?"

"I'm whatever you need," I purred over the loud, throbbing music.

"I don't need any fast-talking jock underestimating me. I'd make sheet meat out of you."

My hands twitched nervously. Needing a cigarette or a succulent breast, I raised a hand to lay a gentle palm on her shoulder.

"You touch me, I'll slap you flat," the woman said, smooth and serene. Then she turned her head and said, "Gin and tonic," to the bartender, who hastened to get her a refill and place it in on the bar in front of her stool.

"I might enjoy a slap," I said with a grin. But I lowered my hand, deciding not to touch her…yet. "I may not be the best looking, but I'm the only one talking to you."

"Oh, please," she said in a withering tone. "I'm not alone." With that, she stalked off, disappearing into the bathroom.

I bounced on the balls of my feet, still grinning. I called out "Hey!" to the bartender, who leaned close, wiping a glass. "You know someone named Darcy?"

The bartender nodded and did a cursory scan of the patrons. "Ain't here yet."

"Okay, thanks." I started on my third beer and ambled to the pool tables. Three women had just finished a game of cutthroat and they let me in to play partners for eight ball. I paid for the game and we slapped each other on the back and exchanged names. I picked a stick, the best of the sadly curved and badly bowed pool cues that were in a stand on the wall.

Just as I leaned over the table to make my first shot, the woman emerged from the bathroom, freshened in some way that I could not detect. I flubbed my shot badly and my partner groaned. The woman took her seat at the bar behind me and watched, sipping her fresh drink. I tried to concentrate and stay focused, wishing I hadn't joined this game. I missed my second and third shots.

I aggressively ignored Raven Red, who was obviously alone. No one else dared approach her either. Suddenly, I felt my back prickle from the nearness of her as she stood behind me on tiptoe and whispered, “Play the shadows.”

I whirled around to say, “Femmes don’t know shit about pool,” but she was gone. I got a scent of perfume and damp air as the door closed. I shook my head and with a smile, regained my composure and made every shot.

“Play the shadows, my big black dick,” I muttered.

By the time I finished playing at nine o’clock, the bar was standing room only. I fought my way back to the bartender and yelled, “Darcy here yet?” Only in a gay community could you count on this intimacy of strangers. The barkeep nodded and pointed vaguely to the other end of the bar before getting caught up in more drink orders.

CHAPTER SIX

"Great," I said without enthusiasm, slicing my way sideways through the crowd. I was the tallest woman there so I could see easily. I was relieved that there were some sistahs here. I nodded courteously to each. Like kings and queens, each met my gaze regally and inclined her head just right in return. I reached the corner of the bar and noticed a group of four, three women and one man. I evaluated the group and made instant judgments just on posture and appearance. Darcy had to be the one in the middle, and she was a self-important stocky butch wannabe with the sort of swagger only a huge ego and massive insecurity could cause. The other two women were both blond, one built like a bear and the other one like a stick. Hoping to be proven wrong about Darcy after introductions, I approached. Holding my beer above my head out of harm's way, I stuck my hand out. "Darcy Tate? I'm Nora."

Darcy looked me up and down and finally shook my hand. "We're drinking slippery nipples," she announced, grinning at the blond stick, who giggled. "'Cause they're better in pairs."

"So true," I murmured, wondering just how fast and far to run.

"This is my lover, Ava-Suzanne Morgan-Frazier," Darcy said. She pronounced the second name "Sue-zAHn." My mouth twisted. I supposed Ava-Suzanne played the pee-AH-no and put dah-zies in a vahse. I did not offer my hand because Ava scowled at me with such disdain. I wanted to snap this skinny white twig in half. She was plain enough and bony enough to be a supermodel.

"This is Jhoaeneyie Crosswaithe, quite the capable egg," Darcy continued, introducing the bear.

Jhoaeneyie and I shook hands, and I was surprised to find my hand engulfed in a firm grip. "How you doin'?" Jhoaeneyie boomed in a strong twang within a foghorn voice. "My name is pronounced Joanie, but if you ever write me a letter, it is spelled," Jhoaeneyie touched her cheek and winked, "quite unconventionally. You see, I am a nonconformist. Definitely not a traditional type." People sitting close were startled by Jhoaeneyie's voice and stared for a moment. She continued. "No offense, but I'll never remember your name."

"None taken. I'll never remember yours or how to spell it," I replied.

Jhoaeneyie was seized by laughter that bellowed out of her throat. "Touché, touché, touché," she replied, pronouncing it "toosh."

"And this is Jack Irving." Darcy indicated the man who was busy doing shots of Black Jack. He smiled merrily at her, his brown eyes warm, and shook my hand.

"Here, come sit here, I'll give you my seat." Jack slid to a recently vacated stool and patted the one he emptied.

"Thanks, Jack." This was unusual. Gay men rarely hung with dykes. The rule is gay men with straight women, period. Fraternization between the two homosexual cultures was the rare exception. I sat and observed the bar in comfort. There were lots of jocks here, some attractive femmes, and all ages and colors and class ranges.

A bunch of good-looking butches too, but they made me uneasy. It was as if butchness was not okay here, so women naturally butch worked hard to soften it. Some wore makeup!

Some wore earrings or other feminine jewelry. Some wore women's clothing. Some had ludicrously long hair. Some carried purses. "Oklahoma butches," I said to my beer as I drained it. Another appeared immediately.

Jack, obviously drunk and liking it, leaned his shoulder in to mine and said slushily, "Love your head."

I grinned at him and ran my hand over my smooth scalp. "Thank you."

"Don't get much of that here," Jack continued, "Too conswer, uh, consper, conservative. But me, I love it."

Jhoaeneyie, eavesdropping, said, "I used to have real long hair. Down to here." She indicated her rear. "But I had to cut it off. I simply had to." She ran her hand through her blond pompadour. "I just adore it now."

"You two are practically twins," Jack muttered to his drink.

"Yeah, no offense, but that's real different. *Real* different." Jhoaeneyie studied my gleaming head that I had freshly waxed after my shower.

"Yeah, what's with all the bad hair?" I picked out poodle perms, old feather dos begging to be retired, mullets, fried, frizzy bleach heads, women who had ponytails on their crowns and the rest of their heads shaved, and incredibly, women proudly sporting a tail or a single long thin braid down their backs with otherwise short hair. I wanted to come through here with electric shears.

Jack guffawed. "Tell me about it, honey. This," Jack indicated the bar, "is my worst nightmare." He shivered and threw back another shot. "Buy you another too, sweetie?" Jack peered into my beer bottle.

"Sure, but how about some real beer? What the hell is this piss?" I swigged the dregs of my drink.

"Oh." Jack giggled. "Welcome to Oklahoma. Weird blue law. Bars can only serve beer with 3.2 percent alcohol. Ain't that some shit?"

Jack and I toasted Oklahoma's senseless restrictions. Darcy, who had been talking to her girlfriend, now turned to me.

"So, what do you do?" Darcy was aggressive, like a little pug.

"I'm a college basketball coach for—"

"That's nice. I make tapestries. I weave my own cloth. You should come see it. I'm an artist, really. 'Course my day job is at the Ford Glass plant, but I just have that to support my BMW."

Astonished, I nodded.

"Ava-Suzanne, my lover, is a musician. She's also an incredible artist."

I looked at Ava-Suzanne, who smiled a prim, tight smile with hard eyes.

"What do you play?" I asked politely, not caring at all.

"I'm a flutist," Ava-Suzanne said icily.

I was busting to say, "You're not pretty enough to be so hateful," but I didn't. "Oh, really." I sipped my beer, staring at the bar. This was a dead end and a boring one. Maybe I could forget this Jessica Fletcher detective work and pick someone up and make that hotel room useful.

"I'm a therapist," Jhoaeneyie boomed. "But I play guitar on the weekend. You know, to unwind. My job just shatters me. Isn't it ironic?"

Jack and I stared at her.

"My IQ is one forty-five, but I'm as forgetful and clumsy as a two-year-old. You know what I mean? Isn't that ironic?"

"That is ironic. That's so ironic, it borders on metaphor," Jack quipped.

Jhoaeneyie laughed again, causing several couples nearby to move away uneasily. "Touché."

"Now look at that." Jack gestured to a man across the bar. "Men should never wear pinkie rings. That's just obscene."

I looked over at the man in question. "Oh, that's just the beginning of his problems."

Laughter burbled out of Jack and we clicked drinks.

"Say, Idgie—" I began.

"Jhoaeneyie."

"Jhoaeneyie then," I said, "Do you know what all this cloak-and-dagger Michelle stuff is about?"

"Well, you see," Jhoaeneyie trumpeted. "I did know Michelle. She came to me as a patient. *I know all about her.* I'm afraid I'm not at liberty to tell you anything." Jhoaeneyie touched the side of her nose. "Client confidentiality, you know."

"But I don't want to know—"

"Sorry." Jhoaeneyie winked. "Can't help you."

"All I'm asking is why am I—"

"That's enough." Jhoaeneyie shrugged. "I've drawn a boundary. You must respect that."

I blinked. "Uh-huh." I lit a cigarette to burn disgust out of my mouth.

Jhoaeneyie put both of her thumbs into her nostrils simultaneously and dug around for a few seconds before removing them and wiping whatever she found on her pants.

"Idgie's famous double dip," Jack murmured. I coughed on a swallow of beer. Darcy and Ava-Suzanne were on the dance floor jerking stiffly like spastics.

"I have spot-on intuition," Jhoaeneyie said. "I can see into people right away."

"Is that so?"

"I'm a complicated lady."

"She's a complicated lady," Jack echoed.

I looked her up and down. "Nothing is complicated."

"Oh, you're a black-and-white type," Jhoaeneyie said, then embarrassed, added, "No offense."

"No sweat," I said.

"Good." Jhoaeneyie laughed. "Glad you're not uptight about that stuff. You know what I mean? Glad you're laissez-faire." She pronounced it "less-sez fair."

"And?"

"Well, FYI, Darcy and Ava-Suzanne are real super ladies. They're something special."

"Oh, I can see that," I said. Jack sipped his shot.

"So, I just want you to be careful." Jhoaeneyie double-dipped again.

"Why?"

"Because I don't want you to get off on the wrong foot in a new town. See, I'm an encourager. I see what people are about and I encourage them in the proper direction. Know what I mean?"

"No clue."

Jhoaeneyie laughed and laughed at that, scaring several passersby. "You…" Jhoaeneyie gasped. "You are amazing. You're hilarious. I knew we'd hit it off."

"I've got to go change," Jack announced, standing up. "Save my seat, will ya, precious?"

"Wait! Don't leave me." I clutched his arm.

"I'll be right back. Don't you worry."

"Why do you have to change? You look fine," I persisted.

Jack looked down at himself. "I cannot *hope* to meet anyone as superfine as I am in this raggedy, wilted shirt. This tragic outfit is *so* eight o'clock. And just look at me!" Jack admired himself in the mirror behind the bar. "I am a mess." He grinned seductively.

"Come right back," I commanded.

"Of course, bobbin. My other shirt is in my car. You smoke as much as you need." He left.

I glanced at Jhoaeneyie, who double-dipped, her eyes twinkling. Darcy and Ava-Suzanne were headed back to the bar to sit.

"I'm a witch," Jhoaeneyie said, trembling with excitement as if presenting me with a gift. "Yep, Jhoaeneyie's a witch," she repeated, grinning. More patrons glared at the foghorn voice.

"Is that right?" I stirred the bowl of peanuts.

"Doesn't that shock you?"

"Not particularly." I shrugged and tossed a few nuts into my mouth, which made me thirsty enough to finish my beer. The bartender replaced the beer with a new, frosted one.

"I really am," Jhoaeneyie added. "Although my daughter, Journey, isn't sure she wants a pagan life, I've encouraged her to make her own choices."

"Because you're the encourager." I laughed. "That's beautiful." I smiled so hard it hurt. "Journey, huh?"

"Yes, you'd love her."

"I doubt that."

"No, you would, I'm serious." Double-dip. "She's exceptional, you know what I mean?"

"Darcy. Ava-Suzanne. How's it going?" I clapped Darcy on the back.

"I'm exhausted." Darcy sighed with a smile. "I don't know how I do it. I really don't. With everything I do, I should be dead."

I said nothing.

"You're amazing," Jhoaeneyie said.

"You're a goddess," Ava-Suzanne added.

Darcy put a hand on her left breast and addressed me. "There's a lot going on in here, you know what I'm saying?"

I sank onto my bar stool and hugged my beer.

"Between my job," Darcy continued, counting off on her fingers, "and supporting Ava-Suzanne, and my spiritual work and my art and then helping this one"—Darcy gestured to Jhoaeneyie—"with her music...I am done in. See, I'm real visual. That's my medium. So music is more of a challenge."

"A guitar is a moody mistress, you know what I mean?" Jhoaeneyie said. "See, I'm not like that. I flunk all simple stuff. Tying shoes, flushing the toilet. Give me something intricate and difficult. That's my métier." She pronounced it "may-teer."

"Jack!" I shouted, seeing him come inside again. "Jack's

back." I noted, with a little envy, how fresh and crisp he looked. I vowed to copy his changing clothes idea.

Jack grinned and sat. Everyone drank in silence for a few moments.

"Darcy's done time," Jack murmured in her ear. "Funny, huh?"

Interested, I turned back to Darcy and said, "Jack just told me you've done time. Is that true?" I wondered if that had served Darcy's artistic purpose.

Fake modesty made Darcy smile archly and say yes.

"What for?"

"Forgery."

I turned back to the bar and said to my beer, "Forgery's a woman's crime."

"What?" Darcy heard me but seemed stunned. "Ava-Suzanne, my lover, has played in Europe. We'll probably go back there soon." Darcy sniffed. "Better class of people."

"Is that so?" I asked Ava-Suzanne, whose nostrils curved into a snarl.

"Oh, Darcy, please don't brag on me. You know I hate being an ornament. I have issues with being shown off," Ava-Suzanne said, simpering.

I dared to put my hand reassuringly on Ava-Suzanne's cold forearm. "Don't worry about it. Really."

The infidel voice of Jack slipped into my ear again. "She was third chair in Bumfuck, Arkansas, or some such mishbegotten place."

I smothered my laughter by draining my beer. I hadn't planned to drink so fast, but I had no other way of keeping a straight face. Plenty of time later to laugh out loud. I needed a cigarette badly.

"So, Ava-Suzanne, where have you played?" I asked.

"Oh," Ava-Suzanne replied airily, "Europe, various places in the U.S. In different orchestras."

"Do you play here?" I didn't even know if Tulsa had an orchestra.

"No, she can't anymore," Darcy interrupted. "She has a serious energy blockage in her right hand. We're getting alternative medicine to treat it, but until then, it's agony for her to play."

"You see," Jhoaeneyie began, "emotions are connected to the body. I've seen it. Ava-Suzanne is gifted, but her obstacles from trauma forbid her playing."

"Bullshit," Jack cooed tipsily into my ear.

"Have you been to a doctor?" I asked.

"Yes, but they say I'm fine," Ava-Suzanne answered haughtily, shaking out her right hand for emphasis as if it hurt to even talk about it.

"Allopathic medicine is worthless. That's why we're going to the womyn's holistic natural healing clinic and have Qiu Qu with Cinnamon Moonbear. She's the best. I'm learning her trade so that I can do it."

"Ladyfair Moonbear is *amazing*!" Jhoaeneyie interjected.

"Cho Choo?" I asked.

"Yes." Darcy warmed to her subject. "It's a process of clearing nasty, thorny storages of pain."

"Ask how." Jack giggled.

"How?" I asked.

Darcy sat up straighter, clearly loving her own voice. "A qualified practitioner immerses Ava-Suzanne into specially supercharged ionized clear fluid...You know what that is?" Darcy asked smugly.

"Expensive water," Jack whispered.

"And Ava-Suzanne remains there for a specified amount of time depending on what you're clearing and how deeply." Darcy smiled. "After which she is released and the first big breaths afterward are vital to the healing. That is what moves the blockages, those first powerful gasps."

"You are shitting me," I said.

"No, why would I? The results are well documented with research and case histories on their Web site. And I've seen it work wonders for Ava-Suzanne."

"Yeah, the Chappadick treatment by inches," Jack whispered in a slur. "I say, heal her all at once." Jack and I clinked drinks again.

"Plus, I was a mess before I did it. It made me a whole new person," Darcy added.

I waited to see if Jack had anything to say about this. He didn't. He was smoking, though, and in glee, I took one and lit up, flicking one wooden match of my perpetual pocket collection with my thumbnail.

"Oh, baby, that's cool," Jack said. I grinned and set several more matches on the bar in case I needed them.

I pulled on the cigarette in ecstasy. Oh, God, the sweet, hot dryness that caressed me deep inside where no woman could get. I held the smoke inside, nestled in every crevice for over a full minute. I kissed the cigarette as I wrapped my lips around it for another long drag. I could keep a straight face now, no matter what Darcy and Ava-Suzanne said. Paradoxically, my career as a jock and a coach kept me in such great shape that I was a better smoker, try though I might to quit annually. With a smile, Jack watched me smoke and offered me a sip of his shot. I took one and followed it with a long drink of beer. God, I loved things on my lips and in my mouth. Cigarettes, suckers, bottles, pens, pencils, straws, toothpicks, women. I offered my beer to Jack, who drank happily. Darcy and Ava-Suzanne were staring in distaste. I hadn't noticed before, but under the calming influence of tobacco, I saw that Darcy was nervous and fidgety. Her lips were raw from continual licking, and her cuticles were bloody shreds. I wanted this over.

Darcy was pinching the bridge of her nose.

"What's the matter, kitten?" Ava-Suzanne crooned.

"Just a second." Darcy pressed her temples. "I have a

headache, but I'm not a headache person. There." Darcy smiled with all her teeth as if she had done a trick. "All gone. With all I do," she began, Ava-Suzanne and Jhoaeneyie nodding sympathetically, "all my tension goes right to my neck and shoulders. That's where all my tension goes. Right there. I carry a load of stress because of my multitasking."

"Right now, she's cleaning her oven," Jack muttered.

"I need to find a good massage therapist. One who will take my special requirements into consideration. And work with me on many levels and simultaneous therapies. One who is exceptional because I like it deep. But till then," Darcy smiled wistfully, "sometimes I get a little headache and I have to treat and heal myself. Thank God for me, huh?" All three laughed and raised their glasses. I had to shut my mouth, for it had fallen open. Jack winked at me.

"I'm hungry. Where can we go for a bite?" I asked, knowing it would end the interview.

"I'm a vegetarian," Ava-Suzanne said prissily.

"Of course you are," I said. "I didn't fight my way to the top of the food chain to be a rabbit. But you might know where is a good restaurant for all of us. Do you eat milk, eggs, and cheese?"

"Yes."

On a hunch, I asked, "You eat fish and chicken too, don't you?"

"Yes, but not every day." Ava-Suzanne pursed her lips and patted her short, messy, dishwater hair.

"Mostly, I cook for her. I'm a great cook. Chicken, fish, whatever, I can do it. We should have you over some time. We're both vegetarians, but it would be delicious. And fun." Darcy seemed sincere. I rolled my eyes in disgust. I knew animal rights activists and true vegetarians and militant vegans and vegetarian chefs. In Los Angeles it was very common. And *nobody* there had the temerity to admit she ate meat while claiming to be vegetarian. Even I knew fish and chicken were meat. Hell, milk was just liquid meat. Around the college where I coached, the vegetarian places were on every corner. What was uncommon, however, was a femme who would mix a stiff drink and eat a slab of meat. But I understood Darcy. Some people were poseurs and didn't know it. What's more, they didn't want to know it.

"Sure, let's do that some time. Suppose you tell me what you know about Michelle?"

"Let's rock and roll!" Jhoaeneyie exclaimed.

Darcy flew through her nervous tics, which seemed odd for this wall of a woman. It would've fit her flyweight girlfriend better. Jack had gone to negotiate with the DJ for some better songs.

"All I know is, you better talk to Max Abbott. The number is in the book. Max can tell you everything."

"Max Abbott." I wrote it on a napkin wondering why in the hell Darcy couldn't have told me this on the goddamn telephone. What a motherfucking waste of time. It didn't occur to me until later that Darcy was lonely and wanted to be the first in town to lay claim to a new friend. I never considered that Darcy just wanted a night out and used me to get it. I continued, "Okay, what about this character…" I dug in the pocket of my navy sport coat for the scrap of paper I had saved since Michelle's desperate call. "What about this Sloane Weatherly?"

Darcy motioned for me to shut up. Then she looked around and shook her head. "Don't go looking for Sloane. Nobody wants to be found by Sloane. Leave it. Let that be, okay?" Darcy gathered my unused matches and tried, with her thumb, to light them, one after the other.

"Sloane is *baaaad newwwwws*," Jhoaeneyie said, then held up her hand. "But I can't tell you why." Ava-Suzanne just clenched up angrily, like a fussy fist.

I shrugged. "Okay. Listen, thanks for everything. It was nice meeting all of you. I can't tell you what a help you've been," I lied. "I'll buy the next round. I've got to go." I sucked the remaining foam from my beer and helped myself to another of

Jack's cigarettes, automatically flicking my thumbnail across the head of a match I removed from my pocket and applying it to the tip. "Not as easy as it looks," I murmured. I motioned the bartender over, gave her the money for my own tab, a large tip, plus the next round for Jack, at whom I winked before sliding off the stool and into the night.

CHAPTER SEVEN

I struggled to get a deep breath. It had been easier to breathe in the bar. The atmosphere was like being under the ocean, the heat was like the center of a volcano, and the air was heavy and sodden. I called Max Abbott. A woman answered and told me that yes, Max would still receive visitors at this time of night. I hung up and even though I had been told she was dead, I tried to call Michelle. Still nothing. I wiped my face, which was slick with oil and sweat. I asked someone in the car next to mine how to get to Max's address. Oklahomans were nice, obliging people and I liked most of them so far.

After continually wiping sweat from my face just to have it reappear, I fidgeted in the marble entryway of Max Abbott's house. Maybe I should just leave this alone and go home. What the hell was I doing, anyway? A fool's errand. Michelle would laugh at me. I was just removing the keys from my pocket to leave when a noise at the top of the stairs startled me.

As the woman descended the stairs, I felt two things: one, a flash of shocked recognition. This was the redhead from the club earlier tonight! The one who had called me a pickaninny and blown me off. So, she was in a sham marriage to this dude Max Abbott and liked lesbian action on the side. Well, I wouldn't play that. The second thing I felt was a flush creeping over my body. It was especially prickly where my slacks met.

The woman was the sort who had three expressions: about to have sex, having sex, and just finished having sex. She was the kind whose hair was always mussed and tousled just right, her sloe-eyed glance more sultry and sparkling, her lips fuller and redder, her cheeks pinker and her voice huskier than anyone else's. She was the sort who loved a good roll in the hay and good food, and anything else in the world was a bothersome bore. More than that, she was beautiful. To many, God gave a bounteous, voluptuous body. To many, God gave a pretty face. To very few did he give both, and Lord have mercy, she was one. She looked as if she had just stepped out of a painting.

She wore a floor-length black filmy robe cinched so tightly at her waist, the knot was disciplinary. She had legs to her throat and long auburn hair to the small of her back. The voluminous fabric that belled out around her on her descent revealed nothing but emphasized everything. She had a bosom that rose off her chest like a young boy's bottom. Her breasts swayed and pulled against the thin gown, seeming as if they would climb up her neck any second. I kept my eye on them in case they did. She stood in front of me, waiting for me to look up and meet her eyes. I knew it and didn't. I stared straight at her breasts. I watched two spots of material on her chest gather, harden, and protrude as if pouting. I realized my mouth was dry and I swallowed with difficulty. Oh, God, for a lollipop, a sucker, a pen, a pencil, a straw, a cigarette. I would smoke ten at once. My heart beat faster as I restrained myself from grabbing this woman and knocking her to the floor. My mouth would fasten hard onto one of the pouty nipples, pinching the other to silence it. I would quench that nipple with my saliva. Deep sucking and a silvery kiss left on one, as I would switch to the other, biting it, chewing it like an eraser and—

"Come in." She twirled, turning away and walking into the living room.

I silently coached myself. Snap out of it. Don't go slobbering and drooling all over Max's wife. This chick is as straight as they come. Calm down, she's just a woman. I breathed. I fondled my matches. Just a woman like me. With that thought, I laughed out loud and smothered it by saying, "Thank you."

Okay, so she was dangerous. But she's Max's and where is he? And what the hell was she doing at the club earlier? I must have a certain attitude with a chick like this. Don't let her get to you, I coached myself.

"Sit down." She gestured to a tiny footstool before seating herself languorously on a chaise. I rejected the footstool and chose an overstuffed wingback and cleared my throat. I was thinking of her big, ripe ass, like melons bouncing on two strings. I had admired it as she walked toward the chaise. Oh, what I couldn't do with an ass like that. Smacking, slapping, spanking, grabbing, fucking, licking, biting, maybe I would just spread it and dive in. Just imagining the fragrance made my breath catch. I cracked my knuckles, feeling my fingers throb. A cigarette, goddammit. Please, please, just one and all this would be okay. I watched her open a box on a side table and extract a cigarette and put it in her mouth. Dunhill cigs. Poseur. Show smoker. But still, it was smoke. I leaned forward to catch a whiff. Obligingly, she blew smoke right into my face, never showing a single sign of recognition from the bar.

All right, I can be cool. "Aren't you going to offer me anything?" I asked.

She smiled. "You have to really, really want it."

I needed my mouth to close around a cigarette. The dry, smooth roundness of a good cigarette. The weight of it on my lips, its shape expressing my anticipation, its readiness to surrender itself to smoke in my mouth as I sucked on it with my breath, the firm balance it had, the fire in the tip… My mouth was dusty and my lips were aching, but I shrugged and said, "I don't want anything that's not given to me."

She grinned approvingly. "Then you must have very little."

"On the contrary, I have more than I need." I removed my lip balm from my pocket and smoothed it over my mouth. I let my hands rest on my knees. I caught her glancing greedily at my strong, graceful, square hands.

"Guess you're the furniture," I said. Our eyes met.

"Guess you're the Negro," she answered tranquilly.

"Why don't you go off and do your girly stuff with some of your little friends? Go study your vaginas, have a tickle fight in your panties, play with hair bows, whatever. Just leave so I can talk to the man of the house. Where's Max? I came to speak with Max."

"Who are you, Shaft?"

"Damn right. Can you dig it?"

"Shut your mouth, fool." We shared a brief laugh.

She stretched her legs in front of her on the chaise and then crossed them delicately at the ankles, causing the gauzy robe to split and fall open at the tops of her thighs. "I'm Max."

I stood angrily. "You're shitting me. Everybody in town has told me to talk to Max Abbott and *you're* Max?"

"Yes, sit down. It's a family name that I'll never tell you what it's short for, and don't *ever* call me Maxine."

I sat, trying to calm my mind. "I didn't expect you to be a woman."

"I didn't expect you to be African American."

"So what now?"

"I offer you a drink and you stay awhile…Suzy Q?"

"The name's Nora Delaney." I growled in response to the lighthearted insult. "And no…no…I can't drink right now. I need to smoke too much already."

"All right then, you ask me your questions and I bat my eyes and tell you I know nothing."

"Nice place you got here." I needed to change gears. Stay in control. I noticed even here inside an expensive home that the room, though cool, seemed marshy. I saw magazines that must have been exposed to the outside sitting on a counter curled into rolls and fat with wet swelling.

"Yeah, I'm a kept woman."

"Kept? Really? I didn't know anybody still did that."

"Yes. Find any butch dumb enough and rich enough and a girl can have everything and great sex too." Max inhaled on her cigarette slowly and deeply, stretching as she exhaled.

"How fortunate for you," I said woodenly. "I sure can't think of anything else to do with you."

"Oh, so you've thought of it?" Max said, all satin.

"Isn't that arrangement sexist? And archaic?" I didn't care if it was or not. I just wanted to keep talking.

"Tell that to this." Max opened the top of her robe to reveal two large scoops of breast barely sheathed in a black lace bra between which lay a diamond and emerald necklace, winking lasciviously. Max closed the robe again, clutching the neck as if she were a prude schoolmarm.

"So what does a girl like you have to do to get a cubic zirconia bauble like that?" I grinned, baiting her.

"I'm sure CZ is all you're familiar with," Max said. "Why, all I had to do was smile." To prove it, Max smiled.

I rolled my eyes. "Bitch musta been outta her fuckin' mind," I muttered.

"Butches are easy. Even easier than men. Remember how easy butches are?" Max said, laughing genuinely, making her one and only reference to our previous meeting at the bar. She then inhaled so her chest lifted and the rosy curved tops of her cleavage were visible for a few seconds.

"I imagine the butch who would cough up for that would extract a mighty high payoff."

"Yes, why don't you imagine that?" Max stretched her toes. "What else can you imagine?" She tipped a grin to me.

I bent and retied a shoelace. Then I cleaned a smudge from my shoe with a wet thumb. I shook my trousers as if they'd picked up dust and I stroked my damp scalp. All devices to betray the evidence of my imagining. Sure, I imagined it; I imagined it all: Max's legs wrapped around me, urging me on, faster, faster, harder, harder, Max's breasts bouncing like punching balls as I made Max beg me, as I made Max contort like a monkey, as I grabbed fists full of Max's hair and Max straightened and curved like an archer's bow. I imagined the wet gliding, the slipping and sliding, Max's full white bottom pink, her nipples hot and puckered, her mouth dusky and calling out to me, please, please, please more. I imagined every muscle in that lush body taut, reaching for me, for what I could do. I saw Max laid out before me, frosted with sweat and glistening, the entire naked whole of her, Max's belly completely exposed and poised for me to do as I wished. I saw Max quivering and trembling and panting and growling and finally… No, not yet. Not quite yet.

I checked my watch and turned the ring I wore round and round my finger. I cleared my throat again and said acidly, "I'm just disappointed that a strong, liberated woman would prefer this sort of arrangement." Dumb, but when lacking any words, falling back on righteous feminist outrage always worked.

"Where are you from, 1979? Lesbians as a collective are experiencing a new wealth. And with new wealth, the dykes who are collectors collect bigger and bigger treasures."

"So that makes you a ho—"

"*Trophy*," Max corrected, her eyes snapping. "Believe it or not, it's a full-time job. Shopping, getting my hair done, getting my nails done, facials, massages, waxing, plucking, working out, getting made up and dressed up, it's exhausting." Max turned and laid on her hip, facing me. "And that's just the behind-the-scenes work before the job really begins."

"I'm sure," I said dryly. "So you can do this, what else can you do?"

Max licked her lips and made her answer heavy. "Nothing."

"Ohh, your life is so hard, I bet you'd trade it all in for a doctorate of your own."

Max's laugh was like the tinkle of ice in a glass of gin and tonic. "Don't be silly. Skilled femmes get everything in the end."

I shifted impatiently. Watching Max suck luxuriously on her cigarette was almost unbearable. Time to ask the hard questions and get out of here. Get some fresh air. Pull it into her lungs like a drowning woman finally breaking the surface. It would be good enough to just get some Max-free air. Who was I kidding? I would run to the bar and decompress with a pitcher of beer and a binge of cigarettes. I would nick a bright red cherry out of the garnish tray. Then I would exorcise Max with that cherry I would crush between my teeth. I would enjoy the smashing, feeling the pop. Feeling it burst as I bit down. Grinding the soft flesh to pulp and feeling the slippery fruit slide down my throat and tasting the lingering sweetness. To be drunk. Seeing Max twirl a lock of her hair as she stared at me, I realized there weren't enough cherries in the world.

"Did you know Michelle?" I asked roughly. Get out fast.

"Only briefly."

"What do you mean?"

"I mean, I had an affair with her long ago."

"An affair?"

"Yes, we slept together once."

I continued before my mind could wander. "Only once?"

"Yes, you know, sometimes you need someone." Max folded herself in half and rested the side of her face on her shin. "But you only need her for the night." She blew smoke and blinked. "You know what I mean?"

"Michelle doesn't seem like your type. Isn't she a little…soft and feminine?" I reached over and cupped Max's chin playfully. Max sneered and jerked her chin away.

"You don't know me," she sniffed.

I smiled all the way to my toes. "Oh, but I do. Whatever happened, you two never slept together," I said and let it drop. "Then why is everyone in town saying you knew—"

Max shrugged, but her eyes glittered angrily. "Everybody," she snorted. "Who? Two people? Three? Lesbians can be vindictive, Nora." My name crawled out of Max's mouth like a pornographic picture. "What do you think of our petty little Tulsa community so far?"

"It was like meeting an angry bear. I just played dead and prayed," I answered.

Max laughed. "So you see what I mean."

I nodded. My breakup with Michelle had been cataclysmically ugly. I shuddered just remembering it. It had been like a small personal disaster.

"So you really don't know anything." I shrugged.

"Nope." Max grinned. "Just a kept woman, sheltered and pampered and utterly naïve."

"Oh, please." I stood, ending the interview and dismissing Max's preposterous remark. Without a further word, I strode to the cigarette box and snapped it open. In a split second, I closed my eyes and was lost in fantasy. Legs sliding apart under my commanding black hands, creamy, magnolia white skin yielding under my grip. Max's curly tangle of auburn pubic hair offered up in supplication. Please, Nora, please. Open me. Spread me apart, explore me. I am Braille, I am your food, I am your water. Pull my lips apart ever so slowly. Where do your fingers fit? What if you put your mouth on me? Red on red. Can you fit inside? All of you? Let my cunt suck all of you in and hold you there, your entire body, until I am satisfied. Tell me about myself. What can you do with me? What will you do to me? And when, when, when, *when*? I opened my eyes and took two cigarettes and put one in my pocket and the other I perched unlit on my lower lip. "No one keeps anything from me that I really want," I growled. I snapped my thumbnail over a match head and it obediently burst into flame. I lit the cigarette. Max lowered her eyes and smiled. Then Max stood, preparing to see me out.

Suddenly, I pinned Max to the wall, my cigarette smoking itself in my hand. I pressed with my weight and stretched to my full height. Max let out a tiny gasp of surprise. "You move just like a panther," Max whispered. I stared down at Max with smug satisfaction. I brushed a curly red tendril of hair from her face.

"Say you don't want it. Look at me and *say it*," I hissed, passion forcing the words into Max's ear.

Max looked up very slowly. She seemed to be struggling to veil the snapping fire in her eyes. Finally, she tilted her mouth and said, "I don't want it."

I laughed. I could feel Max's curves through our clothes. I leaned down again and spoke to Max's collarbone. "Keep saying that over and over. Maybe you'll convince one of us." Then I stepped back, regarding Max, looking for the crack, but there was none. Triumph and defiance mingled in her manner as I replaced the cigarette in my mouth. Max watched all of this silently, absorbing all, revealing nothing.

We talked as we walked to the front door.

"But perhaps those people you spoke to wanted us to meet." Max's tongue trembled at the corner of her mouth. Its seductive pinkness…its shining wetness… "For numbskull reasons of their own. But then we hit it off…and we—"

I shook my head. "I don't need any more trouble."

Max approached, desire rising from her robe in hypnotizing waves. "No trouble at all." Her voice was smoky and swirly.

I jerked open the door, surprised at my own force, and pushed it into Max.

Max just smiled, her eyes dark and twinkling. "Kissing a black man is just like falling face first into a velvet pillow. I wonder if kissing a black woman is the same?"

Max's lower lip hung open, and to me, it looked like a dewy slice of peach. I gripped the doorknob and walked out, after first leaning into Max and whispering, "You'll never find out. I came here for *nothing*." Then I slammed the door without meaning to. I looked back and saw Max watching from the window, her robe untied and open, exposing her bra and black panties. Perspiration pooling in all my hollows and creases, I got in my car and before I drove away, I looked again at the house. Max was gone. Because of her absence from the window, I had to clench my fists to keep from returning at a run. But I was angry. And upset. Angry because Max hadn't offered me the simple relief of a cigarette. Upset because I knew that if I succumbed, this Max would be no casual piece of ass. She would be a wild ride. The kind of ride that you know is dangerous but you get on anyway thinking you have the guts and the strength to do it and when you get off, you're changed. Maybe weaker, maybe stronger, maybe destroyed completely, you're different than the you that climbed on with such a gaming spirit.

Before I backed out of the driveway, I had to wait for pedestrians to pass. A group of white women out late. I watched them in the rearview. I shook my head noticing their butts. Oh, how I despised anemic, flat asses. I hated when Michelle would put on clothes and ask, does this make my butt look big? I always wanted Michelle's butt to look big. To say no to a woman asking that question was an insult. An insult enough to mean that that woman was sexless with no juice, life, or appeal. Women should fatten their asses and parade their succulence proudly. I would personally guarantee that such an action would result in more and better sex. Women should always want the answer to her butt looking big to be a resounding *yes!* Then, a tumble into bed. I glanced again at the house where that round, ample fruit of an ass still called to me.

I drove down the one-way street and when I was sure Max couldn't see, I put the car in park, pulled the emergency brake, and turned off the lights. I gripped the steering wheel like a life preserver, relishing the ice cold air blasting into my face from the air conditioner, and I breathed deeply for several minutes. Ducks quacked on the lake as they floated in the darkness. I considered slipping a hand into my trousers for some relief, but something told me that I needed a sharp edge for this business. So I concentrated on my breathing and banishing Max from my mind. How could Max have gotten to me? It's not like pussy had just been invented.

After perhaps twenty minutes, I was ready to leave. Just as I was reaching for the lights, something caught my eye across the lake at Max's house. With the landscape lights in her yard, I could see her garage door opening. Then headlights. Next, a car pulled from Max's garage onto the one-way street and started to slowly coast its way around the lake toward me to leave. I ducked out of sight. As the car passed, I caught a glimpse. It was Michelle's car. I was sick of these mysteries already and decided to follow it.

Chapter Eight

The driver was a lone black female. Following, I kept what I hoped was a safe distance. I had never tailed anyone. We drove and drove through deserted streets. The prettiness of the town evaporated, grew industrial, then abandoned, then ugly.

At last, the woman parked at Tisdale's Barbecue, a quaint white bungalow with big windows and hand-painted signs. It was open until three a.m. when things around here must really jump. I pulled into the gravel parking lot of the tiny A-frame bar next to Tisdale's. Then I walked toward the barbecue place, suddenly feeling queasy and scared. What if there *was* real danger here? I shrugged. All would unfold in due time.

"If a nigga could just get a motherfuckin' breath!" I shouted, leaning on the car for support, filling my chest with soaked air. I pictured my lungs blooming with mold, my armpits growing slidy with moss, tadpoles burping out of my mouth, my skin dripping saltwater. When I felt calmer, I lit a cigarette. The air was drier when I smoked.

I imagined lying on my back, Max's ample weight pressing me flat as Max straddled my eager face. I looked into the seed of heaven and strained to reach it. Max teased me, remaining out of reach as I got madder…

Compelled by my impulsive nature, I entered Tisdale's and was embraced by warmth and the savory smells of wood smoke, tender, juicy meat, and sweet, spicy sauce. There were several busy, loud groups, laughing and eating, enjoying their glorious mess. The woman I followed sat alone in a corner, eating ribs. I stepped up to the counter and ordered the same.

"Sweet or sour?" the enormous woman behind the counter drawled. She was the color of milk chocolate and had beautiful glossy skin that was clear and shiny with oil. She wore a head rag and a stained white apron.

"Sweet or sour what?" I asked uncomfortably. This was the first time I had been anywhere in the South and also the first time I had ever had what I suspected to be authentic barbecue. I felt the woman in the corner staring at her.

"Sauce," the counter woman answered.

"Sweet."

"It's mighty hot." The woman eyed me, full of doubt.

I regained some composure and smiled seductively. "Just the way I like it. Hot and sweet."

"Uh-huh." The woman rolled her eyes and took my money. "No refunds. I'll bring it when it's done. Have a seat."

I walked over to the person I had tailed and asked if I could sit with her. She let her eyes wander pointedly over the two empty tables nearby, then back to me. I resisted any explanation and just stood silently. At last, the woman shrugged and shoved a chair out with her foot. With a nod of thanks, I sat. The woman picked up another rib with both hands.

"I'm Nora Delaney." I gave my power smile.

The woman let go of her rib with one hand and without wiping it, she stuck it out for me to shake as she growled, "Sloane."

I shook her sticky, greasy hand briskly. Sloane had big muscular mitts thick with yellow calluses on the palms. I swallowed, just slightly uncomfortable. I remembered taking dates to Ethiopian restaurants in LA so I could check out their hands. Ethiopian food came without any utensils, so I was free to observe my dates' style and grace as they ate. This woman's hands told me: caution.

"Sloane Weatherly?" I asked.

"Yep."

"I've heard of you from a couple of people."

Sloane looked up, grinning unpleasantly. "Ah, my reputation precedes me."

I laughed, unable to relax. Usually, I was the intimidating one, the strongest one, the predator…in my game, in my job, in my love life. But this bulky-bodied butch was a little scary. She was built like a fireplug and every ounce was muscle. The way her shoulders bunched over her plate, Sloane reminded me of a grizzly devouring a salmon. I was solidly muscular too, but I felt like a toothpick in comparison.

"Places are open later here than I would've expected. I thought you'd roll up the sidewalks at six," I said, attempting humor.

Sloane studied me without blinking. "We only leave open the places we need. The absolute *essentials.*"

"Here's your dinner." The counter woman set a tray of ribs and sauce, coleslaw, potato salad, white bread and butter, whole jalapenos, a slice of raisin pie, and a strawberry soda on the table. "Enjoy."

"Thank you." I smiled again, and again, got nowhere with it. The woman harrumphed and switched her big ass tantalizingly all the way back to the kitchen.

"You got the same thing I did," Sloane observed.

"Yeah, I figured you would know what is good."

"I sure do," Sloane answered. I got a picture of Max in my mind and thought of the two of them together. A sick wave of jealousy washed over me, and suddenly I wasn't hungry, in spite of the delectable aromas. My hands itched for a cigarette. I longed to dash this plate to the floor and grind my heel in it. I needed a drink. A strong one. What had Max been drinking? Gin and tonic. My mouth ached for something to pull on. My lips needed to close around something and suckle it.

"Aren't you going to eat?" Sloane asked, dropping a rib bone.

"I guess." I picked up a rib, fat with meat and glossy with sauce. My teeth crunched in the crispy flesh that was saturated with smoke and sauce. The meat was chewy and tender. Ah, yes, this was the Real. The counter woman/cook had thrown in plenty of burnt ends. Mmmm, mmmm, goddamn, this was holy. It felt good in my mouth. I thought of Max's thighs, as ivory and milky as dogwood blossoms, as pink as fresh roses with a blush, and I tore into the ribs with ferocity, alternating with bites of spicy jalapeno and peppery onion that flared fire into my sinuses and cleaned my tongue. I devoured everything before Sloane had a chance to finish her coleslaw. I looked up, my face wet with grease, grinning big. I threw my last pepper stem into the carnal wreckage.

"Enjoy that, did you?" Sloane asked with a tiny, wry smile.

I laughed, suddenly feeling at ease. Darcy was wrong to advise against seeing Sloane. "Sure did. This is some *fine shit.*"

"Funeral is tomorrow," Sloane said casually, putting a toothpick in her mouth. I cleaned my hands the best I could.

"Whose funeral?" I lied.

"Oh, come on, I was there when you saw Max. I know you followed me. I heard you came from LA. Some hotshot coach."

"So?"

"So, I'm telling you. Funeral is tomorrow at the main Methodist downtown. Three o'clock."

"Did you know her?" I gulped my strawberry drink, enjoying the afterburn of the sauce and the acid of the bubbles. I wished it were a dry beer that was so cold it would hurt going down.

"Only a little."

"That's what everyone says," I mused, still shocked at the mention of Michelle's funeral.

"She couldn't keep herself out of trouble. I helped her out a couple of times. She was staying with me when it happened. I know you're her ex. I've got her parents' address if you'd like to check it." Sloane reached into her breast pocket and handed me a slip of paper. "I've got some of her sorry shit if you want to go through it. Mostly just trash, though."

"Yeah, Michelle said she came from a really poor family and never got over it. She was really into poverty."

With an inscrutable expression, Sloane rolled her toothpick from one side of her mouth to the other as she studied me. "Poor? You don't know shit."

"Really terrible, huh? Like South Central? Compton? Worse?" I asked, trying to picture soul-numbing, never-ending poverty in this clean, pretty toy town.

"Michelle? You got her all wrong."

"How's that?" My mind creaked back painfully to our relationship and late-night confessions and after-sex storytelling.

"She really sold you a bill of goods, didn't she?" Sloane shook her head, laughing huskily.

"What do you mean?" I asked, feeling like kicking something hard. We were together three years. Not long, but long enough to learn a few things about each other.

"Y'all ever come back here to visit?"

"No, why would we? She's from Oakland. I never knew why she came here after our breakup."

"Where'd she say she grew up?"

"Madison."

"*Wisconsin*? Oh, Lord." Sloane slapped her knee.

"What? Sloane, tell me."

Sloane got serious. "Listen, I don't know you and all and I don't know if I should be the one to tell you, you get me?"

I nodded.

"Okay, but since you're here now with all your questions, I'll do it."

I pushed my plate away and leaned forward, tense. A large family entered: grandparents, parents, aunties, uncles, sisters, brothers, and cousins. They were evidently familiar to the counter woman and the cook in the back because suddenly the little house rang with happy shouts. There was much hugging and laughing and slapping. The high-pitched greetings of the women rolled away from them in concentric circles, rippled through Sloane, me, and the other customers, touched all four walls, doubled in volume, and rolled back. Sloane and I watched, Sloane smiling sleepily, me irritated. The family's order was placed, with a lot more loud joking and joyful patois.

After a couple of minutes, against my better judgment, I was just getting ready to stand and take Sloane outside when Sloane touched my sleeve. Eventually, the group settled, dragging tables and chairs to form their tribal table.

In a fever of impatience, I turned back to Sloane to demand information when I saw her rise and throw her trash away and get a refill on her strawberry soda. She sat and took a long gulp.

"You got a cigarette?" I asked desperately.

"Don't smoke."

I sighed. "Neither do I. Okay, what don't I know about Michelle?"

"More like, what *do* you know?"

"Nothing?" I guessed.

Sloane grinned and touched her nose. "The chick is nasty. She's a liar." Sloane let that sink in. "She's never even *been* to Oakland or Madison. And she *ain't poor*. Her family is one of the wealthiest in town, maybe the state. The McKerrs. Heard of them? Oil dynasty. She disowned them long ago over some scandal and has been grifting ever since. They disowned her right back. I think everybody was after Michelle for one reason or another. I heard she tried her hand at some powerful blackmail. A senator or something. Blood to her daddy. She's never worked a day in her life, just a scammer. She lived off you, didn't she?"

"Yeah, but she was going to school, she worked part-time, she was gonna—"

"No, she wasn't. That's played. Check it, man. She's a student who ain't never spent an hour in class. She fed that line to every girlfriend she's ever had. She gets some old textbooks on the cheap and she stays gone at the same time every few days and nobody is the wiser. Why did you break up?"

"She stole from me, I cheated on her."

"Nice. Guarantee she cheated on you too. While she was supposed to be in class, she was hooking up and gettin' her freak on."

"How do you know all this?"

"Been knowing her and her family all my life. We went to school together."

"You went to school together? She's that rich and went to public school?"

"No." Sloane appraised me coolly. "I went to private school. Hated every minute."

"How do I know you're not lying?"

"You don't." Sloane shrugged. "Like I said, I don't think it's my place to tell you. But you can always check on what I've said and it will hold up. Just like anything Michelle ever told you will break down if you look."

"I'm kind of doing the amateur sleuth thing. Is there anyone else who might know more?"

"A regular gumshoe all the way from LA." Sloane leaned forward. "What do you think you're gonna find out? Where your money is? Who she sold your soul to?" Sloane laughed. "Her roommate might have something for you."

"Roommate?" My eyes sharpened. "Roommate or *roommate*?"

"What do you care? You broke up. She's dead, and you're on to better things. Am I right?"

"Well…"

"Her name's Amber. She works at this freaky bookstore, Light and Love. The landlord kicked her outta her place 'cause Michelle didn't pay the rent, so I don't know where she's staying, but you can catch her at work."

"I thought Michelle was staying with you?"

"She was because she had moved out of their place and stiffed Amber, which I did not know. With everything that has happened, my old place gives me the creeps. I won't live there anymore. Amber is flaky about living quarters, so try her at the bookstore."

My head was reeling. But when Sloane stood to leave, I had the presence of mind to grab her solid arm and say, "Hey, I might need to get hold of you again. Can I get your number?"

Sloane grinned and said, "You can reach me at Max's." She patted my shoulder and left. I gritted my teeth. Was this the butch who kept Max? Was Max all hers? Images of their sex haunted me and made me miserable in a million ways and completely oblivious to the large family behind me. I pictured Sloane's strong, dark hand sliding up Max's plump, pale, parted thighs. I imagined all the things Sloane would make Max do. Take that off; no, let me rip it off you. Come here. On your knees. Sloane getting a handful of Max's hair and making her arch until her raspberry nipples reached for the ceiling. Chocolate fist, auburn hair, the colors in my mind were intense. The two of them mixing their colors, blending their palettes, blurring… Max's soft sighs of surrender, her nails scratching Sloane's wide ebony back, Sloane growling in triumphant possession. Hers. Max was hers. Oh, God.

I absently bummed a cigarette from one of the men seated at the table behind me. I put it in my breast pocket without even noticing the brand. I thumbed the match with practiced ease, needing its tiny fire even without applying it to a cigarette. Was Sloane there now, telling Max all about me and how pathetically deluded I was? Then Max would laugh her sultry, tinkling laugh and Sloane would reach for her, her black eyes full of desire.

"Enough talk," Sloane might say. Sloane could park at Max's without an excuse. She could go into a room with Max and close the door. I crunched ice from my cup to cool my sudden dryness, my sudden anger. Sloane could beckon Max and Max would come. Max would come to her, just like that, anywhere, anytime, in front of everyone. I needed to let off some steam. I would cruise and cruise until I found someone to drown myself in tonight.

CHAPTER NINE

I threw my trash away and sauntered out the door without a backward glance to head back to the bar for some filly fishin'.

Once in the car, I wiped the sweat off my head and face and looked at my map of Tulsa to reacquaint myself with where I was versus the bar and Max.

Max's was so far out of the way to the bar from Tisdale's, in no stretch of rationalization could I just casually swing by on the way. The barbecue joint was north, the club was south and east, my hotel was downtown, and Max's was midtown. So I gave up trying to justify it and was grateful I was alone. "If I'd known Max was here, I would've moved long ago," I said, fumbling out of my pocket the extra toothpick I had taken and placing it between my lips. Nothing like a cigarette or a nipple, but it would do. Hell, a leaky ballpoint pen would do.

I drove off, scattering gravel and grinding the toothpick to soggy splinters as I headed for Utica Avenue and south. Then I lit the bummed cigarette and smoked it as if it were Max.

There it was, Max's street. I turned right onto Swan Drive and pulled over immediately to let the full effect come slowly. I hadn't paid much attention the first time I was here.

Max's house was Asian-inspired. It was a long, low, angular deep orange brick house with black accents. It could have been an antique Chinese lacquered box in some precious shop. It had marvelous huge lattice gates, a privacy wall, and its only adornment, a balcony with an awning that flapped invitingly in the breeze. The house, like most on Swan Drive, was set far above the street, so any open curtains were an invitation for the wandering eye to intrude. The house was moody and dark, and mystery clung to it like a mist. Even the way the huge trees that shaded the home rustled in the wind made my heart beat faster. I turned off the car and rolled down the windows. The air rolled in like a steam bath. I could hear the quiet chattering of the ducks on the lake as they swam in the moonlight, creating silver Vs of flashing brilliance. I thought all birds slept after dark, but obviously, I was wrong about so much. I suddenly felt at home with all of this: Michelle's death, Tulsa, Sloane, Max, and even my own spying. I breathed deeply, enjoying being here in this strange, wet city, on this bizarre errand.

My gaze sharpened at the turning off of some lights in Max's house. From this angle, I couldn't tell if Sloane was there or not and it didn't much matter. This was my time with Max. I felt an improbable intimacy and bittersweet aching that was mine and Max's alone. I got out of the car and closed the door quietly, as if Max would be listening and discover my presence. The air smelled so good, I stopped and closed my eyes and just enjoyed the summer scents of cut clover, mown grass, watermelons, and petunias. Sweat broke out on my brow like beads of anger. I let two pedestrians pass before I ambled to the sidewalk surrounding Swan Lake. This was a charming area for a romantic stroll under the old-fashioned street lamps, or for a thoughtful meditation on one of the many benches. There were lots of big trees, flowers, and tall ornamental grasses waving a welcome among the lily pads over which stretched a handsome wooden pedestrian bridge. The lake itself was home to a pair of majestic great blue herons that studied me without blinking as I passed. There were only two swans but they ruled the lake, floating regally from one end to the other. I neared the house and saw with disappointment that

Sloane's car, which had been Michelle's car, was indeed parked comfortably next to Max's shiny Lexus. I stood alone on the street, an unrequited Romeo sending darts of desire up to the house.

I hid behind a tree as I noticed movement on the dark balcony. It was Max, alone and smoking. My mouth watered at the prospect of both. Max paced and finally leaned over the front toward me, her silky robe shimmering and parting delectably.

With Sloane nowhere in sight, I had to battle the temptation to call to Max. I would rather die than look a fool in front of this woman, so I didn't. Instead, I tolerated the sweat dripping off my body and breathed the clenched knots out of my knuckles and relaxed into being a voyeur.

Oh, to be invited in, to be *beckoned* into the inner sanctum, even if only for a drink and a smoke. Just to be held in her eyes would be enough. The sensual prospect of just stepping over the threshold at Max's request made me shiver. I stunned myself by realizing I would *rather* talk to Max first than bed her. I actually wanted to *know* Max. So far, this had never happened to me. It was always sex first, talk later, and in the case of Michelle, let her move in too soon. In my experience, it paid to fuck first. It was an easy sorting system. I was horrified at the idea of spending hours, days, weeks, or *months* pursuing some woman chastely, getting attached and involved, and then having a dud in bed. Then I was stuck and it was always a mess to extricate myself. It was so much simpler to clarify the rules in the beginning and start off right. If the woman was good in bed, which I determined ahead of anything else, then I would consider giving more of my time from my mind and my heart. Then would come the dinners and dancing, the movies and parties.

Max was different. She was a contradiction to me. *Because* she had hooked me so deeply in her sex and *because* I breathed Max in like a drug and needed more and more, I wanted to reverse my modus operandi. This was too intense for me not to know Max. I felt an unfamiliar pang of guilty conscience as I remembered the soft femmes protesting with those same words to me, scornful and passion hungry, five minutes before I dumped them. So this is what it was like to be the girl. Maybe all women wanted this? These thoughts whizzed through my fevered mind as I watched Max take the breeze on the balcony. Even Her Majesty's skin shone wetly. Max was utterly oblivious to the pedestrians who walked by, some staring. Or she knew and didn't care. She stood proud and indifferent, her diaphanous robe swelling and shrinking with the current. I had relaxed, noticing that Max and I shared the same rhythm of breath. I could see her half-exposed, taut breasts rising and falling as she sent her thoughts into the night. Mesmerized by those plump globes, I wistfully wished she were thinking of me. Oh, how I wanted to reach up to her, to shout…but that was the kind of thing someone did in high school. And here I was, a respected professional, thirty-five years old, stalking a stranger. Max lifted her heavy curtain of hair and held it with one hand as she fanned her neck with her other hand.

At the sound of a car coming down the road, Max turned. I was tense too, dreading the sloppy reunion of someone, anyone, arriving, claiming Max, kissing her and leading her inside. In spite of that painful image, I couldn't tear myself away. Even if a lover fucked her there on the balcony, I could not leave.

It was just a random car. I sighed. Max sighed. Then she went inside the house flapping the robe for air and I waited to see where she would turn up. I saw a lamp go on in a huge glass room in the lower right corner of the house. Good God, it was her bedroom. My excitement at seeing this was tempered by anger that everyone else could too. How dare she live this way! Not only no curtains on her bedroom, but also walls of glass on a highly trafficked public street. How could she sleep on a stage? My horror deepened as I realized Max probably would've had sex in bed too. Lord have mercy, to be such an exhibitionist. To have all the wild, nasty, acrobatic, jungly, tender, sweet things happen under a microscope. Well, that wouldn't do. No, it certainly wouldn't. If Max were mine, those glass walls would have blackout draperies installed first thing. I was so shocked by the idea of dominating, taming, and changing Max that I ignored it completely and instead focused on the moment with her. I panted, trying to get a good breath. My eyes filled with tears and I sneezed, surprised by this occurrence like a horse seeing a snake. I was appalled and fascinated as Max removed her robe, slid into her four-poster canopy bed, arranged herself, and picked up a book and began reading. In the heat of my idiocy, I even strained to see the book title. After a few minutes of nothing else happening, I was a little exhilarated to see that Sloane wasn't joining her. Where was Sloane? Why wasn't she drinking her fill from the silken Max fountain? Why was Michelle's car here? I was confused and even more emboldened to climb the wall and knock on the glass. But I didn't. Like a vampire, I must be invited inside.

Finally, the park and the lake were quiet. I broke the spell by shaking my head and doing deep knee bends. While Max still read like a mannequin in a store window, I went for a run around the lake. I didn't care that I wasn't dressed for it. I didn't care that the mugginess was like a smothering sheet wrapping me in a cocoon. Without a cunt or a cigarette for comfort, I needed this. I loved feeling the slap of my feet on the pavement. No matter how hard I pressed, the earth always pressed back, supporting me. I paced myself, breathing slowly and deeply, struggling to acclimate to the syrupy air. I felt strangely at home while running. I loved my strong, lean body and everything it could do so easily.

I ran hard. I ran until my lungs heaved and my body streamed with sweat as if I had stepped through a waterfall. I ran to outrun my sex, but it kept up. I wished Max could watch me play ball. I sprinted the last hundred yards, collapsing into laughter on the trunk of my car, overcome with my own dementia. I stretched for a while, figuring I had done four miles, four times around the lake, and that was okay. I enjoyed being an athlete. A jock or a hardbody is what others have called me, but I couldn't bear to describe myself that way. I gasped, trying to catch my breath. My lungs felt tight and gummy and full of paste. My eyes were still weeping and I felt congested and sneezy. I glanced at Max's bedroom, wishing only to bum a cigarette, but the windows were dark now. It gave me a thrill to think that maybe Max had noticed me and was pressed to the glass in the blackness, watching me lustfully.

I shook off the silver beads of sweat and pulled roughly at my crotch, deciding I would return to my hotel alone. Max was alone, so I would be. We'd be alone together. I liked that.

Once in my hotel room, I tore off my clothes and collapsed into bed, asleep even before my skin cooled.

Chapter Ten

For unclear reasons, perhaps best not examined closely, I had decided to follow the Amber lead. I had curiosity and time—two ingredients that could result in any outcome. So I had arranged for the wake-up service to call early so I could talk to this bookstore woman, have a nice run, eat lunch, and get to the funeral.

I fought my way out of heavy layers of sleep to hear the phone ringing. My genitals still throbbed and twitched from last night's spying. I derived a perverse pleasure from this teasing torture. Was Max calling? I couldn't find the lamp switch, so I groped for the phone, knocking it from the nightstand. I had what I guessed to be a sinus headache.

"Hello?" I croaked.

"This is your eight a.m. wake-up call," a computer voice said. I hung up and stretched.

I turned on the television and saw that the local weather people were issuing dire warnings. "Don't go out at dawn or dusk because of the mosquitoes; don't go out in midday; check on neighbors and relatives; watch children and the elderly; make sure pets have shade and water; do not exert yourself in any way if at all possible; stay hydrated; allergens and smog are strong; use sunscreen if you must be outside, and these are the warning signs of heatstroke…" I turned it off, flopping back on the bed, yawning.

I needed information. Sloane might know. Darcy might know. I sat up and scrubbed my eyes. I called Max's number and the woman who answered said neither Max nor Sloane were home. Take a message? No. I hung up and rummaged through my pockets for Darcy's number and dialed.

"Darcy, go!" Darcy barked after half a ring.

I laughed, still not used to the way she answered the phone. "This is Nora."

"Yeah, what's up? What's going on?"

"Well, I don't know anything about this city and I want to go for a run." The thought lazily crept across my mind of just running around Swan Lake again. "In a pretty place. And then I need to eat. Know any restaurants?"

"Going to the funeral later?"

"Yeah." I squinted at the clock, wanting a cigarette. The smog of smoke would cushion me from Darcy. I also needed some aspirin. This woman put me on edge. I hoped fervently that Darcy, Ava-Suzanne, and Jhoaeneyie would be busy and I could eat by myself or try Sloane again. I dreaded calling Sloane because I was so afraid of seeing her, fresh from bed and sex-rumpled, happily giddy and deeply satisfied and smelling like Max. And if anyone in the world could recognize that, it was me.

"Well, Riverparks is the place to run. It's miles of paved path on the riverbank. I used to run there all the time."

I tried and couldn't picture Darcy's doughy body running anywhere.

"But I'm into isometrics now. You know what that is?" Darcy continued.

"Yes, but where—"

"I do it twice a day and it really shows. Ava-Suzanne can sure tell the difference." Darcy chuckled. "I would come run with you, but I get shin splints. I really miss it, though it can be bad on your joints. Are you sure you want to run?"

"Yeah, I'm used to it. So how—"

"Well, suit yourself. No more of that high-impact stuff for me. I'll be starting Pilates soon. Ever heard of it?" She pronounced it "Pie-latts."

I rolled my eyes. Ain't this some shit, I wanted to say. Instead of opening the drapes onto the criminally bright, scorching day, I switched on the dim bedside lamp and studied the Tulsa map. The city was bigger than it looked. "Yeah, I've heard of Pilates." I pronounced it correctly. "Now," I said as I would to an ornery freshman on my team, "what river is that?" I scratched my stubbly head. I'd need to shave my scalp before the service.

"Arkansas River, can you find it?"

"Sure."

"Okay then, now, where to eat…you like Tex-Mex?"

"Sure."

"Oh, hold on." Darcy covered the receiver and I could hear her talking. Then she said, "Ava-Suzanne says why don't we all meet at Café Kokopelli around one?"

I rolled my eyes and groaned inwardly. I had asked for it, hadn't I? "That would be fine."

"Then we could share a ride to the funeral."

"Oh, I've already promised Sloane," I lied.

Cool silence. "Sloane? Sloane Weatherly? Not a good idea, but whatever. Café Kokopelli is at Thirty-fifth and Peoria. Can you find it or should we pick you up? I'll be in the BMW."

"No, no, I can find it. Is it near Swan Lake?"

Darcy paused meaningfully. "It can be if you like."

"I'll find it, don't worry," I said hastily. "See you there at one o'clock." I laid out my funeral clothes, put on baggy shorts and T-shirt and headed out.

I reached my rental car and there was heavy moisture and condensation clouding the windows. I had missed the fog as it had gathered during the night and spread through the streets, touching everything before it melted. I snapped on the air conditioner and turned on the wipers. I drove to the bookstore, which was midtown and close to Max's. I had to exert all my will not to dump the game plan and just drive over to Swan Lake, bust in on Max, and roll all over her, tangling both of us in body-warm bedsheets, laughing, breathless, rubbing skins. I was home at last. Later, I promised myself. Later.

The bookstore was in part of an old foundry that had been lovingly restored and that had kept the original exterior. There were spectacular oak and sweet cherry trees all around the building. Their leaves were turning brittle and yellow and falling into heaps on the sidewalk. The ornamental lawn was crisp. Some marigolds in boxes were the only plants thriving. The foundry had been converted to shops. I went inside. It was a huge space, nicely cool and dim. I heard the phone ringing insistently over the New Age music. All I could see were bookshelves. Hundreds of them. Mismatched and packed to bulging. The smell of incense was overpowering.

"Look out!" A woman whizzed by on Rollerblades and stopped at one of the phones. She wore a tiny gauzy skirt and a tight half shirt. She had short straight brown hair, closely cropped. She had tattoos on her arms, her legs, and her belly. She wore fifteen rings on each hand, five earrings, and a navel ring. "Light and Love," she snapped, thoroughly put out. "Yes, I do readings over the phone, but I can't right now, I'm swamped. You need to call back either after I've closed or before I open tomorrow." She hung up.

The phone rang. I stood next to a shelf that was labeled "Ouspensky and Gurdjieff." I was fascinated and wanted to watch. I noticed the heads of many other browsers among the shelves.

"Light and Love," the woman barked. "Yeah, we have the Ephemeris. What year and type? Uh-huh. Rosicrucian? Yeah, we have that. Until nine p.m." She glided to a customer service area that was in the center of the enormous room and raised three steps. She went up and sat on a stool. "Bear, are you still here?" She was exasperated.

"I told you, Amber," a man whined. My look sharpened.

Bingo. That was the woman. "I'm dating a faerie. Is that weird?"

"No, we've all done that a time or two, am I right? But I can't help you."

"Don't you have *anything*? Any book about this that would show me where her head is at? I need to get into her headspace."

"Well, I know an alien abductee you could talk to."

"Whoa." Bear laughed, holding up his hands. "That's a trip."

"Other than that I don't know. Like I said, the faerie section is over there. Everything we have about faeries, headspace and otherwise, will be there." She pointed and added, "Perhaps a therapist could help more."

A woman approached the counter and held something out to Amber. "Can I use black tourmaline for anger?"

"You bet."

"But what about for creativity?" she persisted. Bear wandered off to thumb through the faerie section again.

"For creativity, you want this," Amber said, handing the woman a stone. "Tiger eye. They also come in blue, but those are rare. This will work fine."

A large golden retriever wandered past me, followed by a little boy, barely a toddler. I noticed the poured terrazzo floors slightly streaked with Amber's wheel skids.

I began browsing. In a glass case, I saw embroidery sets called "Stitches for Witches." Next to that were tiny cast iron cauldrons no larger than a tennis ball. On top were elaborate candleholders bearing likenesses with their names: Cat Wizard, Wolf Council, and Wizard Retreat. On the wall were mounted dragon sconces for sale. I stopped short when I reached a locked deep glass cabinet filled with wands. They were all types, from simple dark wood to elaborate, gem-encrusted with their own purple velvet carrying cases. On the end of each wand was a very sharp crystal. I sucked air at the price tags—$1,500!

Amber skated to my side. "Who are you?"

"I wanted to ask you—" I began. The phone rang.

Amber bellowed, "I've got someone needing a Scorpio pendant *gift-wrapped*, someone else wanting to look at Tarot decks, another one needing a new moon goddess pentagram, a guy wanting to buy that sarcophagus, and now this. She better get me some fucking help around here." Then she rolled off to get the phone. I waited. Amber skated back.

I smiled. "Do you have a minute?"

"Does it look like I have a minute?" Amber said. "You want to know about the wands and if I'm single, right? I can always tell. I have a gift for insight." She clattered around to the rear of the case to unlock it. "Which one do you want to see?"

I was almost speechless. "Well…I…"

Amber addressed the ceiling. "That's all I need, another damn magician. You know what happened last time. But if that's what is in the cards, then make it so. Blessed be."

I laughed. "No, no, you got me all wrong."

Amber smirked. "Sure I do."

"Hey, listen, I'm just standing here. I don't give a shit about all this crap."

The phone rang. "Stay here," Amber commanded. She skated off to answer it. I gazed at various titles on a display table. *The Dumbass' Guide to Wicca and Witchcraft*, *Gunilla's Guide to Massage*, *The Tibetan Book of the Dead*, *Zen and the Art of Motorcycle Maintenance*, *Be Here Now*, *666* by Aleister Crowley, *Tantric Yoga*, *Easy Vegan Recipes*, *Magical Herbs*, *The Gospel According to Thomas*, *How to Levitate*, *The Qaballah*, *What You Should Know about Gnosticism*, and *Natural Childbirth.* I was about to pick one up, I didn't know which one, when Amber returned.

"You're a Capricorn, aren't you?" Amber said, nodding.

"What? No. My birthday is in May."

"I can always tell. Cappys are so stubborn." Amber laughed.

"So listen up. We can go out, but there are some things you need to know first. I am devotedly bi and I like it. I only do open relationships. Monogamy just kills me, you know what I mean?"

"I only came here to ask you—" I spoke slowly from shock.

"Amber," someone called. "I need two grams of dragon's blood."

Amber squeezed my arm. "Don't go away."

A customer nudged me over so she could look more closely at the wands. My skin was beginning to crawl.

"Aren't these beautiful?" the customer said reverently. "I wish I could buy all of them."

I just watched, feeling so alien, I might have grown horns or sprouted tentacles.

"I'm a light worker," the woman said and at my look of bewilderment, she added, "I work in the light. I work *with* light. And you're someone with immense fire and energy. I could tell immediately."

I cleared her throat. "Can you tell me…"

The woman smiled, looking eager.

"Where is Earth and how do I get there?"

The woman laughed and walked to inspect the mortar and pestle sets. Amber skated back, a lit cigarette dangling from her mouth.

"What's that?" I sniffed, suddenly interested.

"Clove cigarette. Try it." Amber placed it between my lips. I got a strong whiff of patchouli from Amber's skin.

I smoked and smiled. It was good. I started feeling a little buzzed. "You sell these here?"

"Yeah. That and American Spirit. No, keep it," Amber said when I tried to return the smoke. Amber removed another from her skate boot and lit it from a lighter she stowed in her skirt. "Really mellows me out. You know what I mean?"

"Sure. Now listen. I came to ask about Michelle."

Amber smiled wryly. "You don't really want to pull on that thread, do you?"

"Why wouldn't I?"

"It sounds a helluva lot better than it lived."

"What does that mean?" I was loving the luxury of smoking in a shop.

"Capricorn, why don't we go out for a drink after I close so many hours hence?" Amber grinned, tapping her ashes to the floor. The phone began ringing. "I gotta go. But think on this: The easiest person to lie to is the one who wants to be deceived."

"What does that have to do with me?"

"I know who you are." Amber smiled, skating backward. "And I will enjoy trying you on for myself. See you at nine sharp tonight." Amber reached the phone.

"Aren't you going to the funeral?" I called.

Amber shook her head, the phone ringing underneath her hand. "I said good-bye when I kicked her sorry ass to the curb. I gotta work. A funeral is for the people who care." Amber licked her lips and air-kissed me. "Light and Love," she yelled into the telephone.

I shook my head. Another dead end. I dropped my butt and ground it out. This crazy place, Amber talking in riddles and trying to seduce me, which left me cold. I left to go for my run.

CHAPTER ELEVEN

I drove to the river just because of my unfamiliarity with the town. Had I realized how close to the hotel it was, I would've jogged to it.

Instead of parking right away, I drove farther down on Riverside Drive, from Southwest Boulevard to 121st and back, just admiring the scenery. Tulsa was a beautiful city. It was bursting with trees. Like a city had been built in the forest. I saw seagulls, which I didn't expect to see away from the beach, and herons gliding gracefully over the water. The entire stretch of track was pretty and made me consider moving here. There were lots of people out, *white* people to be sure, but that didn't faze me. Even in these cremating temperatures, people were jogging, biking, blading, playing Frisbee golf, rugby, and volleyball. Families, couples, and singles were strewn on blankets in the grass. Dogs barked and ran with the joy of life. Children shouted and screamed from the playground equipment, and vendors were selling water and juice and ice cream and pretzels. I pictured myself here…buying a house close and running here every day.

When I returned to Southwest Boulevard, I did a U-turn and parked, thinking I would run seven or eight miles if I watched the time. Once out of the car, my sunglasses fogged, I began sneezing, my eyes began watering, all in a flash. I stretched and I forgot all my miseries and discomforts as my spirit soared. The upcoming funeral did not bother me now. I took off, loving the feel of my feet hitting the ground, propelling me. I pulled air into my lungs greedily, speeding past joggers and walkers and even some slow bikers. I loved my legs that were as strong and dependable as iron. I felt I could jump any hurdle today. I nodded, smiled, at everyone I passed. Birds sang, locusts buzzed, crape myrtles bloomed, squirrels chittered, and I ran through it all, the river and I running silently together. I even loved the soggy air that wilted me. In the car, I drank and drank of the water I bought on the return run. But my cottonmouth persisted. I threw the empties over my shoulder into the back. I stopped at a drugstore, and to my everlasting irritation, like a failure or a defeat, bought a sinus and allergy relief medication and dry-swallowed two before I left the store.

Back at the hotel, my clothes wringing wet, I checked my messages—none—showered and shaved my scalp with practiced efficiency. Then I admired myself dressed in the mirror. "I am so, so *fine*. Max should be so lucky."

I found Café Kokopelli with no trouble. Again, when I stood, rising out of the car, my sunglasses fogged me blind. The restaurant had sheltered outdoor seating with ceiling fans, several floor fans, and an overhead mister that hissed cool microscopic water droplets onto the diners. The restaurant also had twinkling lights and jazz grooving softly in the background.

Ava-Suzanne, Darcy, and Jhoaeneyie were waiting, having saved a table nearest the cold, black outdoor fireplace. Ava-Suzanne wore two mothy sweaters and she rubbed her arms and hugged herself continually as if she were cold. Darcy, when she had a chance, sandwiched Ava-Suzanne's hands between hers, trying to keep her warm. Jhoaeneyie was booming, woofing, and gesticulating about something. I watched this little show from the parking lot with distaste.

After I was seated, I felt Darcy's gaze penetrate me in a particularly disturbing way. I ignored her and reached for the chips and salsa.

"See that?" Darcy gestured to the parking lot full of expensive cars. "I like to keep an eye on her."

I guessed she was bragging about her BMW again, so I just nodded absently.

"So, I hear you met Max," Darcy said snidely. As she sipped her herbal tea, Ava-Suzanne scowled at me. Jhoaeneyie whistled.

"Is that what you heard?" I replied smoothly.

"She's something else, isn't she?" Darcy asked, her voice low. Ava-Suzanne knocked one of her sharp elbows into Darcy's ribs. "Oh, honey, I'm just talkin'. You're my sweet pea. Here, take your tinctures." Darcy removed two bottles from her bag and handed them to Ava-Suzanne. "Yeah, Max and I almost hooked up."

I turned my gaze to Darcy. "What?"

Darcy grinned. "Max and I were almost a couple." Ava-Suzanne squirted tinctures under her pale tongue, blew her nose on a used tissue, and buttoned her bulky sweater.

"Yeah, you and every other butch in town," Jhoaeneyie added with a wink. "She's a dirty skirt. When she's single, it's every dyke for herself because that one goes on a trampage."

"She wasn't like that when she and I were together. I had a calming influence on Max."

"Is that right?" I crunched angrily on a chip. I stared at Ava-Suzanne, who had leaned back in her chair with her eyes closed to catch the sun on her pallid skin. This chick must be a riot in bed.

"Yeah, it was years ago, before my sweet pea. Didn't Max mention it?"

I grinned, feeling like a shark. "Nope, sure didn't." I wished Jack were here to whisper the truth in my ear. What would he say about this?

"She has *issues*, you know. Made her run away. Maybe it still hurts her too much." Darcy shrugged and sipped her iced tea.

The cubes had dissolved and the glass had sweated a lake on the table. Ava-Suzanne stared at us for a second with one cold eye.

"Hurts *her*?" I couldn't resist asking. Then I gave up. I really didn't want to fight about what had to be a fantasy and so just agreed. "I know you're right. Max carries her wounds deep."

"That's so true," Darcy said dreamily.

Jhoaeneyie laughed like a horn blatting. "I *know* that's right."

"Lay off Max for a while, okay?" Darcy barked.

"Yeah, Jhoaeneyie, let her go already," Ava-Suzanne added, showing fang.

"Hey, she's nothing to me anymore. I've *moved on*." Jhoaeneyie leaned forward with her face all sincerity. "I *hate* being right about her. I really do. It hurts me."

"Well." Darcy pointed at Jhoaeneyie. "That would be true if even one speck of it were true."

"Whoa," I interrupted. "Time out." They all looked at me. "How are the margaritas?"

CHAPTER TWELVE

Our food arrived and we began eating in silence. I enjoyed the place. Tiny sparrows pecked at crumbs at the feet of the diners. I crushed a chip and threw it to the birds. I luxuriated in the low mumble and laughter of others around me. The jazz and the shade from the burning sun and the warm breeze transported me to a contentment I hadn't known off the court since before I let Michelle move in.

"Excuse me," Darcy barked to the waitress. "This isn't right. I ordered blue corn tortillas, not white. And I wanted fruit instead of black beans. And I want extra sour cream." Darcy thrust her plate into the hands of the waitress, who mumbled an apology and strode off. Darcy rolled her eyes and wiped sweat from her forehead. Ava-Suzanne picked anemically at her food, piercing tiny pieces with her fork and then smelling them before returning each bit to the plate, rejected. Her food looked as if she had taken a big spoon and stirred it all into a quagmire. I ate of mine, relishing everything. It was hot and delicious and spicy and pleasingly Tex-Mexy. Plus, if I finished quickly, I would leave sooner.

"How was your run?" Darcy asked, twiddling her thumbs. Ava-Suzanne shoved her plate away with disgust and nibbled a chip, her sallow skin emanating unhappiness. Jhoaeneyie just kept shoveling it in.

I spoke with a full mouth. "Oh, it was beautiful. I—"

"I used to run ten miles a day when I was single. I'd run every year in the Tulsa Run, you know. Really big deal. But Ava-Suzanne convinced me to give it up for the good of my healing. It was just too much stress on my joints. Plus, it's more time for us together." Darcy smiled and patted Ava-Suzanne's leg. I chewed madly, trying to keep the laughter down. Where were Jack and gin and smokes when you needed them? I swallowed fast and sneezed into a napkin and dabbed my eyes.

"Allergies? Us too." Darcy studied me as if I were a specimen. "Oklahoma will do that to you, worst state in the Union for—"

I protested, my face clogged, "I've never…I don't…"

Darcy waved me away. "Doesn't matter. Natives can suddenly develop them. No one knows why."

"You see," Jhoaeneyie blared, "Oklahoma has the worst air quality with regard to pollen and natural allergens. Let's just say that if you come here, it will make you sick."

Ava-Suzanne smiled and sparkled.

"Here, I've got…" Darcy searched her pockets. "Love puppy, what do you have with you that we can give to our friend Nora here?" Ava-Suzanne rolled her eyes and made an ineffectual gesture and shrugged, leaning back and closing her eyes again.

I was never sick a day in my life, but I held my stuffy head. "No, no, I'm okay. Forget it." I didn't want to incur debt to Darcy. So I acted fine and began eating again. "So, I met Sloane Weatherly and she was cool," I said.

"Well, she may seem that way at first, but she's bad news."

"Yellow means caution," Jhoaeneyie added.

"Why? What happened?"

"I'd rather not say," Darcy said in such a way that she rather would say. "Aside from the little run-in she and I had, she's also mixed up in this Michelle murder along with Max, probably."

"Sloane? You think Sloane killed Michelle?"

"Shh!" Darcy ordered as the waitress brought her second plate.

"For God's sake, have some discretion," Jhoaeneyie said, motioning for me to tone it down. In response to Jhoaeneyie's loud demand, several nearby diners quieted.

"I think you're mistaken," I said loudly.

"And what do you know? You've been here, what, two days? I've been here all my life," Darcy said.

"You just don't know the score around here," Jhoaeneyie said.

I drank my water, wiped my mouth, and stood. "Well, we'll see. I gotta book." I left more than enough money for my share and tip. I hoped Darcy wouldn't pocket the excess and stiff the waitress. The funny feeling that in this strange land, I should use foreign currency rather than U.S. dollars swam briefly in my mind. But I shook it off to allergy medication.

"See you at the funeral, pal," Darcy called. Ava-Suzanne waved, wincing.

"Take care," Jhoaeneyie said.

Once in the car, I blew my nose and consulted my map to find the church. The dread was suddenly upon me like a straitjacket. Michelle had been a woman I loved, or thought I had. She was a woman I had frequently fucked. This was a woman I had argued with just days before. And she was dead.

This dead Michelle was the one who smiled so sweetly and yielded so often. I was going to say good-bye to the body of Michelle, who pushed me to take risks and be more daring both on the court and in my profession. Michelle, who made me coffee every morning of our lives together. Even if we had passed out from fighting so long the night before, just the smell of the coffee brewing was like the scent of reconciliation. This would be the Michelle who always taped the right NCAA games for me when I couldn't be home, the Michelle who left silly notes in my briefcase, and the one who made blueberry muffins from scratch. This would be my final farewell to the woman who had charmed me into letting her move in too soon, who had turned me on to sushi, who had introduced me to rock climbing and sailing, who surprised me in the shower, sudsy and slick, and who had a passion for lilies. Michelle was the girlfriend who came to all my games whether I was coaching or playing, and who folded my briefs and boxers just right after they were laundered. Michelle, of the brown hair and brown eyes, supple waist, and tiny ass. Michelle, whose breath was hot in the night, who loved crossword puzzles and collecting glassware. Michelle, who rubbed my shoulders and called me "daddy."

I stared into space. The map lay forgotten. The funeral was forgotten. I must have a cigarette or die. I was so used to cadging smokes, I lowered the car window abruptly and ordered a passing man to give me a cigarette. He complied eagerly, reaching into his shirt pocket and extracting a single from the few he had left in the paper pack. I assumed he was afraid of my bald, aggressive blackness. Or maybe everybody is just extry-nice here in Oklahoma. I thanked him and closed the window again. It was sizzling outside, and smothering in the car with my dress clothes on and no air. I didn't care. Michelle was dead; it seemed little enough to suffer in the car awhile. I thumbed the match, lit the cigarette, and sucked it all the way to my tailbone. Fucking shit, it was a menthol. I despised menthols, but was grateful for the smoke anyway.

I dashed my hands across my wet eyes and felt calmer as I smoked.

This was also the Michelle who used her soft sex as a weapon and bargaining tool. I slept indignantly on the couch for countless nights, proudly refusing to play that. This was also the Michelle who had pawned my bicycle without asking, and who bought a book on lethal, undetectable poisons. "I won't visit you in prison," I had said, joking to cover my fear. This was the Michelle whose cell phone constantly went off like an irritated cricket, and when pressed, Michelle insisted it was "college stuff." Michelle never let that phone out of her sight, so I never had a chance to look at it. I had never needed a phone when I was in college, but I just assumed that times had changed. Michelle was several years younger, after all. This was the Michelle who also was a little crazy and cruel when we fought. Michelle started arguments regularly, I came to realize, so that she could storm out and stay gone. This was the woman who never spoke of a past or any family at all, and only the thinnest of stories, in hindsight, about Madison and Oakland to cover spans of years. This was the woman who had *stolen* from me. *Stolen!* Oddly, of everything I was willing to take and even hitting such a low as to cheat on Michelle, the stealing was the last straw. I was glad that I had never given Michelle access to my bank account and credit cards, though Michelle had angled for them repeatedly. This was the woman who, as I was finding out, was a heartless, filthy liar and possibly a deranged psychopath who was murdered for her trouble.

I finished my cigarette, finally turning on the a/c. Not feeling sad anymore, but tall and clear, I drove to the church.

What happened to you, Michelle? I thought. I arrived at the church and was startled by the presence of several news crews in the parking lot, but then realized this might be a big local story. I took the program an usher handed me. I was early enough to get a back-row seat. I was the most recent lover, usually a position of honor at the front and carefully tended by hovering grief divas, but Michelle was an ex and there had been no time to achieve peace and no one here knew me anyway. This was not Michelle's and my shared community.

It was a large Christian church of some kind; I paid no attention to what kind. Methodist, Sloane had said, whatever that meant. To me, organized religion was for fools. This church was a glorious, tremendous tribute to the Lord that wealthy white men built. The church was *so* big, in fact, that I knew they would never fill it for the likes of Michelle. A celebrity, maybe. Perhaps I should move up twenty or thirty rows. How did a little town like Tulsa support a church of this size? It was fearsome and oh, so somber. Someone played tastefully on the enormous pipe organ that was raised above it all at the front of the church. At least for the time being, the press was respectful enough to remain outside. Or they were kept out, as I remembered the rumored wealth and assumed there to be a matching power of the family.

I looked at the program: *Michelle Wilson McKerr, born June 10, died July 23. Services: July 30, three o'clock at Main Street Methodist Church.* I tried to swallow the pincushion of shock at seeing these words. These words in print, in black and white that Michelle was no more. This was it. This was real. I needed so many drinks, I vowed I would actually buy cigarettes after the funeral and get poisonously drunk and then flee this town as fast as I could as soon as I was sober enough to return the rental car. Forget all the mysteries, forget Max, forget Michelle, forget all this trouble and grief.

"I need to play ball," I whispered fiercely.

Movement caught my eye. Max came in, looking tragically beautiful and fetching in gray. Very nice, I thought, forgetting just as quickly about leaving town. Very tasteful of her to attend and to wear gray, not black. A gesture of respect to be here, yet she had nothing to mourn, so no black. Let the family wear black if they would. Max's riotous raven red hair was pinned in a French twist and her dress was high-collared and form-fitting like a military uniform. One strand of pearls lay on her chest and she wore sensible flats. But for all that, to me, she just looked like a naughty librarian with breakaway clothing that could only disguise her temporarily before her true sensual ripeness came busting out.

I pictured that, smiling a little. Hairpins flying, buttons popping, zipper ripping, nylons slipping, and there was my fragrant Oklahoma peach.

Someone I didn't know escorted Max to her seat and I felt indignant. I saw Sloane bringing up the rear, wearing sunglasses. I decided to sit next to her and so unfolded my big body out of the pew and greeted her. She gave me the butch nod and we traded handshakes. She was sitting in the row directly behind Max and whomever, which suited me just fine. Once settled, over the throbbing, melodramatic strains of "How Great Thou Art," I whispered to Sloane, "Who's that?" and pointed discreetly at Max's companion.

Sloane, who hadn't removed her sunglasses, leaned close to hear me, her black leather pants squeaking agreeably. As an answer, she shrugged, shook her head, and put a finger to her lips. Offended at the implied scolding, I withdrew. Max's neck was right in front of me, her silken white skin begging for a mere brush of my fingers. I imagined how startling yet perfect my dark hand on her ivory throat would look. Max would crumble and be mine, leaning back against my strong solidity and surrendering everything as she relaxed her head to rest on my shoulder. Did Max even know I was behind her? I was accustomed to dominating, so I spread my legs wide and leaned back, drawing myself up and sending Max vibes of definite intention. Was I mistaken or did I see her twitch? I longed to caress the curly tendrils that escaped the severe updo. I saw her sigh and whisper something to her companion. Sloane read the program. I was going to burn in hell for having these thoughts in a church at my ex's funeral, my new conscience chastised me. I saw Darcy and Ava-Suzanne and Jhoaeneyie wave. I wondered where Jack was and wished he were here. He would certainly talk to me and maybe share a secret flask. Jhoaeneyie, Darcy, and Ava-Suzanne sat far away once they saw Sloane, who wasn't aware of them. I now noticed the pews filling gradually. Not filling more than ten back, for each pew was fifty feet long, but filling, nonetheless. The organ played "Sweet Hour of Prayer." Finally, I noticed the coffin. It appeared to be mahogany. It had gold, carved angel and cherub figures flying up to heaven perched on each corner. The tens of ostentatious sprays of lilies had almost obscured it. There were lilies of every type everywhere, including a massive arrangement on the casket. Apparently, her favorite flower was a consistent truth on which everyone agreed about Michelle. I felt remiss that I hadn't sent any. But to whom? I just found out Michelle grew up here. This family had no idea who I was. "Send them out of respect," my mother said in my head, "and it might mean something to them even if they don't know you. Lord knows if I lost one of my babies, I would want to see who all cared." Yeah, okay, Ma, I vowed.

At "Amazing Grace" my tears rose again and I chewed my cheeks hard to stop them. I heard the doors close and the crowd get quiet. I struggled to see the family, but they were hidden out of view in a private chapel to the right of the minister.

A string quartet seated themselves in front of the pulpit and I realized how expensive all this was. The coffin gleamed of money, as well as all the finishing touches like black crepe draped in swooping arcs behind the minister, an oil portrait of Michelle in a gilt frame on a gold stand, all the music and flowers. My mind reeled. Hadn't Michelle hated these people enough to estrange herself?

The minister was in full formal robes and as his mellow, comforting voice filled the church, I retreated, observing my sadness. How difficult it must be to do a service for a wretch who was murdered, I thought. Then, tuning everything out, I relived my Michelle mistake. In the spaces between my breathing, I realized with a jolt that I never really liked Michelle. And that I only thought I had loved her. Michelle was a difficult, unfulfilling pain in the ass, in spite of the sweet, genuine moments. Then why? Why did I do it? I knew better, didn't I? As I retreated deeper, my grief became larger and my struggle for control more desperate. I mourned for the loss of the dream that Michelle had been right for me. I mourned all the fantasies that had kept me stuck and were now shattered. I mourned that I had no love in my life and maybe never had, other than my family and friends. No deep, intimate marital love. I had never loved anyone. Maybe I couldn't. I liked a great many women: Cherisse, Tonya, even Sloane, but never love. I respected and admired them and loved them in an affectionate, general way, like an entire species. So why Michelle? What had possessed me? I never did an irrational thing in my entire life. It was becoming clearer and clearer to me exactly how obviously wrong that entire relationship had been. It's as if the answers were buried in deep, black, murky water and the longer I examined the questions, the closer to the surface the answers rose, eventually popping fully formed into the clean bright air of my mind. Why had I done that foolish thing? I asked myself. The preacher droned on about tragedy and potential being cut short and God calling us when He needed us and what lessons can we draw from this? He used the phrase "in our midst" every few minutes, as was required of clergy. Sloane shifted, adjusting her collar. She left the sunglasses on. She reminded me of a black Schwarzenegger.

Why had I allowed Michelle in my life? My merciless mind persisted. Because I was so lonely, the answer came in bold. I was so lonely, that's why I did it. I felt such profound relief at the truth finally being named, a tear almost squeezed out of my eye. Instead, I clenched my fists and every muscle of my body and breathed raggedly. It had been desperate hope and misplaced longing that permitted me to act against myself. I willed the damn tears to stay back, deep in my dry sockets, my eyes red and bulging slightly. And why then? Why did I fall for that one at that time? I was scared, getting older, and so unconsciously lonely. And why Michelle? She was just next in line. Someone handed me tissues. It was permission to cry. Well, I wouldn't. Not until later. Maybe not ever. Sloane put her hand on mine long enough to squeeze gently, and then it was gone. And I, who worked through everything with the swiftness and efficiency of a strategic game plan, went further.

As my grief slowly ebbed into containment, I realized I knew what I wanted. I wanted a wife. A wife who was tailor-made. I wanted a real woman who lived with courage and gusto. A woman with authentic appetites. Hunger for great sex, great food, great love, and great fun. One who was big and generous and who could stand up to me but could also melt. One who was beautiful without vanity and without trying. A woman who could dress up or down and had confidence no matter how she looked and didn't depend on me for forced praise, fishing for compliments. One who didn't always ask, Do I look fat? Does this make my butt look big?

Yeah, I would say with a grin, get all your clothes like that.

Someone who was juicy and ripe and luscious and large and knew the value of such a thing. One who could fight with me and play with me too. Someone who commanded respect and fidelity just with her breath.

Someone who could soothe me and make me laugh. Someone I could make to laugh too. A laugh like ice cubes tinkling in a glass…

Most of all, I wanted a woman who didn't emasculate. Someone who treasured the sort of butch I was and adored me for being so. Someone for whom the complexities of butchness were as precious as they were to me. A woman who appreciated the perfect balance of male and female in the female body of a butch dyke. I cringed inwardly as I thought of my many misunderstandings and disappointments at the hands of truly well-meaning women who wanted me. A lot of femmes took their power from shrillness, bossiness, controlling, disdain, and contempt for the butches they desired and showed no respect for the gift of difference. How many women had I dropped cold after they tried to dress me? How many femmes had I abandoned, heartbroken, when they tried to get me into a skirt or a frilly blouse or other article of women's clothing?

They came into my life like entitled matriarchs and I was the fixer-upper. They proclaimed I should wear my hair thus and so or wear just a little makeup to soften myself, or a little jewelry or carry a purse. Then they were traffic cops in bed and I was done with it. And that was just the beginning. What were these women thinking? Why were they attracted to me if they just wanted to change me? I decided long ago that women like this didn't want love and harmony in their lives, they wanted aggravation and dissatisfaction and frustration. Maybe it gave them something other than their empty selves to focus on if I was their pet project and I was never completely acceptable and therefore never finished. I was their busywork.

Meantime, there were fights and unhappiness. Tantrums. I took to saying to a date first thing, "If we hook up, this is how I am, period. Cope or die." But they were sly and manipulative, those sorts of femmes. They were all eyelashes and smiles, nodding and agreement, then, *wham!* Their faces came off and the battles began. I was excellent at walking out. Femmes like this were always from the South or from the Midwest. Who knows why they were like that? Was it because they needed to be in perpetual self-denial of what they really wanted? Or was it that they were ashamed of my butchness about which I had fierce pride? Or were they threatened? Could be a million things. I sighed and mentally listed what I *did* want.

A rare femme. Someone who—

I was startled from my reverie by everyone standing. Sloane gave me a small smile. Hymn books were removed from their shelves. To conclude the service, the congregation sang "Softly and Tenderly." The minister announced the reception for one hour later at the family's home; all were welcome, after a brief, private graveside service for the family only.

Everyone remained standing as the front rows filed out first, passing the now open casket. I surmised the family would stay and pass the coffin after the church was empty. Max and her escort edged out with their row and I had to stop myself from touching Max's shoulder. We were separated again and she would be lost in the crowd and leave before I could speak to her. It took so long for my row to be ushered out, I was twitching in my skin. We approached Michelle and I braced myself, debating about walking the other way or closing my eyes. But with Sloane ahead of me, I knew I could do it. I should do it. The casket was lined with pink satin and velvet. There was an elaborate silkscreen of lilies inside the lid on the fabric. Michelle looked heavily made up and plastic. It was still shocking for me. A few days ago, fighting with her and blink, now this. Michelle's hair lay in big, graceful curls around her face on the satin pillow. A way she *never* wore it. I sneered. Straight hair, no paint, just all grin. Depending on where Michelle was shot, the embalmers must've used some powerful putty to disguise it. Though, to me, it would've been gentler to see Michelle's injured, bloody body as it was when she died than to see this repulsive, pretty fakeness. This false mannequin Michelle was too creepy to inspire sadness or a good-bye caress.

I closed my eyes and wished blessings to Michelle as I passed.

When we reached the exit, an usher was handing a stem of lilies to each guest. The press was packing up their gear.

Sloane took hers and went out into the blinding sun and drenched air of the parking lot and waited for me. I stared at my own lilies, counting the cost of that too. So it was over. So much was now over. The dread of the funeral, the funeral itself, Michelle and me, all of Michelle, and in a way, lots of old me too.

Sloane clapped me on the back and said, "A lot of us are going to Queenie's now. Drinks are free."

"What about the family reception?" I wanted to get a look at them. Shake hands, murmur condolences, look Michelle's mother in the eyes. Maybe hear a few Michelle stories. Maybe tell a few.

"Naw, naw, that's just for the rich white folks. They're not wanting Michelle's *gay* and nigga friends up at the big house. Just their own friends."

"Okay, where's Queenie's?"

"Thirty-sixth and Peoria. Want me to drive?"

"No, I can find it. Is it near Swan Lake?"

"Yeah, everything is near Swan Lake." Sloane laughed and walked away.

I stood in the sizzling parking lot alone, watching the people all around me leave and get on with their lives. They'd go home, kick off their shoes, take off the stiff clothes, and turn on the television. Suddenly, I was angry. It wasn't this easy, I wanted to shout. An hour isn't enough to say good-bye to someone. Even someone like Michelle. I threw her lilies down to wither on the searing pavement and walked to my car to consult my map. I would stay in the background, but I wanted to watch the graveside service. Then I could go to Queenie's and try a gin and tonic.

Chapter Thirteen

In the car, it had to be two hundred degrees. Panting, I turned the air-conditioning on high. I checked the address of the cemetery. Park Lawn was just down the street on Peoria. Good. I could find that easily. The more I navigated Tulsa, the more I appreciated its logical layout. So Queenie's would be roughly three miles from the graveyard. I sped down to the cemetery to get there well before the family so I could position myself in a good hiding spot.

It was a forested graveyard, though not so large as the acres and acres of dead cities I had seen on the West Coast. I turned in and saw there were several services happening today. I drove by the quaint stone cottage where the caretaker lived, searching for the correct tent.

In the distance, under a spread of live oaks, there was a huge crypt. With grim certainty, I drove to it, parked, and stared in awe. The crypt was a massive marble structure with pillars in the front, statues of angels at the four corners, stained glass windows, and an ornate wrought iron door. There were redbud and dogwood trees, as well as forsythia and azalea hedges along the edges of the family plot. The name McKerr carved about the door boldly announced ownership and glory. Wealthy, ostentatious, and superior even in death, I mused, wondering if the hedges were there for beauty or to separate the rich corpses from the other dead losers. Oklahoma pharaohs. Surrounding the crypt was an immaculate lawn of headstones used for the family once the crypt was full. There were even marble memorial benches provided for peaceful reflection. I approached Michelle's grave, but not too close as workers were preparing for the service. It was as far to the left as it could fit and still be on McKerr land. I only knew it because the tent and chairs were set up. I nodded to a couple of workers who stared at me.

"The service won't be for another few minutes. Why don't you go get a cool drink and come back then?" one muddy man asked me as he poured water on his head and shook it off in a silver halo.

I shrugged and replied, "I need to be here now. I'll stay out of the way."

I felt such a sense of peace under the deep shade of the trees; in a flash I understood why people had plots. It was serene and beautiful and everywhere I looked I saw a nice view. City parks bordered the graveyard on two sides and the third view was the rest of the cemetery and the fourth was the downtown Tulsa skyline. Small though it was, its skyline was reassuring somehow.

I strolled among the headstones, some aged, worn and comfortable, some soft and crumbly, others hard, bright and new. There were many mighty patriarchs whose likenesses were chiseled in relief onto their tombs.

"Vanity, vanity, vanity," I muttered. I noticed the dates went back more than a century, to the 1870s, right after the Civil War and roughly at the time of the Oklahoma Land Run. Right? I couldn't remember. I sighed. It didn't matter; these men made their money from oil, not land. Why didn't Michelle ever tell me the truth of her origins? I saw squirrels cavorting through the trees. I saw the news vans pulling up, so I decided to find my place. I picked up a couple of acorns and walked to my car. It certainly came in handy today that Michelle's family had never known me. I parked my car in the opposite corner of the graveyard and walked to within one hundred yards several plots over and sat beside a tree. I felt dizzy, wondering if I had heatstroke. My skull only perspired this much in the fourth quarter of a game when I had played the first three really hard. The wet air pressed from every direction like a vise. I sneezed five times in rapid succession, and because I was without tissue or handkerchief, I did the Farmer's Salute: pressing one nostril closed at a time and blowing out of the open one like a power jet. The family was beginning to arrive.

The wind rustling the cottonwoods and the sycamores almost fooled me into believing it wasn't sweltering. Even hiding in the overwarm shade with the torrid wind, I expected to grow gills on my neck. Who knew a landlocked dustbowl could have the weather of a rainforest? I thought it would be a desert like California, but this was the wettest air I had felt outside of a shower. Oklahoma continued to surprise me. No wonder it would be a short service. Even the natives must hate this, I mused. Why would anyone stay here long-term? I then remembered the quiet, intensely blue twilight, the marshmallow air, and the pearlbone moon hanging heavily over the maples; hearing the ducks mumble to themselves and the breeze bringing the scent of petunias and wisteria from somewhere. And actually hearing crickets and locusts and little frogs singing. The concrete of Los Angeles, perched though it was on the ocean, seemed so hard, fast, and lifeless in comparison. The birds chirped and warbled around my head. It was as if Tulsa had lifted her skirts and settled carefully into the earth, not disturbing habitat or wildlife.

I absently plucked a blade of grass and put it in my mouth. The family had arrived and the minister was present and I could hear, above the locusts and birdsong, his rich and fruity voice rolling over the headstones, even though I couldn't understand the words. I squinted, trying to get a look at Michelle's parents, who were among those seated. But between the shafts of sunlight over the distance and the gray shade of the tent, I couldn't make out much. There were roughly twenty people at the service, a much smaller group than I expected. There was a man who looked familiar, as if I had seen him on C-Span or CNN, and off to the right…on the outside edge was someone I knew. Who? I sat up sharply, the grass falling out of my mouth. It was Jack.

Jack Irving, whom I'd met and liked at the bar when he was tagging along with Darcy, Jhoaeneyie, and Ava-Suzanne. What in the hell? The more I found out, the more mystified I was. One of the news cameramen fell over a stone cross. Security guards for Michelle's family kept them at a distance.

The clan all bowed their heads simultaneously. Then, in turn, each came forward and dropped a scoopful of earth on the lowered casket. Then there was lots of hugging and gradually, they all drove away.

I sat in shock for a few moments, trying to puzzle everything out. I wiped the wet off my face with my sleeves. Next, I saw a Ford Crown Victoria pull up. I crouched lower even though I was out of sight.

An old black woman with a good, strong build got out of the car. She wore a crisply starched gray maid's uniform. She walked to the casket. She carried a large white cloth that could be a diaper or a towel and wiped her eyes continuously. I edged up to a shrub so that I might hear better. What I heard was copious wailing. The woman was talking to Michelle and sobbing. Ashamed to witness such a private scene, I turned away. The woman eventually calmed herself. Perspiration dripped from my nose and as I pinched it away, I resumed watching. The woman opened her great pocketbook, removed a small Bible, read from it, then threw it in the hole and walked away, head high, without looking back.

I waited a while longer and stood with a groan. My knees popped. I began limping back to the car, working the kinks from my body and trying to breathe. Instead, I fell into a frenzy of sneezing. I decided to take another capsule.

As I approached her vehicle, a marker caught my eye. I was incredulous. No way, that just couldn't be. I read and reread the name to make sure I wasn't seeing things.

"Billy Bob Pigman," I whispered, shaking my head. "Unbelievable."

I had to drive around the entire cemetery because the little road was one-way. On the way out, I was surprised to see a beautiful monument to the blacks who had died in the Greenwood riot, a large Jewish section, a Greek section, even a small what I guessed to be Cherokee section. Again, Tulsa amazed me.

I decided to freshen up quickly at the hotel before going to Queenie's. I counted on seeing Max and wanted to smell good. I rinsed rapidly in the shower, used lots of deodorant, and put on khaki shorts and a tight white T-shirt. I posed in the mirror, pleased with my muscles, hoping not to sweat too much.

CHAPTER FOURTEEN

Driving up to Queenie's, I discovered that there was no parking. The cars filled the lot and lined the street. Why weren't there any valets? I finally parked in a church lot and cursed the block I had to walk because doing so, I was soaked and my crisp fresh shirt was limp. But the ever-present wind baked me a little dry before I went inside.

A quadruple blast of dark, cold, smoke, and music assaulted me as I pulled open the heavy door. After having been blinded by the brightness outdoors, now I was blinded by the darkness within. There was a live band playing and I listened and watched until my eyes adjusted.

Someone yelled in my ear, "Delaney!"

I turned around and grinned."Weatherly!"

"Where have you been?" Sloane was smiling dopily and carrying a bottled beer by its mouth. I shrugged, the music momentarily rendering me thoughtless. The lead singer was a lovely woman with a sexy overbite and glossy black hair cut in a swingy pageboy that swept her jawline in time with the music. She writhed and groaned to the blues the band played.

Lila was singing about drinking poison if the judge didn't set her papa free.

"They're good!" I shouted.

Sloane nodded and said, "Our own white Lady Day. Drink?" Sloane held up her beer.

"Yeah!" I shouted, "Gin and tonic!" The drink would secretly bond me to Max.

Sloane met my eyes and grinned before going to get the drink. The song ended and riotous applause and cheers rose out of the blackness that hid the audience. The dance floor was crowded too, I noted. Maybe I could slither over and ask Max to dance and just hold her close because there was no room for anything else. To hell with Max's little friend who brought her to the funeral. Life was too short.

Sloane reappeared at my elbow and handed me a cold glass sparkling with clarity. It was a beautiful drink. I smelled it. Tangy, sugary. I tasted it. Gently bubbly, tart, edgy, and sublimely sweet. Mmm, this was very, very good. I felt a snap inside as if I had found a part of myself as I swallowed. Max's tongue would taste like this at first, then as we went deeper, I would get Max's real flavor. Maybe at the back of her throat she would taste like honey. Like pecans. Like milk. And her red, swollen, slick cunt when I finally, softly put my face there would taste like pineapple. Then, as I went deeper, it would taste dark and meaty. Her backside would be rich and fragrant and earthy like fresh truffles. "Thanks," I told Sloane, "I'll get the next round."

"Sure, pal. Lila's got deep pockets. It's all free today, so you buy me as many drinks as you'd like."

I was sure Sloane deliberately waited for me to take a big gulp before casually announcing, "Max wants to see you."

I barely escaped choking and spitting all over the floor. I put my napkin to my mouth and coughed, but not too much. Could've been a coincidence. Sloane watched. I looked at the stage as the singer announced a break before her next set.

"Oh, she does? And she sent you to tell me?"

"Sort of." Sloane swigged her beer. In anticipation of my thoughts Sloane said, "She's not here. She's at home, alone, expecting you. I 'spect you can find your way, right? It's near Swan Lake." Sloane grinned.

At her suggestions, I rebelled. “What makes you think I’ll go?” Even as I said it, my mind told me not to make a fool of myself in front of sharp Sloane.

She clinked her beer to my drink. “Uh-huh” was all she said.

“I’m gonna mingle,” I replied in a tough voice and walked away casually. Sloane’s knowing look infuriated me. “I’m gonna mingle?” I cringed at the memory of saying something that stupid. Why didn’t I just give it up and own my obsession? Sloane seemed like a friend…but my pride and fear prevented it. Maybe after a few more drinks, I could drop the ego. Yeah, I’d be an alcohol-infused butch, my eyes rolling with drunkenness, quoting movies, singing songs, and putting my arms around everyone within reach, declaring that I loved them forever, really and truly, I mean it. Never having been a sloppy drunk, I shuddered at that idea too, convinced to my everlasting embarrassment that if I were ever going to be messy, it would be in front of Sloane, and I definitely didn’t want that. First, I must find a cigarette; then I could face the rest.

I looked the crowd over, wondering what to do next. I spotted Darcy, Ava-Suzanne, and Jhoaeneyie, but too late to avoid them.

Jhoaeneyie engulfed me in a bear hug and rubbed my back. I shoved her away, but she held on to my arm. “Hard stuff,” Jhoaeneyie said, her head tilted. “Real hard stuff. Are you okay? Do you feel safe, deep down inside?”

I used my stone cold stare to glare Jhoaeneyie to silence.

“Stay healthy. We need you.” Jhoaeneyie released me.

“Here.” Darcy thrust a big colorful drink into my free hand. “It’s a juicy pussy.” Darcy swigged hers. “Try it,” she urged me as Ava-Suzanne tittered and sipped her own.

“I prefer to get mine on the outside. I like them better on the hoof.” I smelled the drink. “Hmm, tropicale.” Cloying, canned, oversweet fruits. Well, I could pose with it for a while.

“So, what have you heard?” Darcy asked eagerly.

I shrugged. “Just part of that last song.”

“No, no.” Darcy frowned. “About *us*. What did you hear?”

“Tell us everything,” Jhoaeneyie said.

“What?”

“I figure the entire community is buzzing and you would’ve heard something by now.”

“Yeah, your hotel isn’t under a *rock*, is it?”

I stared down my nose at Darcy and Jhoaeneyie in disbelief. Ava-Suzanne licked her lips.

“We’re really private, so I thought I’d get your version and then tell you the true one,” Darcy continued, trying to smother her eagerness.

“We really hate these messy lesbian rumors, but what are you going to do? It is the system we live in,” Jhoaeneyie said. The band announced a break and cleared the stage.

“I ain’t heard shit.” I cocked my head. Darcy was pale and deflated.

Jhoaeneyie shook her head. “Unbelievable.”

“Oh, well, never mind. I guess you’re just out of the loop.”

“Uh-huh, that’s it,” I agreed.

Ava-Suzanne sucked a cantaloupe chunk. She looked like an albino tree frog.

“Well, what do you think?” Darcy gestured to the empty stage.

“Just great. They’re going places, I think.” I put my face in my drink as if it were an oxygen mask.

“Yeah, I’ve known them for a hundred years,” Darcy boasted. Ava-Suzanne simpered on her shoulder.

“Oh, they’ve been struggling for so many years.” Jhoaeneyie puffed. “I’m glad to see them finally getting off the ground. We’re real proud. I’ve watched them come up for a long time. Poor dears.” Jhoaeneyie tilted her head and smiled ruefully. “But we’ve been their number one supporters cheering them on just *forever*.”

“Really?”

"Yeah, I'm the one who told Lila to start singing in the first place," Darcy said. Ava-Suzanne nodded in agreement. Darcy continued, "We are real tight. I can introduce you if you like. Sometimes I sit in with the band." Then, she added with false modesty and a bad British accent, "Sort of like the fifth Beatle, you know?" Ava-Suzanne and Jhoaeneyie laughed. I stared. "Lila tries to get me to sing, but I tell her, look, that's your thing, not mine, understand? See, I'm real visual. Music isn't second nature. At least not yet." Darcy searched my face for a response.

"Where's Jack?" I blurted, desperate to derail this line of talk. Darcy, Jhoaeneyie, and Ava-Suzanne turned together and gestured to the bar where he sat alone, smoking and drinking thoughtfully. He was still in his cemetery suit.

"I think I'll go over and say hello."

I pulled away, but Darcy said, "Good idea, we'll join you."

"Hey, Jack." I clapped him on the back and put my empty glass and the juicy pussy on the bar, shaking my head for the fruit drink and nodding at the bartender for a refill for Jack and me, saying as if experienced, "Tank and tonic." I also sent a beer to Sloane, pointing in the smoky darkness. Jhoaeneyie, Darcy, and Ava-Suzanne sat on Jack's other side.

Darcy leaned in with an approving smile. "Good choice, girl. That's the best of the British gins."

"Yes, I know," I stated indifferently.

"Hey, baldy. I remember you. You're the…the…" Jack grinned impishly and shrugged. "A lot going on for me right now. So sorry. Whass your name? Mr. Clean?"

"Nora," I said, delighted. The bartender slid our drinks toward us. "Thanks." Free drinks or not, I knew to tip well and passed Jack his bourbon.

"Oh, thass right, you're the generous charmer." Noticing my hungry look that only another smoker recognizes, Jack passed his pack. I thumbed the match into flame and inhaled with a grateful sigh.

"You gotta teach me that," Jack said.

"Any time." I smiled, blowing smoke to the ceiling. I lit another match for Jack as a demonstration. Ava-Suzanne pointedly began coughing. Jack rolled his eyes and lit a fresh cigarette himself.

"You know, Ava-Suzanne grew up with Michelle. Lived right next door. Silver spoon up her twat." Jack giggled. I stared at Ava-Suzanne, who glared imperiously. Jhoaeneyie watched, her eyes sharp with prurient interest.

"We were estranged at the time of her death," Ava-Suzanne said frostily.

"You know, Jack is Michelle's cousin," Darcy said to me across Jack. Jhoaeneyie smiled with satisfaction. Stunned, I looked at Jack for confirmation; he stared straight ahead. He lifted his shoulder, nodded imperceptibly, and drained his shot. Then he leaned close to me.

"You know, Darcy Tate used to be plain old Roberta Johnson before she changed her name," he whispered.

I felt loose and goofy and I laughed. "Figures."

"And Jhoaeneyie hasn't been a therapist for years. She had her license revoked for inappropriate conduct," Jack continued.

I laughed again. "Naturally," I said. "So, you're Michelle's cousin?"

"Yeah." Jack grinned, turning to me, his eyes red. "We go… we went way back."

"You were close?"

"Used to be. Before she burned *all* the bridges."

"What does that mean?"

"She shat on everyone but me, and I thought it would never happen between us, but it did and I ended our relationship. About that time, she also shat hard on Sloane and had to leave town. I heard she went straight to Los Angeles." He said it in a tone that implied, I heard she went straight to hell. "And she hooked up with some sucker there. Maybe that's who killed her. Either that or the governor's men. She died there in some dump apartment."

I was impassive. "She died in LA?"

Jack frowned. "Oh, you didn't know."

"No, I did not."

"How did you know Michelle, anyway?" Jhoaeneyie demanded.

"I was the sucker in LA."

Jack stared. Darcy stared. Ava-Suzanne stared. Jhoaeneyie stared. It was as if the bar got silent.

"I guess none of you knew *that*," I added.

"No, no, sorry, I just didn't." Jack shook his head.

"*You're* the ex?" Ava-Suzanne asked derisively. Darcy elbowed her. Jhoaeneyie smirked.

"Yeah, what of it?" I asked angrily. I was ready to wipe that twig.

"Nothing," Ava-Suzanne said, venomously sweet. "I just didn't realize Michelle was so…*diverse.*"

I snapped to Darcy, "You want to control your mannequin's mouth before I have to get ugly, you get me?" Then to Ava-Suzanne, "I don't know what your problem is and I don't care. You just shut up and stay out of my way, dig?"

Jhoaeneyie held up her hands. "Let's just turn down the volume here. We're all hurt and vulnerable. Remember we're sisters and we love each other."

I tasted bile and took a breath to speak but before I could, Sloane cupped my elbow. The tension rose within the little group. "N? Whassup? Doin' okay?"

I sighed. "Sure. I believe I'll have another candy drink, though."

Venom fairly dripped off Ava-Suzanne. Darcy's jaw muscles were rippling, and a vein throbbed in Jhoaeneyie's forehead.

"Darcy. Ava-Suzanne, Jhoaeneyie," Sloane said easily.

"*Sloane*," they said icily, in unison. I looked from one to the other: Sloane, an affable grin on her face, Ava-Suzanne appearing constipated and unhappy about it. Darcy was angry, and Jhoaeneyie was upset but supplicant.

"I want you to meet Lila and Reese," Sloane said as the singer and another woman entered the group.

"Excuse us," Darcy said loudly and she, Ava-Suzanne, and Jhoaeneyie turned back to the bar. Jack, his eyes closed, held his forehead in his hands and was now surrounded by the three.

CHAPTER FIFTEEN

Lila, may I present Nora Delaney, fresh from the sticks of LA. And, Nora, this is Reese Montgomery, Lila's partner."

"Oh, thank God the skank bitch is *dead*!" Lila cried, shaking my hand and trilling laughter.

Stunned, I said, "What?" My shoulders were starting to bunch. Reese was heavyset but dapper in khakis, loafers, and a severely pressed, starched shirt. Lila wore a swishy, voluminous black skirt and gold sequined blouse with leopard-print pumps. With her flashing black eyes and saucy grin, she looked like a gypsy.

"I don't mean anything, darling. It's just such a marvelous *party*. And I love any excuse for a good party, don't I, Reese Angel?"

Reese said nothing, but smiled, her face tense.

"Oh, poor dear Michelle, she will be so *deeply* missed." Lila overanimated a sad clowny face.

"Did you know her?" I asked.

"Not a bit, darling." Lila laughed into my face and swirled around me. I was dizzy trying to follow Lila and decided to shrug her off as a ditzy diva.

"Let's have a look at you." Lila held my face and turned my head this way and that. She growled and barked, snarling hungrily. Sloane took a step back. Then Lila said, "You're a beautiful, strapping buck, aren't you?"

"Watch it, El, you're gone make my dog, Nora, blush," Sloane said.

"The hell you say." Lila rubbed noses with Sloane.

Reese pulled Lila back and wagged a finger in her face. "Lila, my queen, you mustn't arouse suspicion. Remember whose girl you are."

"What a bore. But as you wish, Reese Cup." Lila grinned at me but then stood straight and solemn with a pouty mouth to face Reese. "I'm a harmless flirt. Simply everybody says so. You're such a square."

"Now, now, Lila, I'm sure you don't mean that." Reese smiled uncomfortably and stroked Lila's arm.

"Hmph. I am and I do." Lila pulled away and clung to me.

"Well, well, looks like Nora caught the big fish," Sloane said. I gave her an exasperated look.

"Don't worry about me, Reese." I tried to be soothing. Reese's dead shark eyes turned to look at me. "I'll protect her from salacious influences. She's safe with me."

Reese looked as if she would like to strangle both Lila and me, but she smiled and said, "Of course you will. I am grateful." She made an awkward little bow. Reese's malevolent gaze remained on Lila, who was oblivious.

"Oh, will you? Will you take care of me?" Lila blinked up at me and feigned a faint, forcing me to catch her. She snuggled against me and cooed, "An oldie but a goodie."

I tried to step away, but Lila's grip was like a claw. Jack pushed into the group.

He and Lila screamed and hugged and air-kissed.

"That is a fabulous dress. Does it come in small?" Jack asked.

"There are no small women, just small faggots," Lila replied.

They bumped hips.

"Meow, Jack, have you met our latest import? She makes me crave deep, dark, rich chocolate, doesn't she?" Lila pressed us together. Jack saw the look on my face and burst out laughing.

"Yes, doll baby, I've met her. Go easy. She's an amateur at you," Jack said.

"Amateur, schmamateur, have you seen those hands?" Lila asked. Everyone looked at my hands, which I promptly shoved into my pockets.

"I declare, Lila, you are a married woman. You've been settled so long, you'll finally have something fun to tell at confession," Jack said.

"No, she won't," Reese said.

"She might," Sloane added.

"Hell, no," I stated.

They all turned to look at me. Lila's chin was trembling, Sloane and Jack were grinning, and Reese was thunderous.

"She's not available…I'm not available…you do the math," I said.

Sloane raised her eyebrows. "You're not available?"

"Last night she was," Jack said. He and Sloane slapped palms.

"Oh, Nora, don't break my heart wide open right here before my last set. Don't make me sing the blues for real."

"Don't break her heart," Reese said to me, her teeth gritted.

I shrugged. "I'm somewhat available." I wished I had gone immediately to see Max. *My* Max, as I was already considering her.

Lila smiled. "Just look at that face!" Lila made fish lips and grabbed my jaw. The group sighed in relief. Lila was charming and flirtatious, throwing back her head to laugh and touching my biceps. Lila had a gaudy cigarette holder that she sucked on frequently for effect. When she smoked especially hard, she looked like Betty Boop.

I put down Reese's careful stare to Lila's aggressive behavior. Lila squinted at the bar where Darcy, Jhoaeneyie, and Ava-Suzanne sat, talking.

She pointed her cigarette holder toward them. "Reese, dahling, I see those three boors everywhere. Who are they? How do I know them?"

Reese raised Lila's free hand to her mouth languidly and kissed it, Lila's other hand still being caught on my arm. "Fans, my princess. They're fans of yours."

"Oh, of course." Lila laughed, squeezing me again and tilting her head and tossing her short slinky black mane. Reese's eyes smoldered. I moved away from Lila, closer to Sloane. "You know what I say, if you're a hugger, hug me twice, bitch, but don't ever touch my butch," Lila exclaimed, referring to someone approaching to embrace Reese. Lila and Reese ignored Darcy, Jhoaeneyie, and Ava-Suzanne. Jack air-kissed Lila again and returned to the bar.

I watched Jack nurse another shot and cigarette. A man approached, nudged Darcy over, sat down next to Jack, and patted his shoulder. I turned back to the sound of Lila's voice.

"—know that Reese is an artist?"

I groaned inwardly. There were more artists crawling out of the woodwork in Tulsa than were contained in the whole of the Los Angeles Museum of Art.

"Let me give you a tour." Lila grinned, her luscious overbite making for a spectacularly schmoozy smile. She took me by the arm and led me to a wall of the club. Reese and Sloane followed us.

"Of course by day, you know this is my *incredibly* chichi and tiresome restaurant. And at night, it becomes my *sanctuary. I just live to sing, you know*."

"Don't we all," I said.

Lila tittered. "You are *delicious*." Lila pointed with her cigarette holder, the smoke trailing delicately after her hand. "Here is one of her earliest paintings. I was so skinny then. I hadn't yet come into my voice." Lila batted her eyes and tipped her head. "But Reese saw my potential, didn't you, darling?" Lila said over her shoulder. "And she encouraged me and painted me and put meat on my bones and a voice in my throat."

I tried to extricate my arm from Lila's firm grip. When I still couldn't, I tried to engage Reese in the conversation. "Is that true, Reese?"

"Every bit of it. But what my humble princess doesn't say is that she made me grow as a painter too. These early works are too sentimental. They're positively puerile."

I studied the paintings. Lila in a garden, Lila on a couch, Lila at a microphone, Lila just standing. As they progressed, I did note a certain density becoming present in the pictures. A color complexity and mastery of brush stroke emerged over time. An ambience coexisting simultaneously with a focused objectivity developed that wasn't present in the early works. I grudgingly admitted that I was impressed. Reese was good. Sloane just smiled, staying silent.

"You make a living at it?" I asked.

"Oh, hardly." Reese chuckled.

"Don't listen to her, Nora!" Lila crowed. "She is ever so popular. Always in demand is my Reese Cup." Lila seemed to make this remark sincerely, but her eyes shone hard.

Reese smiled, pleased, but she was still unsettling like a sheathed knife. "It's an avocation that I'm hoping to nudge into a vocation. I have a few shows, I have a few dealers," Reese added with a shrug, then continued with deliberate lightness. "I have one in LA. I go there on business frequently. What part is your stomping ground? Perhaps we could dine."

"Oh, I'm sure your business doesn't take you to my territory," I answered, wanting to win this contest.

"All the nudes are at home," Lila whispered conspiratorially, pulling hard on her cigarette. "Couldn't show those here, of course." She laughed.

"Nudes?"

"Yes, Reese paints mostly nudes. Something about integrity in the human form and that it must be naked to appreciate properly. When I sit for her, I find it just so *sexy*. She's always looking for models. I believe she must've painted every femme in town, haven't you, darling? Her studio is in our home and there, I can keep an eye on her. She has women coming and going all hours, don't you, my naughty imp?"

"Yes, but only for work. You are my one and only passion, princess," Reese answered.

Sloane winked at me.

"And here is her latest painting!" Lila announced. We had made a circuit of Queenie's and now stood at the stage where the musicians were tuning up for the next set. The painting was of Lila at the mike, singing so ferociously, she looked like a tigress after an antelope shank.

"Oh, forgive me, I must fly. My band awaits and they are impatient for me."

"Isn't everyone?" I smiled, all smooth sex.

"Oh, I love you, you dirty scamp. Reese Cup, can I keep her as a pet?"

Reese glowered but made her voice light. "Whatever my princess wants, she gets."

"I would never survive in captivity. Perhaps just part-time?" I answered.

"Oh, darling, you are a hoot and a half. If you enjoy art and would like to see more, I…*we* must insist you come for dinner at our house tomorrow night. We won't take no for an answer, will we, Reese Cup? You must come. I love entertaining, especially new blood. About seven thirty, Winthrop Tower, nineteenth floor, bring Merlot." Lila kissed me on the cheek and turned and glared at Reese, who stared at me with a sly smile and flat eyes. Sloane kept her eyes on the ceiling, smothering a laugh.

"Reese, come, I *need* you," Lila said. They both went backstage.

"What was that?" I asked incredulously.

Sloane smiled and offered a small plate of finger food. As I ate, Sloane made excuses about having to leave, then asked, "Aren't you going to see Max?"

I swallowed hard and shifted my gaze from staring fixedly at the newest Lila portrait to stare miserably at Sloane. "Why bother? Aren't you two—?"

"Oh, no." Sloane laughed. "Best friends. I've been staying in the guest quarters until I can find a new place. Michelle stayed with me for a while, you know, and now I want fresh digs. Bitch wrecked my damn car. So I'm driving hers."

"Oh!" I said, an enormous weight falling from my chest. "But the dyke who escorted her at the funeral..."

"Friend. You want me to draw you a map to Max's cootchie? Nigga, be a *man*."

I gazed at Sloane nakedly. "I don't know a fucking thing, do I?"

"Nope, but don't let that stop you."

Sloane and I laughed together. Then she moved away, saying she had spoken to someone at the bar that she needed to finish getting to know.

The band swung into "Night and Day" with a flourish and it was so loud that I decided to finish my drink out on the deck before racing over to Max's. I stopped at the john. In the humidity, the door had swelled, so I kicked it open. In the stall, there was standing water, I thought the toilet leaked but soon realized the tank had so much condensation it pooled on the floor. I checked my watch: Six p.m.

I hung my head over the sink and spooned handfuls of water over my scalp to cool my head. My sinuses complained by stuffing up immediately. I cried out and jerked upright when a hand crawled under my shirt and up my back.

Amber was grinning at me in the mirror. She was shorter without her skates on. "Hello, lover."

"What are you doing here?"

"I got someone to cover for me at the bookstore. You and I have unfinished business."

"*Why* are you here?"

"We shared a moment. I've come to collect on the promise."

I shoved Amber's arm away from me, turned off the water and let my head drip. "What promise?"

"The promise of your hands." Amber put my hands on her buttocks. "And the promise of your mouth." Amber stood on tiptoe and caught my mouth with her own. I let my reflexes take over and kissed Amber, who then hovered near my mouth and murmured, "I see you. I see what you are. You're an animal. You need me. Are those not promises loud and clear?" Amber batted her eyes.

I stepped away. "But those promises are not to you." Thoughts of Max tipping a grin to me. Max on her knees, fondling her own breasts, arching back, opening her throat, pinching her nipples, her hair brushing her back, her legs parting, parting, parting, revealing her swollen slick cunt, untouched by anyone but me, all for me, only mine forever. Max splitting wider and wider, her clit nourishment, her cunt drink, her breasts hors d'oeuvres, her ass dessert.

Amber pressed me against the bathroom wall. "Well, where is she? Why aren't you with her? Looks to me like you're ripe for the plucking."

I imagined Max's mouth…Max's tongue exploring my skin, all her curves and straight edges, all her taut tendons and her potent hairlines, leaving clear tracks of desire. Max's hot breath, her lips raw, damp, and puffy from my kisses, Max's voice sliding out only in groans and gasps. My hand sinking into Max's hair and twisting it in a knot around my fist as I brought Max's mouth to my own…

I pushed Amber back a couple of steps. "Listen, if there's anything I want from you, I'll let you know."

"Hey, magician, you want this?" Amber retrieved her purse

that she had dropped on the floor, removed a clove cigarette, and lit it.

My mouth watered. "Maybe just a drag."

Amber rested against me. "You can have all you want." She gave the cigarette to me and I closed my eyes and pulled hard. I felt her move away and heard fumbling. When I opened my eyes, Amber was stark naked in front of me.

"What the fuck? You are one crazy bitch." I laughed.

"Oh, you Cappies and your conservatism. Let loose." Amber shook her breasts. "Live a little. It would be a big healthy step for you."

I could hear Lila wailing another song. If Max had done what Amber just did, I would've smacked her bottom right smart, dressed her double-quick, hustled her out of there, and given her a lesson she would never forget in the privacy of her bedroom. No one could have the privilege of seeing even one extra inch of my precious Max. But this chick was on her own.

Amber was spare and lanky with long legs, high, small round breasts, and a decent ass for a white girl. She was so comfortable with herself, she looked like a marionette: all loose joints just waiting to be directed by a stronger hand.

"If I know you, Cappy, this doesn't give you much choice, does it?" Amber grinned.

I finished my cigarette, enjoying the dizzy little buzz, and flicked the sizzling butt into the toilet. "Nope," I said, jumping on Amber and biting her throat.

Amber's laughter gurgled. "I knew it," she whispered.

"Shut up," I said. I picked up Amber and put her on the sink where she squealed with delight at the touch of cold porcelain. I jerked her knees apart and brushed her bush with the back of my hand. Amber leaned her head back. She closed her eyes. She tilted her pelvis. I rummaged in my pocket and removed the latex gloves and dental dam I always carried. I snapped on the gloves like a surgeon going to work. I stepped in between Amber's knees spread oh so accommodatingly wide.

I took one of Amber's dark red nipples in my mouth. She moaned. I sucked harder and harder still. She began gyrating slightly. "Yes…yes…" she whispered.

"You are one nasty cunt, aren't you?" I muttered.

"I'll be whatever you make me. I get what I want," Amber answered, gasping when I tweaked her clit.

"Maybe you should be my pony. Get on all fours and take it up the ass while I whip you."

Amber's eyes sparkled. "I'm a wild pony. It will take a lot to break me."

"Oh, I'll break you right now." I knelt on the floor. I heard clapping and cheering outside the restroom. Then the music began again. I placed the dam on Amber's cunt and sucked her clit.

"Oh, my God, oh, my God, oh, my God." Amber went limp and still. "You are so good…you are so good…yes, yes…"

"Shut up," I commanded. Amber nodded and closed her mouth. She opened her legs wider and curled her hips farther to me. Amber gently pulled her lips open, steadying the dam. I nipped her thigh, then moved to her ankles and bit a ring around each. I nibbled my way back up her lean legs to her thighs, where I sucked and left two matching bruises. I kissed her navel and tugged on the belly ring with my teeth. She was panting and pulsing. I began licking my way down to the dam. I placed my lips ever so gently around her turgid clit. She grunted and sighed.

The door slammed open and Darcy, Ava-Suzanne, and Jhoaeneyie all pushed in together. I expected Amber to clap her legs closed and hide in the stall, horribly embarrassed as she dressed quickly and ran home in shame. I stood, waiting.

Instead, Amber remained where she was. She didn't even close her legs. She grinned big and stretched her arms. "Hi, guys. Having a good time?" she asked. "I know I was."

"Amber," Darcy said. "Love your outfit."

"This old thing?" Amber laughed.

"Amber, I've been meaning to ask you if you ever got in that book on Numerology that I ordered," Jhoaeneyie said.

"Jhoaeneyie, honey, I'm a little busy. Call Light and Love tomorrow."

Ava-Suzanne stepped in between Amber's knees and rolled Amber's nipple between her finger and thumb. Amber wrapped her legs around Ava-Suzanne and held her close.

"You look absolutely appetizing," Ava-Suzanne said, her voice low and gravelly.

"Care for a go?" Amber, her chest deep pink and her eyes glittering, stared at Ava-Suzanne. "There's plenty," she added.

"This ain't working for me," I said, rolling off my gloves and throwing them in the trash. "Y'all play on through." I searched in Amber's purse, feeling certain she wouldn't mind, found the cloves, and took all of them.

Darcy stepped beside Ava-Suzanne and began stroking Amber's cunt through the dam.

"Come one, come all," Amber said.

Jhoaeneyie snorted and said, "No pun intended."

"Yes, there was," Amber replied. "I need to get off and the more the merrier." Amber groaned as she writhed under Ava-Suzanne's and Darcy's touch.

"You started it, now we'll finish it," Jhoaeneyie, with a quick double dip into her nostrils, said to me. "Guess it was too much for you."

"Yeah, it sure was. Live it up." I left the bathroom, my head clearing at last. I was glad to be out of the grip of that rapacious octopus. Lila waved to me and kept singing. I picked up an abandoned glass full of golden liquid and downed it, hoping to burn the experience out of my mouth and therefore out of my memory. I leaned against the wall, panting.

Sloane came by on her way to the bathroom.

"You might want to wait awhile," I warned, then laughed. "Or join in."

"Amber?" Sloane asked, cocking her head to listen.

"How did you know?"

"I saw her come walking in with That Look. She's famous

for it. I should've warned you..." Sloane laughed. "But I didn't want to."

"Thanks, dog."

"Oh, you're still upright and conscious. Consider yourself lucky."

"Yep, she's getting the full ten point inspection. Lube job, oil change..."

"Fluids check?"

I nodded. "Air filter, tire pressure..."

"Is it the gruesome twosome?"

"Naw, there's three of them in there on her."

"Oh, Jhoaeneyie's harmless. She just watches. She will caress Amber's hair or hand someone a dildo, but she won't do a damn thing. She ought to play piano in the background."

"I don't want to ask...how do you know this?"

Sloane shrugged. "I've heard plenty."

Lila's song ended to raucous applause. Shouts and cries came from the bathroom. Lila heard this and announced, "Is God here? Someone is paging God. God, if you're here, you're needed in the restroom." Laughter rippled through the club. "In the spirit of attaining multiple...ah...states of bliss...hit it, boys!" Lila cried and swung into another song.

"I'll just use the men's," Sloane said and left.

I needed a drink, a proper gin and tonic to put myself right again. I left Amber's cigarettes on the bar. After reflection, I wanted no reminders of that scene, no matter how sweet the smokes. I planned to drink this last cocktail out on the deck and then head to Max's and see what I could get started there. Before I could go outside, the foursome from the bathroom approached me.

"There you are." Amber smiled dopily, leaning on Darcy and Ava-Suzanne's arms. Jhoaeneyie took up the rear. "You and I still have a date with destiny."

"I've had Destiny and she's a bore," I answered. "I'll pass."

Amber tittered. "Remember, I get what I want." She passed her forefinger under my nose. I grimaced and slapped Amber's hand down.

"Not this time. You let somebody else play that squeezebox, hear?"

Amber set her jaw and then spied her cigarettes on the bar. "There you are. Funny, I don't even remember putting them down here. Brandy? Courvoisier?"

Ava-Suzanne stepped to the bar and said, "Two juicy pussies."

Jhoaeneyie and Darcy giggled. "Cause they're better in pairs!" they crowed in unison.

Jhoaeneyie ordered two slippery nipples. She and Darcy repeated, "Cause they're better in pairs!" And fell out laughing.

Amber lit a clove and stuck it in my mouth. I spat it to the floor. "I'll get my own," I told her. "Cigarettes and poon… *and drinks*," I told Jhoaeneyie, who tried to hand me a slippery nipple.

"Oh, is my girlfriend cranky because she gave up the sweet thing tonight?" Amber cooed.

"Girlfriend! Bitch, you are deluded."

"Amber is never deluded," Ava-Suzanne retorted.

"You're my world now." Amber grinned, taking my hand and kissing my fingers.

I jerked away. "You and I never even met, got it?"

"No, no, it's in the cards and in the stars. You resist as long and hard as you like, but you're mine. I think it's cute. All that fighting. I like a warrior," Amber said, sipping her drink.

"Well, I don't like crazy. And you don't do nothin' for me. I told you. This," I gestured between us, "ain't gonna happen. If you were the last woman on the planet, I'd kill myself and you could hump my dead body. If we were trapped on a desert island, I'd take your cigarettes and then use you for fish bait. Is that clear enough, Amber?"

She winked at me. "Not quite." She turned to Darcy and Ava-Suzanne. "She doesn't get it, does she?"

Ava-Suzanne laughed. It was a chilling sound. Darcy laughed too. "No, she doesn't. Not even remotely," Ava-Suzanne answered.

"Not a clue," Darcy said.

"No way," Jhoaeneyie added.

"You see, Nora," Amber propped her arm high up on my shoulder and twirled her fingers next to my temple, "all of this is so Earth. You need to expand your perceptions. There's a lot at work here."

I patted myself down and found a stale, forgotten Marlboro in a hidden pocket. I lit it and Ava-Suzanne coughed pointedly.

"Could you blow that somewhere else?" she demanded.

I drew so deeply on the cigarette, the end burned brightly and crackled with heat. I pursed my lips and blew hard right into Ava-Suzanne's haughty face. Her wispy bangs lifted with the smoke. She closed her eyes and smiled, all ice.

"Thank you." She nodded. "Thank you for showing me who you are."

"Oh, I'll show you a lot more than that, baby doll." I grinned and shrugged Amber off my shoulder.

"God, I love this woman!" Amber cried. "She's so refreshing."

"She's just what this town needs," Jhoaeneyie said.

"Yes, Tulsa needs another hole in its head," Ava-Suzanne said.

In spite of myself, I laughed and slapped Ava-Suzanne on the back. As if they were monkeys following the group, everyone else laughed too.

I tried again to remove myself and go out to the deck alone, but Jhoaeneyie grabbed my arm.

"What's the best thing about coaching college basketball?"

"The pussy," I quipped.

Jhoaeneyie looked uncertain about whether I was joking, so she sort of choked and coughed, halfway to a laugh. "What I love most about being a therapist is *helping*." Jhoaeneyie smiled angelically. "The helping," she repeated. "I'm a helper. It just feels so darn good to know you make a difference. Don't you find that?"

"No, I just want to win." I smiled.

"Hmm. Mmm-hmm. Well, anyway, like I was telling my roommate Joan, that's really why I do what I do."

"Hold it. You live with someone named Joan? And you're name is Jhoaeneyie?"

"Yeah, isn't it ironic?" Jhoaeneyie grinned. Then she baby talked, "My widdle darlin' wuvs that we have the same name. She is my baby Joanawoan. I wuv it too."

I was thunderstruck. I didn't know whether to slap Jhoaeneyie upside the head or puke on Jhoaeneyie's shoes. I drained my drink.

"My tweetie butter britches would jus wuv to meet you—" Jhoaeneyie continued until I grasped her arm.

"You've got to stop that *now*."

"Oh, Nora, you've got to excuse me. I'm just a big spoiled brat. Isn't that ironic?"

"Do you mean stupid?"

Jhoaeneyie blinked at me.

I rolled my eyes. "I meant to whisper that."

Jhoaeneyie narrowed her gaze. "Have you ever been in really good therapy?"

"Fuck no."

"No need for expurlatives. I would like to invite you to sit with me. Put the can opener to your head and really open you up. Would you be willing?"

"Oh, hell naw. Nigga, please." I shook with laughter. "Counselor, heal thyself."

"I'm a therapist."

"That ain't what I heard, okay?"

"So I'm pumping gas now, so what? There's no shame in that."

I stiffened my spine righteously. "Ain't no shame in any job."

"That's what I'm talking about. I keep trying to tell Joan that, but she just keeps yelling at me, 'You're Phi Beta Kappa. You're summa cum laude. You need to do better.'"

"Joan is your roommate? What the hell does she care about what you do?" I was being deliberately obtuse.

"Well…she's…" Jhoaeneyie blushed, swaying from side to side anxiously. "She's my *roommate.*"

"I'd tell her to go straight to hell and mind her own damn business."

"No…you don't get it…she's my…" Jhoaeneyie cleared her throat. "You know, *roommate.*"

"What? Roommate. Yeah, she pays half the bills, so what?" I delighted in baiting Jhoaeneyie.

"Forget it," Jhoaeneyie snorted. "You know, for a successful lady, you're not too sharp." She pointed to my head. "Up here."

"I know. That's what Mensa keeps telling me."

"Who? I believe the word is," Jhoaeneyie lowered her voice, "*menses.*"

"Oh, right. Thanks."

"So did you send anything to the family?" Jhoaeneyie ate pretzels. Lila crooned a slow, sad number. Amber, Darcy, and Ava-Suzanne were talking astrology. Amber kept laughing hysterically and squeezing Ava-Suzanne's arm.

"Not yet," I answered. "I want to go by in person."

"We sent a pan of fudge and a six-pack of wine coolers."

"Mmm," I marveled. "That's real classy."

"Yeah, that's what Joan thought. She's from New York. She says I really should be from New York because I'm just…you know…too fast for around here."

"Is that right?"

"Yeah, I'll be telling an antidote and it will just—whoosh! Right over your head."

"Oh, the long, boring stories you must have," I murmured.

"What's that?" Jhoaeneyie swayed, then everyone clapped as Lila finished her number.

"Nothing."

"When I took a leave of absence from being a therapist, we talked about moving to New York, we were this close."

"Uh-huh." I was tipsy and relaxed and therefore somewhat blunted and mellow, so standing here shooting shit was just fine. The music pounded me flat and nailed me where I stood. I enjoyed watching Lila and thinking my own dreamy, buzzy thoughts. As such, I was not overly troubled by having fools surround me, nattering like so many pigeons.

"Yeah, I forget why we didn't. But I need to get back into doing therapy so we can. My earning potential is so great… it's a trade-off. I'm either devoted to clients and working one hundred hours a week and making sweet dinero or I'm sitting on my thumbs making squat at Fast Eddy's. But I get nights and weekends off. It's real hard, though. God didn't make me to answer phones, make coffee, and pump gas. In my last job, I had a secretary do *all* that. She dealt with all those trenial details. She had my car taken care of, hotel reservations, airlines, vacays, appointments, correspondence. She would've sent the fudge to Michelle's family for me and the goddamn phone. Oops, sorry about that expurlative. But I'm just having a period of adjustment, right? I'm just not used to doing those servant-type things, you know what I mean? Joan and I go round and round about it." Jhoaeneyie stuck her pinkie in her ear and jiggled it.

"That's a shame," I said, a mild anger sparking and then dying when I looked at Jhoaeneyie double-dipping into her nose with her thumbs.

Ava-Suzanne, Amber, and Darcy joined us. Amber put her

hands on my shoulders from the rear and hopped on my back. I nearly dropped my drink.

"Piggyback, Daddy!" Amber squeezed me with her legs and bucked. Jhoaeneyie and Darcy laughed; Ava-Suzanne scowled. I tried to pluck Amber off, but she was like a clinging spider. So I shrugged and walked over to Sloane, who was bent over with laughter. A lovely, soft, dark, curvy woman stood next to Sloane, smiling and holding their drinks.

I swung Amber around to be closest to Sloane and said, "Take this, will you?"

Sloane wiped her eyes. "Are you finished with it?"

"I never got started. Just get it *off me*."

"No, no, no!" Amber tightened her legs around my waist and she curled her arms around my throat.

"Goddammit, you psycho, you're choking me!" I cried, my voice strangled. "Sloane, get her before I fall backward and smash her dead," I added, still unable to breathe well. I was pleased that I never put down my drink.

"C'mon, little honey, c'mon, whackjob." Sloane tickled Amber. "Time to get off the ride. It's someone else's turn."

Amber shrieked and kicked, causing everyone to stare. Even Lila faltered briefly in her song. At last Amber was loose enough that Sloane lifted her from my back and set her on the floor where she crossed her arms and legs and became a poutball.

I straightened my collar. "Whew, thanks."

"You owe me." Sloane grinned, retrieving her drink from her date and then kissing her date's neck. Lila finished her song to whistles and cheers.

"I think I saw the face of Satan." I crunched ice cubes.

"You barely escaped the flesh-eating virus, dog."

"Nora, my Black Beauty!" Lila called, squinting into the darkness. "Where are you, paramour du jour?"

I tried to hide in the wallpaper. Some genius with the spotlight guided it over the crowd. Sloane, her arm around the lovely woman, began breaking into incredulous laughter again. "You got the whole town in an uproar, N," she said between gasps. "I haven't seen anything like this since Ellen and kd were here."

Reese came striding over, an unhappy frown creasing her face. She clamped her hand on my arm and escorted me briskly to the small stage.

"Thank you, Reese, my darling," Lila extended her hand and Reese kissed her wrist obediently and disappeared. Then Lila gave the same hand to me to pull me up onstage.

I shook my head and backed away.

"Oh, you simply must. I insist," Lila said, then implored the crowd, "Encourage her."

The crowd cheered and jostled me until I reluctantly mounted the steps.

Darcy, Ava-Suzanne, and Jhoaeneyie were watching. I didn't care that Amber left with someone else and I didn't care that Reese was fuming behind an amplifier, but I did care that Jack slipped off his bar stool and wobbly wove his way outside to the deck.

"At last." Lila sighed juicily. "My dream come true."

"What do you want, Lila?" I felt my scalp prickle. I was veering wildly between being high, mellow, anxious, tired, irritated, relaxed, and aroused.

"I just want to introduce you to everyone. Everyone? May I present Nora Delaney? A big-time college basketball coach with the best hands since…Reese Cup, who is someone notable in basketball?"

"Magic Johnson!" someone called.

"Thank you," Lila answered, "Nora D., this is everybody. Everybody who matters, that is." Lila took her lit cigarette in a holder that Reese crept up and handed her. Lila put a lacquered fingernail in her mouth and said, "Well, almost all are Who's Who." The crowd laughed. "The rest, and you know who you are," Lila pointed vaguely, "can get out of my restaurant and go to hell." The crowd roared. Lila continued. "I just want all of you to keep a careful eye on my sweet black button." She winked at me. "Who needs a drink. How is it that she's on empty here?" Lila squinted into my glass and noted the lime wedge. "Gin and tonic?"

I nodded.

Reese scurried up with a cold, dripping glass and handed it to me and took my empty. "So, everyone," Lila shouted, "please welcome our stranger and see that she comes to no harm. Make sure she feels good. But not too good, you don't want to incur the wrath of Lila."

The crowd laughed and clapped.

"You may go." Lila brushed me off the stage. I stumbled down the steps and, without looking left or right, headed for the door to the deck.

Chapter Sixteen

Outside, the clean roasting air made me need a cigarette. I spotted Jack alone at a table, looking at the burning sky, white and sizzling with evening's approach.

"Hey, stranger, mind if I join you?" I sat next to him and deftly extracted a cigarette from his pack. "There's a church on every corner in this town, what's up with that?" I said after a long silence.

Jack turned to look at me, his eyes red not just from booze. "Did you love her?" he asked plaintively. I nodded. "Me too," Jack said. "Goddamn her."

"So, why aren't you at your family thing?"

"Cause they don't like me and they make me want to vomit. Do you miss her?"

I shook my head. Jack nodded.

"Me neither. Not yet."

"What was her story?" I inhaled and stared straight ahead. I would give Jack space from my gaze, as well as protect my face from anything severe he might reveal. I felt stronger staring ahead.

"You don't know any of it?" Jack asked.

"No. She told me she was from Madison."

Jack laughed.

"And that she was a student. She stole from me," I admitted in a rush. It was an inexpressible relief to air my pain with someone else who knew Michelle. Before now, I had just been angry. But with Jack, I could be hurt.

"She get much?" Jack asked.

"Maybe more than I knew."

Jack grunted. "I think someone in the family murdered her. Or *had* her murdered."

"In the family?" I was astonished. This peerless wealthy white pillar?

"Yeah, and lemme tell you why. Michelle had the goods on a scandal that would ruin the incumbent McKerr's re-election gub…gov…gubernat'rill hopes forever. She was disowned when she came out. Cut off without a penny. She used her considerable charm and wile to dig up this secret and she disowned them right back. I say 'them' because my branch of the family is sort of the underachieving black sheep." Jack sipped one of the two shots he had in front of him. I ground out my butt and bummed another.

"She disowned them?"

"Yeah, she discovered this disgusting skeleton in the closet and it enraged her so much that she was convinced her family and families like it and corporations are what is wrong with the world and she wanted revenge."

"What do you mean?"

"You ever notice her petty theft?"

"Theft? No." I felt more and more foolish. Where had I been for three years? Right where Michelle had wanted me, concentrating on my career.

"Did things just show up at the house, or would she lavish you in gifts?"

"Yes, now that I think about it."

"And she always had an explanation, right? Even though she had no money, she had more stuff than anybody, right?"

"Yes, yes, you're right," I said with dawning comprehension.

"Well, she told me once, stealing from big companies and

cheating corporations was like radical revenge on her family and its sins."

"And what about stealing from those people she loved?"

"Well, she was an asshole and a compulsive liar…just 'cause we loved her and she's dead doesn't take that away." Jack held his head and seemed to be sobering.

"So why would one of the McKerrs kill her?"

"Because she was trying to blackmail them with this secret. And Nelson Philip McKerr wants this governor's race sewn up. A few years in the mansion and on to the White House. He can do it, too. He's a conservative and handsome and charming and slimy. And a liar, just like Michelle. So I have no doubts at all. They had motivation and opportunity."

"Do you know the secret?"

"Yeah, she told me. But number one, they don't know she told me, and number two, I'm completely bought off and an utterly spineless weenie."

"So this is the sort of thing that if you tell me, you might really have to kill me."

Jack laughed and laughed. "Yep. That's exactly it. Do you wanna know?"

"Do you want to tell?"

"I wanna tell if you wanna know."

"I wanna know if you wanna tell."

"Knowing a secret is a terrible, terrible, terrible," Jack seemed sloppy for just a second, "terrible burden."

"I'm strong, I can take it."

"Okay." Jack downed one shot. I sipped my gin and tonic, Max momentarily on the back burner. "Well, you know her family is in oil, right?"

I nodded. "Now I do."

"Big oil. Really big oil. You know at the beginning of the twentieth century that Tulsa was *the oil capital* of the world, don't you?"

I nodded even though I had not known that.

"Tulsa was famous for its rich economy. There was actually a reverse *Grapes of Wrath* thing happening. People from everywhere flocked to Tulsa to cash in. It flourished and grew nonstop until the eighties, when the bottom dropped out of oil. But by then, fortunes were already made. And oil doesn't stay down for long. Look at the prices now, for God's sake." Jack seemed to be growing more sober and alert and eloquent with every sentence.

"Mmm-hmm," I said, wondering how in the hell this tied to Michelle.

"When you have enormous wealth, any town is small, New York, Los Angeles even, but especially Tulsa, where there are primarily two very big oil families and two giant oil concerns. The McKerrs and the Wilsons."

"Yeah, I've heard of them," I said, remembering their ubiquitous logos and wondering at the secret power that was held here in this tiny town's heart.

"Well, our great-great-grandpas or some such ancient history came here to Tulsey Town, as it was then known by the Native Americans before statehood, and our kin started to build their fortunes wildcatting."

"Wildcatting? What's that?"

"Oil prospecting. One who stakes money on very high-risk and probably unsound ventures. The odds are bad, but when they pay off…well, look around."

"Oh. Go on."

"Well, everybody got pretty rich even by today's standards and the ones who emerged as chief competitors were the McKerrs and the Wilsons. The Wilsons had the most, and that just galled old Great-great—or just Great?—Grandpappy McKerr. He was rumored to be a hateful, hard, mean son of a bitch. I'm being almost criminal by simplifying this much, but this is about all I know. Anyway, years pass, oil profits grow, the Wilsons are winning in the oil fortune acquisition and by now, it's about 1905. Naturally, the two families both have a black staff to help around the estates and the Wilsons have a little scandal of their own. Seems years ago, old man Wilson had had a *black* son by their maid. Now you know and I know that that stuff went on all the time and we can be grown up about it. But back then, it was humiliating and shameful, heaven knows why. This son, God help me, was black as night. Not a drop of white in him, it looked like. But I've seen photos. He was Wilson's boy all right. Not the color, but the features and bone structure. It's like you took a transparency photo of the old man and laid it on this boy's face. And the old man was crazy for that boy. Old Man Wilson defied all convention and just doted on his son to the point of making people sick. Apparently, he was infamous for saying things like, 'Love is love and blood is blood.' Anyway, they kept him and raised the boy as a gentleman's butler, which was pretty much as high as they thought he could go." Jack took a breath. I wiped sweat from my face, on the edge of my seat, not knowing how much to believe. He continued. "So because this boy couldn't inherit and the odds were against him having an education or a career, his daddy signed over the rights to one of his own *best* oil fields in Glenpool and gave it to this boy, who was by now a man."

"Are you sure this is the secret?" I asked, feeling tired.

"Patience, woman." Jack sipped his second shot. I crunched ice and smoked. Jack was getting low on cigarettes. "So this grown son now had total ownership of part of the richest oil wells in the world. He left his daddy's house. This was about 1910 or so, and he moved to the Greenwood district. The intersection at Greenwood and Archer was known as Deep Greenwood or Little Africa." Jack laughed, his voice harsh and dry. "It has been called the Black Wall Street, but really, it was the Black Main Street. It had *everything*, all kinds of shops and shit. The son, now financially set, bought a home there, married, started having children, opened his own business, I forget what it was, and just lived his life. He was a rich man, settled and happy. He was well on his way to becoming deacon of his church and maybe his own elected official position someday. The McKerrs watched this drama with vengeful glee. They kept track of the son and his family and waited. By now, it was May of 1921. The Wilsons were way ahead. We McKerrs were floundering. Bad investments, embezzlement, gambling, and inattention to business were bleeding our once powerful, albeit new dynasty dry. Old Man McKerr felt we needed just one push, just one leg up to restore us to previous recent glory. He sank millions into drilling that came up dry. He was desperate. A fanatic maybe. His family never saw him. He went to Texas looking for the next huge well. His plan was to cash in just one more time and then he would make the money inaccessible to the bad elements and wastrels in his family." Jack smiled sourly. "Everyone would live very well, but the principal would stay with the company and the McKerr legend would be set. The name would be mighty forever."

"So?" I looked at my watch.

"So, then, on May thirty-first, 1921, when the race riot began," Jack said, assuming I knew the particulars; though I did not, I didn't reveal it. Jack continued, "The McKerrs, belonging to the KKK, all thronged the courthouse and were eventually deputized by the Tulsa Police."

"*That's* the big secret? There's KKK blood in the family? That's nothing. Most whites probably have a KKK ancestor or two if you go back far enough. No one would kill Michelle for knowing that. Hell, there's probably black blood running in your veins too. Probably Native American blood. Maybe Chicano too."

"Do you want to hear this or not? I'm not finished." Jack drank his second shot and lit up his last cigarette. "Wow, I've smoked a lot tonight."

"All right, go on then."

"Well, when things spun out of control on June first, the McKerr men headed straight for Deep Greenwood. The McKerrs and hundreds of other whites looted and burned, all with impunity because the cops were KKK too. Most of the blacks were disarmed, rounded up, and held helplessly in custody 'for their own safety.'"

"That's sickening." My stomach clenched in rage at this news. I knew of race riots and was no stranger to racism and abuse, but to hear blatant details like this was unbearable.

"I know," Jack said. "It wasn't a race riot at all. Not like LA after Rodney King. The blacks back then didn't do anything. They were *disarmed*. They were rounded up and their homes and businesses and churches were destroyed. It was an assault. A unilateral *war*. Anyway, the McKerrs went straight to the Wilsons' son's house and held his family hostage while they made him sign over his rights to his oil field at gunpoint. The McKerrs swore they wouldn't hurt him if he did as they asked and he did. But…" Jack trailed off.

"They killed him anyway," I finished in a fierce whisper.

"Yes. They got the papers, made it look like it was a sale, shot him point-blank in the head, and left his wife and three kids screaming after they set the house on fire. That oil field was the turning point for the McKerrs. They regained their supremacy and never looked back. They've been the richest and most successful oil corporation ever since. They even have a division that makes *diapers* and one that manufactures *software*." Jack sighed. "The Wilsons suspected, of course, but nothing could be proven. So much happened that night. So many murders. So much waste and confusion. Old Man Wilson just snapped after that. It broke him. The family carried on the business, and to their credit, they are a close second to the McKerrs, but the father was no good after his favorite son was murdered." Jack rested for five beats. "So that's what Michelle was blackmailing about and why they would kill her." Jack lit another cigarette.

"Now wait just a goddamn minute!" I held up my hand. "If this is so secret, how did the families know everything, including Michelle?"

Jack rolled his eyes. "Grow up. The best way to make

something public is to try to keep it a secret. You know that, come on." He puffed furiously on his cigarette. "As for proof, I've never seen any, but Michelle claimed she found plenty when she went through their trash over the years. She loved Dumpster diving anywhere she could. Yep, she was a classy lady." He laughed ruefully.

I sat stunned, stricken, silent.

"She needed money, so she thought she'd make a deal with the devil and get enough to live on. And her secret would keep her safe. But it didn't. And I have this to prove it." Jack opened his coat and removed a letter. He handed it to me, I unfolded it, glanced at the date—six months ago—and skimmed the contents. Of the hysterical scribble, I made out the words "slander," "libel lawsuit," "pathetic, scheming little bitch," "can't prove anything," and "filthy liar." "Troublemaking cunt" was underlined. I handed it back to Jack. "It's unsigned."

He sighed. "I know. She gave it to me for safekeeping. She seemed to think it was incontrovertible proof. But I think it's a slim reed."

I stared into space.

"Well?"

"I just don't know anything, do I?" I asked.

"No, but don't let that stop you. *Knowing* hasn't done much for me."

"That's fucked up. It's *evil*."

"I know."

"How can you be a part of that family?"

Jack snorted, rolling his eyes. "I was born to it. And drinking helps." Jack laughed and raised his empty glass, tipping it for the last drop. "I did change my last name, though. And after Michelle told me all this and showed me the papers, I started donating money every month to the Negro College Fund and sending cash anonymously to one of the survivors I know about. I've considered personally apologizing, but I'm too afraid. What I do isn't much, but it's what I can do. And you know, if everyone just did a little bit, this would be healed. If every white person, not just the McKerrs, stepped up and did just a little bit, if they *took some fucking responsibility*," Jack bellowed, his face red, "racism would disappear. Or if not, the playing field might at least be leveled. Some of the hurt would be healed," he said again.

"Maybe," I said in wonder. I didn't even donate to the College Fund and felt ashamed. "I don't think whites feel much sense of responsibility about these things." I pulled a deep breath of hot molasses air.

Jack turned on me. "*I know*. And that's the problem. *That's the fucking problem*!" he yelled. A couple at a near table glanced over and went inside. "Blame the victim, that's the white man's creed," Jack said viciously, then aped a cracker accent, "I didn't have nothing to do with it. I love niggas, some a my best friends are niggas, spics, chinks, wops, and faggots. Callin' someone 'nigger' don't mean nothin'. A *white* person can be a nigga." Jack was breathing hard. "It happened too long ago to make reparations. It is in the past, we can't change the past. Generations have lived and died since then; the world was different then; now we're much more civilized. That event 'way back then' has nothing to do with us progressives now. It's too late to apologize, it's pointless to make amends, that would be like admitting fault when it probably wasn't even completely our doing, if you take the circumstances in context." Jack stood and began pacing. *"Bullshit!"* he screamed.

I was rapidly going into tipsy shock. Jack certainly was different than I thought. This whole family is a clutch of chameleons, I mused.

"Blame the women for their abuse and rape; blame the gays for the bashing; blame the Jews for the Holocaust; blame the Japanese for the World War II internment; blame the Native Americans for just, I'm sorry, *living* here and trying to cooperate with us and trusting us, and don't get me started on that; blame the Mexicans, blame other Hispanics for not being white; blame the Middle Eastern people for domestic terrorism perpetuated by disgruntled *white men*; blame the African Americans for slavery and everything since then. Have I left anyone out? Oh, my fucking God! It is too much. Thank goodness China has thus far had the sense to keep to herself. Although human rights violations there are a *nightmare*, again, you don't wanna get me started. I'm already on my soapbox." He grinned. I smiled back automatically in response. Jack sat again. "When I drink, I go off. Some people get horny when they're drunk. Me, I get mad. I don't know, maybe that's just how it is with the ruling class. Whoever is in power is corrupted. Maybe if the blacks or the Cubans were the majority in power, there would be terrible civil rights and criminal racism too. Maybe…what is that saying?" Jack peered into my face, expecting an answer.

"I don't remember it just now," I replied.

"That saying…power corrupts perfectly? Is that it? Maybe that's just the way of the world since man stood erect. There will always be evil in power and everyone else is a victim. I just happened to be born now, in this country while white males are in power. I could've been a Christian in Roman times." Jack laughed. "They used to persecute and kill the Christians. Don't you wish they still did that today?" Jack clapped his hands over his mouth. "See? I'm corrupted. I'm no better than Old Man McKerr and all his elitist, murderous, racist, asshole sons."

"What do you do for a living?" I asked in amazement, speculating activist, political consultant, lobbyist.

"I'm an interior decorator," Jack replied with a nelly accent. "Couldn't you tell? It's a biological imperative. I am really good, though. I tell the rich what to buy and how to arrange it. You know, most people wouldn't even know where to put a vase without my help." Jack curled his finger, beckoning me closer. "Sometimes I get a wild hair up my ass and want to completely ruin someone's house. You know, like tell him that he *must* have a lime green polyester covered set of La-Z-Boys in the living room with a gallery of paintings on black velvet and a toilet paper cozy shaped like a doll wearing a ball gown, stuff like that."

I laughed. "Well, speaking as a black person, you're okay by me."

"Are you the spokesperson for your people?" Jack asked wryly.

"Yeah, I won over Chris Rock by just a hair," I said.

"Oh my God, me too! I won out over Tom Cruise. He didn't accessorize properly."

"You are bad." I chuckled.

"I know. Spank me, Daddy," Jack said.

"I'd love to, but I have to be somewhere."

"Oh, you have another date after me? Well, that cunt is just getting sloppy seconds."

"I know, baby," I joked. "Listen, Jack. Thanks for the smokes. And thanks for—"

"Don't mention it. It was a relief to tell someone. Maybe you can topple the family with the information." Jack laughed dryly. "Though I just keep praying that the genes are weak and the dynasty is ending and crumbling on its own."

"Yeah, thanks for that, but not just that. For loving her too."

Jack's eyes got shiny and he nodded, waving me away. "Get outta here, butch."

"Later, Jack."

"You owe me a carton of cigarettes," Jack called. I nodded and smiled.

CHAPTER SEVENTEEN

I sat in the car for a while reeling with this latest revelation. For once, I didn't want a cigarette. I surprised myself by not feeling ready to see Max, but my clit had final word on that and it said, *go*.

I drove to the house and it was dark. If I weren't already a little drunk, I would become so at the heady notion of being summoned and parking behind Max's car like a lover. I pulled up close enough to kiss the bumper and got out. Michelle's car that Sloane was driving was parked next to Max's. Seeing it gave me a shiver.

God, it had been a long day. I had lived an entire year in one day. I checked my watch. Only eight p.m. Sunset was just beginning. The air was sweet with clover and belated wisteria. I knocked on the front door. And waited. It was too dark and too quiet; maybe I should just go back to my hotel and call Max in the morning with apologies. The idea of creeping over to the exposed bedroom and spying on Max was just taking hold when I heard bare feet padding and the door opened at last.

"You got my message," Max said flatly. She wore a white satin dressing gown and her hair tumbled over her shoulders and down her back. Her plump breasts peeped out of the top of her gown. My clit had been right.

"Don't you ever wear clothes?"

"Not unless I absolutely have to. When opportunity knocks, I've found that it pays to answer the door naked."

"You still opening the door for me, naked or not?"

"For you?" Max grinned. "Always. Come in." Her white satin robe rippled as she walked into the living room. "What are you drinking? I know you've been drinking."

"Uh..." I felt edgy that she would know the secret that I had only started drinking gin and tonics tonight to feel closer to her. "Um...uh..." I stammered. Max stared at me and shrugged.

"Beer, probably. Well, I'm out of beer; you'll have what I'm having." Ice clinked into two glasses and she made the drinks. I sighed with relief.

"I don't want some frothy, fruity, femme drink," I growled. I couldn't just remain *in awe*. I had to keep my butch bearings and squeeze a little.

She handed me a glass and looked me languidly in the eye. "Yes, you do. Sit down."

Max chose the couch and I chose it too. Max had to move a cashmere blanket to make room for me. That's when I noticed the reading light on, a book on the side table, candles burning all over the room.

"You were *waiting* for me?" I asked, smiling hungrily.

She looked around. "Don't be ridiculous," she snapped gruffly. "I know you want a cigarette." She extended the box to me, but I was transfixed by the succulent white underside of her wrist and forearm. Oh, if I could just get the nerve to drop my drink and fall on that flesh...I would gnaw and lick and bite all the way to her underarm. Then I would pin her with her arms overhead, to the couch, as I kissed and sucked every centimeter of flesh on her chest and neck.

I wouldn't kiss her mouth or touch her breasts. Her squealing and moaning and writhing would be enough for the moment. I would feast on her armpit; I hoped it was unshaven. I would nip her neck anytime she struggled too hard. I imagined the feel of her hands held above her head in my strong grip. I would feel her heat as she would twist and buck, possibly grinding her hips into me. I could see us: my long, lean, black body prone and her supple, curvy-rich white one. How beautiful that would look. How much better even to release her hands and stare into her eyes as we both knew what was about to happen. I would be propped on my arms, holding myself above her and feel her not fight. See her submit. Feel her luxurious thighs open to admit my angular frame and we would rest there silently, breathing together, anticipating all of it. Max would cradle me between her legs and oh, the heaven it would be to sink down into her at last. To lower myself and be met by breasts, waist, buttocks, and cunt. A cunt maddeningly close and separated only by white satin.

Would Max wear panties? I thought not, but decided the dressing gown would have slipped over her cunt, so I could take my time peeling the cloth away, savoring the fragrance, spreading…but first, I would just press my thigh hard into her, letting her gyrate on my taut leg if she wished. I had business first. With my knee planted possessively at Max's center, I would… Would I rip her bra? No, I would suavely, slowly unhook it and close my hands over those white breasts at last. I would tease them first, stroking and pinching the nipples erect through the cloth, restraining myself until Max closed her eyes and leaned her head back.

When she pushed up against me, thrusting her breasts into the air, I would know she was ready to be naked. And I would strip her, making her shiver with my slow deliberation. Then I would fall onto her bare breasts and devour them. Her head would thrash from side to side, her arms would flail, but she would clutch me with raw need. I would suck her tiny candy nipples into swollen bells. I would feel wetness on my thigh and smile like a wolf, biting her hard to let her know who I was and that I had been here. Only when she began whimpering would I be ready to move on. Then I would put my face above hers and finally, finally, *finally* kiss her. Our lips would meet and match perfectly. Her breath would fill my lungs. We would be tender at first, exploring, nibbling, licking, smothering, then voracious. After that…

"Thank you." I extracted a cigarette, lighting the match with my thumbnail. Max didn't seem impressed.

"Let's go outside, it's so beautiful tonight."

We walked onto the generous deck in the back. The sunset was baking the wood floor and waves rose, shimmering, up our legs. I felt toasted in every way. At least my sinuses were clear. Crisp, yellow leaves fell all around us. The corner of the deck and the lawn were piled with leaves. It gave me the strange confusion that it was autumn. I picked up a dry leaf and looked at it.

"Yeah, by this time, the trees are burned. They shrink and drop everything. Happens every summer," Max explained, noticing my puzzlement.

"What are those?" I pointed to several dark gray shapes huddled together on the lawn as if having a conference.

"Rabbits. What did you think?"

As if to answer Max, one hopped away, flashing its white tail.

The air was blistering and wet and heavy as a blanket. Max bent and flung the cover off a hot tub. Steam rose in the air. She turned on the jets and it became a bubbling, boiling cauldron.

"Care for a soak?" Max tilted her head, her drink in one hand, the ties belting her gown shut in the other. "When the weather is like a volcano, it's good to bathe in the lava."

I nodded my head, smiling. Hot damn. "I'd love a soak." Maybe it would make me feel cool and clean.

"I'll turn the light on so you can see where to step." Max pressed a panel and the tub lit eerily in the sticky bluing night.

I tamped out my butt. "What do I wear?" I growled, braless and removing my shirt.

"Whatever you like. As much or as little as you prefer." Max seemed to busy herself with her back to me. But I stood tall and muscular and proud, wanting her to see. I wanted her to admire my mahogany skin, my Amazon body. I wanted her to see my silken ebony nipples and fall on them, suckling like an albino infant. I wanted Max to turn to me and say something romantic and ridiculous like, "You're glossy, and luminous. Your dark skin barely contains a black fire that makes you glow like an opal. You are sinuous and liquidy, tall like a giraffe, but hard like a bull. Your nipples gleam like chocolate drops on your muscular chest and your tangled mat of black curly pubic hair conceals your animal slickness, but all that is mine now. I get to do whatever I want."

But Max wasn't turning. I dropped my shorts and underwear and stepped into the tub with a sexual groan. I placed my drink on the inset counter. Max turned, and could she have blushed? Averted her eyes?

"I see you're in. I'll turn off the light now. It's nicer to stargaze once it's full dark."

I was comfortably settled, the jets massaging my shoulders, lower back, and feet, and I never took my eyes off Max. Let me see you naked. C'mon, I thought fiercely. It's only a matter of time anyway…

Max set her drink next to mine and dropped her gown where it fell in a radiant heap. And there, like a goddess, a Venus, she stood. Ripe with curves and padding that smoked with sensuality. She had on a white athletic bra and huge white boxers that sagged beneath her navel and belled out ridiculously around her thighs like a skirt. Still, the girl had *stature*, I thought. If a ballerina could actually have a feminine body, it would look like this one. Max's hair fell in fiery waves over her shoulders.

"Come on in, the water's fine." I swung my arms from side to side in the bubbling liquid.

Max carefully immersed a foot. She closed her eyes and arched her neck. "Ohh, yeeeeesss!" Then she slithered gracefully the rest of the way in and sat across from me where we stared at each other, smoldering. The steam that rose all around us seemed an appropriate indication of our mood.

"Kind of modest, huh?" I teased. I watched the water splash

on her penned breasts. The exposed tops were like mounds of puff pastry: white, slick, and soft. Her boxers swelled and swam like bloomers.

"Not really, I just don't know you well enough."

I grinned, sensing I had some power now. "You're full of it. And you knew me well enough to plan this, didn't you?"

She might've smiled, but covered it by reaching for her drink and draining it.

"And that early crock of shit about you being a kept woman. What was all that? What do you do, really?"

"I write software. I create Web pages and am an all-around computer consultant."

"Huh." I sat back, regarding her.

Max shrugged her sparkling ivory shoulders, causing her breasts to pinch closed, then reopen. My lips ached to kiss her breastbone, smack in the center. Against the white of her bra, her skin was rosy and alive. I was swollen all over with desire pumping all through me.

"Don't be too impressed," Max said. "I love it so I do it. Being a high school coach—"

"College," I corrected, laughing sharply. This girl was good.

"Yes, college coach is equally intimidating." Max's eyes met mine.

"I hope so." I kept grinning.

"Oh, you have a leaf!" Her hand reached out and for one buzzing second touched me as she removed a leaf that had fallen from an overhanging tree onto my chest, near my collarbone. My hand closed around Max's wrist firmly. With my other hand, I pushed her against the edge of the tub so she was almost on her back.

"Why don't you let me help you with those?" My free hand floated, as if in a watery dream, down to the waving waistband of Max's oversized boxers. She watched me, her eyes dark. My hand closed on the material and I began easing them off. I got a heart-stopping glimpse of auburn pubic fringe before Max raised her round hips and pulled the underwear back up, the shorts ballooning.

"Not yet," she whispered. "Too soon."

I stared at her and nodded, releasing her wrist, my hunger for Max now trebled by the taboo.

"Let's just enjoy tonight as it is," she said, touching my foot with her own.

"I won't be in town for long," I grumbled.

"We'll see." She leaned her head back and closed her eyes. There she was, floating almost carelessly, taunting me with blithe trust not to ravage her. To have so much confidence that she rejected me and closed her eyes. I gritted my teeth, debating whether or not to take her in my arms and smother her with Noraness. Sloane's words echoed in my mind: "Nigga, be a *man*." I began my stealthy approach when Max lifted her head and stopped me with a wide-open stare.

"Listen. An owl!" She pretended not to notice that I was nearly on top of her. I moved back to my seat, resigned to letting it not be tonight.

"Isn't that a bad omen?" I grunted, irritably draining my glass. Ice clogged my nose.

"No, just the opposite. Good fortune." Max's face was innocent and childlike as the lamp of her smile shone into my face. I was taken aback, not expecting any level of naïveté from this wily seductress. She smiled, staring into the gathering dark, listening raptly to the gentle coos. I concentrated on relaxing now that I wasn't going to get any booty. Why had she called me here? Come quick, I've got to tell you no. Come now, I must tease you for hours and reject you. What had she wanted of me enough to give Sloane the message? Was it to bring me close and keep me at arm's length? If there were games, I expected to be the only player and master of the situation.

"Why did you call me here?" I asked sleepily, sinking into exhaustion.

"Thought you might like a home-cooked meal," she said. I burst into belly laughs, Max joining in.

"You look like a happy seal," she said.

"I am." I grinned.

"Care for some coffee?" She rose, streaming water, and walked to a nearby table where a pot and two glasses sat. "Ruby made it for me about an hour before you came. It takes a while to brew, then I drink it over ice."

"You had Ruby—who's Ruby—make it for you a while ago? And you weren't waiting for me?" I teased, remaining in the tub. Through Max's wet things, I could see it all: the continental shelf of her great, heart-shaped behind, the adorable almond bulge of belly, the triangle of pubic hair, the salmon areolas and even the pinpoints of hard nipple. I leaned back and spread my legs. My hand stroked my cunt, feeling a slick wetness not from the water. I stroked my pussy and swollen clit, wanting to come here in front of Max, in this hot tub, groaning into the inky throat of night.

I wanted her to watch. To begin to ache as I did and to be forced to see me cry out and come. Max's skin would have a fiery fever flush as she crept closer to me. I pictured her approaching me, aroused and ready, straddling me, proudly riding me naked, her breasts swinging and bouncing. Max reaching to pinch and stroke my berry-brown nipples and me losing two long fingers into her ravenous red cunt; Max inhaling sharply with passion and relief for finally being fucked right and filled up all the way, just as she had always needed, I would be the *best*, as she moaned it into my ear. I would grab a breast with my free hand and tell her to ride, ride some more. Her hips and ass would churn a tidal wave in the hot tub. She would shriek and grind and utterly open herself to me. I would be buried up to my wrist in her coral cunt. I would savor that vision: my black fingers fucking this sweet white rose pussy. Then she would lean back and touch me…

"Ruby is my maid" was all Max would say. "Iced coffee with melted ice? Of course you could go fetch fresh." She pretended not to notice my activity, if she could even see it in the dark, so

I reluctantly stopped, deciding again that waiting just might be sweeter.

"That's Vietnamese coffee," I exclaimed, closing my legs with a little regret and settling my breath. "That's like drinking a Jolt and a candy bar."

She rolled her eyes and licked her wine-colored lips. "Yes, it is. I love it. I have a couple pots of this a day. On bad days, more."

"Count me out. I need my sleep. That shit is industrial."

"Okay, then. I'll pass too." She licked the spoon, put it back on the tray, and reentered the tub with a shiver.

I picked up her empty glass and noticed her lip prints. I placed my own mouth over her prints and tilted the glass to capture the ice. I sucked on her gin-scented cubes, fantasizing what she would like to do with this ice all over her slippery wet body. Between her hot skin, the hot water, and my hot mouth, the ice would be a powerful, sizzling shock. Max would arch and gasp. I would brand her with it. And with my teeth. I imagined running my ice-filled mouth up her inner leg to her steaming cunt. There, I would take her slick, engorged clit in my mouth and suck it and the ice simultaneously, melting both. She would surrender everything. Her spine would become liquid, her limbs vapor, and her cunt jelly. I would smear my face with it, drink it and never stop until her coming was absolutely spent. I needed her to come in my face. I *needed* to cause it, to be with it so close. I needed her to buck on my tongue and our flesh, mine textured and hers smooth, to make mind-blowing friction.

I needed her grunts, sighs, and moans more than I ever needed any cigarette. There was a Max-shaped emptiness in my sex. I needed her to flood my face and claw my shoulders, but in the end, relax into it, pearly pink thighs falling wide, wider, wider still, to open and lift to it and take it all in at once and push it all out as she screamed, yes, Nora! Nora, Nora, Nora, fuck me; take me, Nora to the placid, sparkling black sky.

"What are you smiling about?" Max asked, dipping her head

in the water, soaking her hair, which sodden, looked like russet curly satin snakes.

I shook my head, my cunt inflamed and throbbing. I desperately tried to think of a conversation topic. I never wanted to leave her, but I might have to or I would pass out from horniness. "I'm going to Reese and Lila's for dinner tomorrow night."

Three beats of surprised silence from Max. "Oh, really?" she asked coolly. "That should be interesting."

I watched her, knowing femme language well. "How do you mean?"

"Just that. How did you meet to be invited to dinner? Who else is going? Is Sloane?" Max covered her petulance well.

"No, I'll go by myself. We hooked up after the service at Queenie's."

"Oh…after the service. At Queenie's. Did Sloane give you my message?" Max studied her toes.

"Yeah, I got it right away, but I had some stuff to take care of," I said smoothly. Soothing femmes was a natural talent. "You're not all mad at me, are you?" I sat next to her, curving her into an embrace. That surreal Amber nightmare never happened as far as I was concerned.

"No, certainly not. I wasn't home most of the day after the funeral service. It's good you came as late as you did." Max sniffed, lifting her chin.

"Bullshit," I said fondly, and with enormous discipline, moved back to my seat across from her. She was a skittish thoroughbred and I would earn her trust and let her set the pace. Then, before she knew it, she would be peacefully broken to my bridle and loving it. Just what I would do then, I never considered, as I was planning to accomplish this and be back in Los Angeles by the end of the week.

"You can let us both pretend that I'm not lying, if you would," Max said candidly.

I laughed. I suddenly, unexpectedly, respected Max far more

than a beauty and a conquest. "Ah, I could never do that, honey pot."

She flicked water in my face. I splashed back. She shoved an armload of water on me, and I responded by taking a mouthful of water and spraying her with it. Indignant, she leaned back and kicked furiously, churning water all over me. To retaliate, I fell on her, stilling her kicks. I drew her out of the water and held her as high and as close as I could, pressing the length of my body into hers and pressing hers into my own with my arms that were wrapped around her in a tender stranglehold. We were dripping wet and breathing heavily. Her arms hung limply at her sides but I still clung, cradling her like a second skin. Max's boxers and bra, see-through though they were, might as well have been chain mail. I was very conscious of my own nudity rubbing her clothes. We stared at each other for several moments. Finally, I bent my head to her neck, near her ear.

"Why don't you let me make love to you?" I whispered hoarsely. "You're using all these distractions, but we both want it. And we both need it so much." I placed a feather-light kiss on her neck and suddenly her arms were tight around me. She was shaking. She was crying. Oh, my God, I've pushed her too far. I've ruined it!

"Max, Max, baby, come on, what is it, baby?" I rocked her gently. "I put too much pressure on you, didn't I? I do that. I'm so sorry. It won't happen again. Baby, I'm sorry."

Max shook, weeping silently, not saying anything. I maneuvered us to sit and still held her, swaying and soothing. At last, she looked up with a sad but playful grin.

"No, no, it wasn't you at all. It had nothing to do with you. I'm sorry you thought so." Her smile widened. "It's just…it's just this Michelle thing. Just…I didn't know her well…and that she was *murdered* just goes all through me. I feel scared myself as if more of us are in danger. Plus, I've been in shock about it for days now and I haven't had a good cry in a while. It's all so sudden and brutal and permanent. And then, when you took me in your arms, you were so tender and strong and I heard she was your ex and it all came at me at once and…" She shrugged, wiping her eyes and pulling her hair back. "Can you tell me about her? About yourself? About your experience in Tulsa? Let's talk about something so I know you better."

I sighed, relieved. No one here was as she first appeared. Sports was so much cleaner. "It's getting late…"

"I know. Stay just a little longer?"

"Can we go in? I'm growing scales."

"Sure, come on. Will you take me up on that coffee now?"

"Still no. But I'll borrow a robe or a towel or something."

"Of course you will. Come on." She led the way into a mudroom. "Want a shower?"

"With you?" I grinned.

"No." She batted her eyes. "But I'll let you use my shower if you like and you can let your imagination run wild."

"You're heartless."

"Not at all, just smart."

"Uh-huh. Sure, I'll have a rinse."

"Okay. You take the master's shower through there," Max pointed, "and I'll take the guest. Towels and soap are found in the usual places." She disappeared.

I walked cautiously through the dimly lit home, weaving my way through rooms and furniture in the direction Max had indicated. At last, I was in the sanctum sanctorum—Max's bedroom. I was *in* the very room I had spied on from the outside. I stepped back from the doorway into the hallway darkness. What if some other slobbering horndog butch was outside spying on Max now? I hit the light off and proceeded in shadow to the bathroom. Without light I couldn't notice anything about the room, which was just as well, for the temptation to snoop was overpowering. The desire underneath that was to just slide in between the forbidden sheets and settle in. Shower and rejection be damned. Just to lie with Max. To share the night with her. To hear her breathe. To watch her sleep. I stubbed my toe on a chair and cursed juicily, thanking the chair for bumping me out of my asinine longings. This had never happened before. I had never wanted to watch someone sleep, for Christ's sake. Usually, by the time sleep was at hand, I was so exhausted from sex that I was the first to sink into slumber. Let my bevy of homegirls watch me sleep if they wanted. I snorted. Watch Max sleep? Nigga, what are you thinking?

I cracked the bathroom door and felt for the light switch. The bathroom was lavish. All marble with ornate gold fixtures. There was a large whirlpool tub and an enormous glass and marble shower for two with six ominously large showerheads. One on each wall and two above. There was a mini-refrigerator in one corner. There were candles on every surface. Max even had a chaise lounge. There were more floor-to-ceiling glass windows, but instead of the street, they opened on to a private garden. Massive ferns hung in front of the transoms at the top perimeter of the room.

"This is *obscene*." I shook my head, then smiled. "I would expect nothing less. This is a girl who loves her bath time." I warily approached the shower and studied the knobs. "I don't think I can operate that thing, but what the hell, I'll try it." I dropped my towel, startling myself by seeing dozens of my body multiplied in the wall of mirrors. The mirrored door was ajar at exactly the right angle to reproduce my image a hundredfold. I moved to correct it, but stopped, instead posing for a few minutes. I did a couple of raunchy dance moves, a couple of hot basketball court maneuvers, admired my tight butt, and then hiked my leg up, balancing my foot on a counter edge and spread my labia to get a good look at my pussy. Alice Walker wrote that a black cunt looked like a wet rose and I had never found a more apt description. A beautiful wet red rose, tens of them, all reflected back to me. What a sight!

I was suddenly self-conscious, dropped my leg, closed the door, and navigated the shower. The hot spray from all directions was invigorating. The gold clock on the wall said it was almost ten.

"What a hell of a day," I moaned, sudsing myself. Once I finished, I put on a robe I found on the back of the door. Was it Max's? I smelled it. I couldn't tell. Or was it some lover's who left it here? Or worse, was it some "guest lover" bathrobe Max kept for visitors? The style revealed nothing. It was plain, comfortable, and unisex.

Even though it was cool in the house, the wet air caused my skin to grow a sheet of damp.

"Oh, well, I'm in the robe now, that's what matters," I said as I belted it.

I found Max curled up in a cashmere robe on the sofa with her feet tucked underneath her. Her hair was wrapped in a towel and she looked squeaky-clean.

"You have anything to eat?" I asked, patting my belly.

Max stretched languidly. "Sure, come on." She turned on one of the lights on the bank of switches on the kitchen wall. Low-level recessed lighting gently warmed the dark. "What would you like?"

I stared at her until we both burst out laughing. Max lifted herself onto a counter and sat, shrugging. "Why don't you just rummage around and see what you can find? I'm not going to wait on you."

I grabbed a bag of chips, removed the clip and ate a handful. "Shit," I said, spraying crumbs, "these are stale."

"Uh-huh." Max shrugged. "It's the weather. I can barely open my doors, and if I wanted the windows open, I'd have to use a hammer. What is easy the rest of the year now requires a kick and a curse. Sometimes I just turn off the air conditioner, open the windows, and soak a top sheet in cold water and go to sleep with it on top of me."

I nodded and stepped to the gleaming stainless steel refrigerator and opened it. "What do you have in here?" I opened numerous containers.

"I don't know. Leftover stuff. Ruby cooks for me."

I looked her up and down. "You don't cook, huh?"

"Not at *all*, so drop your sexist hopes, you pig."

"You don't know what I was thinking."

"I can read you like a little black book."

"Don't you have any *meat*?" I was leaving containers all over the marble countertops.

"There should be something in there to satisfy you," she said, laughter caught in her throat.

"You've got a couple of steaks. Why don't you just grill those up for us real quick?" I smiled winningly and nudged her knee.

"You've got it all backwards, Leon. I don't do for you. You do for me." She vaulted herself gracefully off the counter, her soft robe parting and legs flashing.

The prospect made my mouth go dry, so I looked into dishes further. "Mmm, mmm, mmm, I like a woman who loves her meat," I murmured into the cold refrigerator. At last, I found some brisket and took that to the table with bread. Max watched all of this, amused. As I settled in to eat, she retrieved the cold coffee from the deck and a fresh glass of ice, poured a cup, and came to sit with me.

"You are something else." I grinned, my mouth full. Max said nothing, her eyes large. She sipped daintily from her cold mug. I did not want to appear too grateful, so I belched, put a toothpick in my mouth and my legs on the table.

"Ruby would appreciate you returning things to the way you found them," Max said. I complied, feeling utterly pussy-whipped, but knowing that cleaning up after myself was the right thing to do. "So a story for your supper?" She smiled after I sat again.

"Yeah, okay. My experience here…my experience here… well, for one thing, Tulsa has got to be the most segregated place in the world. This is such a white town. Where are all my people?"

Max laughed. "Yeah, I know. It's terrible. My neighbors think Sloane is my *help*."

"Not at all surprised." I glanced out the window where the tiny buttery lights from the guest cottage were barely visible through the trees.

Lightning flashed in the distance. "Maybe a storm on the way." Distant thunder.

"Yeah?"

"Spring and fall are our rainy seasons. We have massive thunderboomers, but we almost never have rain in the summer. The clouds just burn up. But maybe you brought stormy air with you." Max bent, unwound the towel, and sat up again, her hair hanging in tousled strings. "You were saying?"

"Can I have a cigarette?" My infernal lung/hand/mouth itch started again.

"Sure, but do let's go outside. Ruby hates a smoky kitchen."

"Who's master, you or Ruby?"

"No question, it's Ruby." She laughed.

I put a hand on the small of her back, marveling at the fuzzy down of her robe. "What's her secret?"

"You take care of my home and me, you can have certain preferences honored too," Max replied tartly, edging away from my hand and giving me a cigarette.

"Not in it that deep," I replied sternly.

"Yes, you are," she said buttery as cream.

"Now I'm certain you want me to be." I smiled. She turned away quickly and we walked outside into the moisture-drenched air. I started sweating immediately, just a prickle at the small of my back, the nape of my neck, and a melting in my armpits.

Crickets filled the night with peaceful song. Max and I sat in a glider that she kept in constant motion. I was convinced that was due to her pent-up desire. On the horizon, cloud banks were piled so high, they looked like the Rocky Mountains. It gave me pause to recognize them as clouds.

"You were saying?" she prompted politely. On the side table, I noticed magazines puffed and curled from moisture, and books swelled and warped by humidity. Max stared straight ahead. I told her all about Michelle and the secret Jack shared. About the McKerrs and Greenwood and Michelle's blackmail attempt. She listened intently.

"So I know it's the family. Some power-hungry asshole offed her and got away with it."

"Could be. What are you going to do?" Max asked.

"What do you mean? I ain't gonna tell if that's what you're asking. I have the information thirdhand, no proof, no suspects, just gossip, a peek at an unsubstantiated letter, and an alleged motive. And I'm *black*. I'm nobody here. Just ask the KKK and all your neighbors and the people of Greenwood."

"You *are* somebody." Without looking at me, Max slipped her hand into mine. It was such a tender, innocent gesture, it almost undid me. My throat tightened around a lump. Lightning flashed closer. Thunder rumbled. The air was thick as treacle. I struggled to breathe, my lungs unaccustomed to percolating in all this wet.

"Well, I guess that's your story for tonight," she said, stretching as she stood. "I can keep you no longer. I'm sure you need your rest."

"Yes, I do. I'm going to the library tomorrow to research this thing."

"What thing?"

"The race riot on Greenwood in '21. I need to know more." I shrugged and added uselessly, "I need to."

"Okay." She walked me to the back door. I stared at her until she met my gaze.

"I'm checking out of my hotel. I'll get my things and come back here. Leave the door unlocked."

Her gaze softened and she nodded, seeming more and more like a demure Southern belle.

"I know there's no lock on your bedroom door either." I grinned.

Max raised her chin defiantly. "The lock is my intention and your obedience."

I ran my tongue over my lips, considering this. I nodded and ignored her ripe, upturned mouth. I grabbed my keys and went to my car, still clad only in the borrowed robe and not caring.

Chapter Eighteen

When I returned, I found, to my suppressed triumph, the door unlocked and the house dark except for one light that led me to the guest bedroom. I locked the front door, dropped my suitcase on the bed, and tiptoed to Max's room. Works every time, I thought. You top 'em right and before you know it, you got a beautiful bottom on your hands.

The door was closed, so I just stroked it and returned to my room. The thunderstorm was growling its way over the city, the rain just beginning. I closed my bedroom door, turned off the light, and collapsed into sleep.

I was awakened by a crack of thunder. Lightning flashed, rain was pelting the windows. Without moving, I opened my eyes a millimeter and saw Max's outline in the doorway. I smiled, closed my eyes, and fell asleep again.

The next morning, food smells awoke me to a sweet sunny day loud with birdsong and rasping locusts. I ambled groggily to the kitchen where Max and Sloane sat with another woman at the table.

"Well, well, well, N. You finally got it together." Sloane grinned.

"Nah, nah, I'm only a *guest*," I replied more bitterly than necessary.

Max and Sloane looked at each other. Max continued eating eggs silently.

"Closer, my man, closer. Closer than anyone's been since—"

"Sloane!" Max barked. "Your burned muffins are stinking up this whole house."

"I know, I'm sorry, Max. I'm just playing. You know me, I play too much. Nora, this is DeAndretta. DeAndretta, this is Nora, just passing through from LA solving mysteries on the PI tip."

DeAndretta smiled shyly, the glow on her walnut skin unmistakable. I nodded to her, feeling jealous and miserable. Somehow, being in Max's house was worse than yearning to be here from the hotel. I had not gone this long without sex since… since I was a teenager. I glared at Max, who was oblivious.

"Nora, Ruby left quite a lot of breakfast. There are scrambled eggs, toast, juice, bacon, cereal—whatever you like. Help yourself. I've got to go get dressed. And did you hear? Electricity is out all over town from snapped tree limbs and severe winds. I bet the roads will be impassable from all the branches."

"Guess we'll go too." Sloane stood, wiping her mouth. "I've gotta get this one home before her husband notices her missing."

DeAndretta slapped Sloane's arm. "She's just playing again." They laughed together. "Nice to meet you all."

"See ya, N. Later, Max," Sloane called.

"So…just us." I looked at Max, who had the gall to look fresh and beautiful.

"Yes, and now, just you." Max rose. "Enjoy your breakfast. Here's a spare key; use it wisely."

"For good and not for evil," I promised, clasping it. Max smiled.

After breakfast, I sat on my bed, contemplating the map. The closest library was downtown so I decided on that one.

I got a cup of ice and crunched it viciously as I dressed. I popped more allergy meds. I left without seeing Max. I drove downtown. I couldn't find a parking space close so I walked three blocks, simmering the whole way. By the time I arrived, I was angry and slimy wet and sunburned.

CHAPTER NINETEEN

The library was four floors, and a kind librarian helped me find the right section.

"You may want to look at the old newspapers too. That's on the third floor."

"Okay, thanks." I settled in with avid curiosity. I randomly picked two books. One entitled *Greenwood: America's Tragedy* and another called *Broken Dreams: The Undeclared War on African-Americans.*

The story pulled me in. Due to segregation, there was a thriving black economy in north Tulsa, the center of which was the street called Greenwood. The blacks were entirely self-sufficient: their own doctors, lawyers, and bankers as well as craftsmen, entrepreneurs, skilled and unskilled labor, grocery stores, a movie theater, restaurants, barbers, retail shops, everything. It was a place booming with success and expanding. Racial tensions had been simmering for years before the riot and there had been beatings and lynchings. But because blacks had served in World War I, they had returned with an intolerance for abuse and there was much more anger and mobilization to fight back.

"We just mind our business and try to get on with life and Whitey just won't have it," I muttered. I was beginning to feel anxious reading this terrible tale.

Then, on May 31, 1921, after a silly, hysterical white woman falsely accused a black male elevator operator of assault, it was gasoline on the smoldering coals of racist hatred.

First, the accused man was put into jail "for his own protection" as there was already a white mob gathered to lynch him. Next, the honorable black veterans and other movers and shakers in Greenwood went to meet the mob downtown at the jail to prevent the lynching. Then every white man that cared to be was deputized, including many members of the Ku Klux Klan, of which the police chief and fire chief were rumored to have been members. That entitled them to be armed against a peaceful, unarmed black population. The majority of black men were systematically rounded up and jailed, also "for their own protection." Included in the sweep were also some women and children carted off to prison when no one had committed any crime. Next, whatever arms the police could find were confiscated, so the remaining residents were unable to defend themselves against the building assault. Then, several hours after many incendiary editorials published in the *Tulsa Tribune* and *Extras*, including one infamous headline that read: TO LYNCH A NIGGER TONIGHT (the original of which has mysteriously disappeared, no trace having been found of it even in the archives), the looting, bombing, and murdering began. Most of the black men were unarmed and helpless in jail while the rest of the families battled it out the best they could, often just hiding until the whites had stolen what they wanted and set fire to the house before leaving. The atrocities were inconceivable. A black man was tied to the bumper of a car and dragged down the street until dead. His head exploded like a melon, witnesses reported. Children watched as their parents were shot in front of them; businesses and shops were looted and destroyed; a whole world, carefully, lovingly built, was annihilated.

Jack was right. Tulsa never asked for help to contain the conflagration or to manage the mob of white people. Tulsa never applied for aid for the remaining black citizens after the massacre.

And it hadn't admitted any fault or parted with one thin dime since. Even the graves remained unmarked.

I slammed the book down, and ran to the bathroom, shaking. Luckily, it was empty, so I was able to lock myself in a stall and tremble and coach myself into calming down.

To put a hasty patch on my broken race heart, I thought of basketball. I ran a series of flashbacks through my head as I gulped air.

I was running to the basket; oh, yeah, I drained it; I'm into the paint; I stroked it; a good one right into the bucket, I hit the tres. Oh, a stellar pass by Nora Delaney and I get it back and drive it to the hoop! Oh, yeah, it's Delaney with the double double!

My breathing started to slow down. Thoughts turned to my team and coaching them, yelling at them as they pounded up and down the court.

"It's your job when you're going for penetration to get square to the hoop. We have no mid-range game; it's either a layup or a free, let's work on that, girls. I used to have a deep team, a Cinderella team, but I lost my seniors, so now I have a young team, a rebuild year, but that's no excuse for how you're playing out there. Now, Lindsay has outstanding execution and feeds to the post well, but she can't carry us. Morgan, you had fifteen rims and eight boards, let's get that number down. Jackson, you're just throwing junk, sit down. Help me out, I can't win these games by shouting; I need you to actually play basketball. Come on, be powerful. Be strong; be invincible; don't think you are, *be* that you are!"

Those last viciously whispered words rang in my head as I finally stood and unlocked the stall. I washed my hands and splashed water on my face.

"C'mon," I said to myself. I strolled outside, my lungs aching for the stinging pollution of smoke, my nerves shredded, my fingers and mouth unbearably empty. The blazing sun hit me like a wall when I opened the door. At every office, there were always legions of exiled smokers, standing around bullshitting and glaring righteously at passersby. I hoped to find them to bum a cigarette. At this library, there were none. Or perhaps I chose the wrong door. I needed a cigarette immediately. Even though I was perpetually quitting, I was ready to buy a pack *right now* if only a machine would rise up out of the concrete. I hadn't bought cigarettes in a year, but Greenwood had snapped me. I had borrowed cigarettes in my briefcase in the car that was parked through the heat so far away. I would rather bribe one off someone now than delay my need any further with an exhausting walk.

There was a homeless man sitting on a bench in the shade. He was smoking. I approached him. "Hey, man, what's up?" The shade didn't help.

The man nodded.

"Listen man, I ain't gonna front. I *need* a smoke and you've got some. I'll buy one off you for a good price."

The man looked at me, waiting. I did some quick estimations in my head. In LA, the guy would probably want five bucks for a cigarette, so here, I should be able to get it for a buck or two.

"I'll give you a dollar for one cigarette." I held out the bill, my back steaming.

The man shook his head.

"Two?" My voice went high.

The man removed a crumpled pack from his pocket and removed one cigarette. "I can't get a pack of these for less than three," he said.

"Bullshit!" I cried. But my jones spoke louder. "Okay, three."

"Twenty." The man smiled.

"Twenty! Are you outta your motherfucking mind?"

"Nope. But you are." The man tenderly replaced the cigarette into the pack and into his pocket. I watched it disappear. My desperation made this bargain okay.

"All right, asshole, here," I held a twenty in my fist. "But I get two at that price." I wiped my face on my sleeve.

The man laughed. "No, you don't. You get one. You want two, I'll give you the second one for fifteen more. Yield marketing."

"Yield marketing," I exclaimed incredulously. My chest was wet.

The man nodded. "What the market will bear. I don't care whether you buy from me or not. I'm not *trying* to sell to you, so that's the deal. Now, with this money, I won't have to eat at Sally's tonight."

"Sally's?" I asked, taking my precious cigarette and handing him the money. I felt through all my pockets. Damn. No matches. They were in my briefcase too.

"Salvation Army."

I was flooded with shame that I had been so stingy. "Here's another twenty. I'll take a second one and a light." I sat on the bench in the shade with him. I smoked my sweet cigarette slowly, taking it in deep and holding on to the smoke. I felt calmer, but suddenly Tulsa made me so sad. Homeless people, Greenwood, Michelle, while overhead, beautiful old trees swayed and waved in the roasting wind, leaves dropping like confetti. Green grass gone brown was underfoot. Flowers nodded in agreement, traffic flowed evenly. It all looked so peaceful.

"Well, look, I gotta go." I said at last. "And I'm sorry—"

"It ain't no thing," he said. "We're cool. Thanks for your business. Come again soon."

I smiled. Once I reentered the library, I walked with shaking legs back to my seat. I felt nasty, like I had just done a drug deal and besmirched the hallowed halls of learning. It wouldn't have mattered what that guy would've asked for a smoke, I would've paid. Do the tobacco companies know that? I sat at the table, flipping idly through the books, becoming freshly horrified at the graphic photos and feeling utterly lost, grief-stricken, powerless, and so angry. I understood Jack's rant and had a lot more to add to it.

I looked up suddenly at the sound of a gentle cough. Practice had told me the sound was a woman, so I wanted to check it out.

Max stood in front of me, looking magnificent in faded jeans, boots, and a white T-shirt. Looking suddenly so *Caucasian*. My entire family seemed to be staring at Max through my eyes. I felt a nappy afro sprout on my gleaming black scalp. In my mind, my grandmother's gnarled, arthritic hands petted me; my mother's soft smile and steely spirit warmed me.

I felt every generation of my bloodline all the way back to Africa. I seemed to be growing darker by the second. And what am I doing, chasing her sorry cracker ass? I thought before I could stop myself. I shook it off when I noticed the worry in her eyes.

"Take you to lunch?" Max held out her hand. Wordlessly, I reached out and took it.

Chapter Twenty

We went to Olson's Buffeteria, where Max assured me the food was legendary and old-fashioned in the very best way. There was a line of businesspeople out the door.

"You have to try the chicken-fried steak. It's required that while you visit, you eat one. It is smothered in homemade cream gravy and it will melt in your mouth. Everything they make is good. And they have mile-high pies. Save room for a piece. Are you okay? You haven't said anything yet."

I shook my head. I was numb. Greenwood was nationally known black history. How had I not known it? Why hadn't someone told me? Why the fuck did I waste all those years in school on the sanitized and revised history of white men when this was out there begging to be known? Why was the world so wrong? If blacks had done it to whites, it would be in every history book. I was revolted at white privilege. At straight privilege. Christian privilege. Money privilege. Power privilege. I wanted to run until my lungs burned out of me, wisps of smoke curling with every exhale. Run until my mind was jelly with no awareness and no memory. Run until I was pure.

The lunch line moved swiftly. Wonderful aromas almost relaxed me. I smiled stiffly at Max and shrugged. My vocal cords were paralyzed. If I tried to use them, I might start yelling instead. I felt as if I had found something new, like I had discovered fire.

How could everyone around her be so calm and nonchalant? Didn't they know what had happened?

The line for Olson's led into a very narrow hallway. There were photos of old Tulsa on the walls. Signs commanded customers to be ready with their orders to keep up the speed. As they neared the food, I noticed it was all older black men serving plates to the white businesspeople. A knife in my throat unlatched my voice.

"No, no, no, no," I whispered, my eyes fixed on the servers. Max stared, trying to guess what upset me.

"That's just Solomon." Max, confused and soothing, gestured to the oldest worker. "He's great. He's been here for a hundred years."

I turned on her. "You call him by his first name? And what does he call you? Miss Abbott? Or ma'am? Does he tap dance for you?"

"What?" she asked. People were beginning to stare.

"I've got to get out of here." I saw no way out other than shoving and pushing people as I fought my way back through the cramped line. Max followed, making apologies.

At the car, Max sat in silence with me. Finally, she asked, "What's wrong?" I stared straight ahead.

"I'll take you somewhere else." She started the car and drove. I noticed we passed Swan Lake. Images and sentences from the books about Greenwood just kept flashing in my mind. It was apropos that the pictures were in black and white. They slid into my thoughts like a drowned savior.

TO LYNCH A NIGGER TONIGHT, the white tourist couple posing in front of a black family's burned-out, destroyed home, black children being held in custody at gunpoint by white police, photos of dead black people merely captioned: victim, victim, victim. A ghostly photo of twisted metal bedsteads, still standing in spite of the homes still smoking ashes; white Tulsans roaming free while blacks were imprisoned for no crime; BC Franklin practicing law out of a tent; black Tulsans forced to spend that winter in tents; cremated dreams, and for what?

Max stopped the car.

"The Savory Spoon?" I asked.

"Yes, we can sit outside in the shade if it's not too hot."

"You say, I'll do." I was indifferent to the scalding weather and molten air.

Max and I went inside where she just informed the hostess that we would be outside. As we turned to go, I noticed bold, brilliant colors everywhere—animal print carpets, and tens of beautiful torsos of nude women all painted vibrantly and hung many to a wall.

"Reese do those?" I gestured to the feminine forms gracing the walls. Max and I found a table in the shade. She laughed.

"No, she didn't. Good guess, though. I'm afraid I don't know what to recommend here since I love everything."

"I really don't care what I eat. Or that I do at all." I leaned back, stretching, thinking I needed a long game and a great fuck to clear my mind. Then a slow cigarette to calm.

After we ate, Max finally asked again, "What's wrong? Something about Michelle?"

I chuckled dryly. "No, that's cool." I shrugged. "I mean, fairly. At least I know how to handle it. But I don't know how to manage this. I did what I told you, I researched Greenwood."

Max sucked in her breath.

"It's as if I've had on blinders and they're gone, poof. It's inside me like a virus. You know all about it, don't you?" I prayed that she did. For some reason, that would redeem her in my eyes right now.

"Yes. I had a progressive education and had very progressive parents. I went through a private integrated school system that was sixty/forty black to white. I memorized 'Lift Every Voice and Sing,' which, as I'm sure you know, is the black national anthem."

A flood of gratitude swamped me. I clasped her hand. "I thought Rodney King was bad. I thought Abner Luima was bad. I thought Amadou Diallo was bad. And those are only the ones we know about. I thought 'Driving While Black' and profiling were bad. I thought being passed over for promotions was bad. I thought not being able to get credit or a loan or a taxi was bad. Shit. I didn't know anything. Now everything looks different. Now I'm different."

Max listened attentively. The sympathy in her face made me weak and weepy, so I looked away. The Savory Spoon's overhead fans and cool water misters barely provided any relief. I licked perspiration off the corners of my mouth. The ice in our drinks was melted, the glasses rested in puddles. After we ate, Max knew to change the subject.

"So, wasn't the food fabulous?"

I looked around and said carefully, "The décor is amazing."

"And the food was great, right?"

"The location is good."

"And the food?"

"Sitting outside is very nice."

"Okay, so I'll take you to your car." Max laughed.

"Yeah, I need some alone time." I walked slowly to her vehicle feeling as if I were an unexploded bomb.

Near the library, we stood next to my rental car and hugged. I was regretful I couldn't appreciate all the erotic possibilities of the hug, but I was too far gone. Max drove away and I got in my car and decided to look at north Tulsa.

As I drove, I admitted my profoundly naïve hope of finding a photo at the library of Old Man McKerr shooting the black man in the head. What I had found was much worse. And it had blindsided me. I knew that race riots were commonplace around 1921, and I knew vaguely about Rosewood in Florida and similar assaults on segregated thriving black settlements all over the nation including New Orleans, Boston, Philadelphia, Duluth, and even Los Angeles, but Tulsa was by far the worst of all. The most destruction, devastation, and death. The *most* hostile and racist aggression to prevent rebuilding or *any sort of restitution*. I remembered the beautiful monument I had seen at the cemetery. Not erected by the city, I realized.

"Probably some old brother bought the whole thing and paid to put it on his private plot," I muttered. I just drove aimlessly through all of north Tulsa, spontaneously cruising neighborhoods, not caring where I ended up, only needing to see these people. Was sorrow stamped on their faces? Would I recognize an ancestor to such tragedy? I fumbled for the box of wooden matches I left on the passenger seat and lit one, watching it burn. I needed to smoke to do this. I extracted my emergency cigarettes from the briefcase full of paperwork and stats and game plans and put the end into the match and slowly sucked the cigarette to life.

What would their homes and businesses tell me? Were they different from me? Were they nobler because they had suffered and I had always been middle class and well insulated from overt abuse? Would their eyes know things? Would they be blacker than me?

I drove by Tisdale's Barbecue again, a place called Southern-style Barbecue, May's Barbecue, and Elijah's Barbecue where the sign out front proclaimed, "Thou Shalt Not Kill, no profanity, open all night."

I saw persistent devastation and struggle present in north Tulsa. Even though I'd read that Greenwood had rebuilt itself and was thriving in the thirties even better than its previous peak years, it had survived by segregation. Once the white merchants realized that a black dollar and a white dollar were equally green, and integration began, Greenwood died. The heart of the black economy dried up. Black businesses perished. The greater segregation began. Put all the successful businesses and shops and services on the south side and abandon the black residents of the north side who were now forced to travel far and wide for goods and services. Weeds grew in the middle of Greenwood Avenue for fifty years. No renaissance for north Tulsa. No resurgence of merchants setting up shop to serve the mostly black dollars.

I noticed all that was absent from north Tulsa. Things that should have been there to bind the community together, but weren't. North Tulsa had no theaters, no grocery stores, where on the south side, there might be three supermarkets all dueling for business on four corners. North Tulsa had no offices, only one bank, no shopping centers or malls, no boutiques, no restaurants other than the four barbecues, no municipal landscaping, only two parks and no mid- to high-range services offered. Hardly any legitimate businesses at all. And the north side had all the train tracks. It was a cultural desert. Blocks and blocks and miles and miles of depressed housing. All the projects were on the north side.

What there *was* and plenty of it: pawn shops, body shops, mechanics, rent-to-own shops, bleak, bland industrial parks and enormous factories, abandoned warehouses, off-brand stores with cheap goods, resale shops, quik marts that accepted only WIC, auto parts superstores, check cashing and cash fast outfits, storefront loans, cheap food chains, a drugstore or two with bars on the windows, filthy, deep discount superstores, bars, bars, bars, and churches, churches, churches, churches.

The poverty was obvious. What was also evident was that the city of Tulsa didn't give a damn. The ugliness of a lot of this part of town tore at me and depressed me.

But also, in a way, north Tulsa was nice. I had the feeling of being in a subculture that was undetectable to the mainstream radar. Like I could do what I wanted and no one would care or tell. North Tulsa was so so far from the courthouse where the cops parked. It was so far from Whitey and his neighborhood covenants and codified behavior.

And some parts were beautiful simply because they had been left alone. There was a Baptist church that was shaped like a huge upright purple teardrop. There were fields and fields of clover and wisteria gone wild. It was quiet and peaceful with no traffic. On the north side, there was personality and individuality. On the north side, there was architectural interest in buildings from eras that believed in design and quality. Homes and yards had actual differences, not that neo-suburban conformist look. In the north, there were open-air fruit and vegetable stands; there was a nightclub painted hot pink; there was a large new university, still isolated by fields; there were beautiful historic homes that had been built in the early oil boom; there were wide, pretty streets and jungles of old urban trees.

I preferred this laid-back area full of real people and real buildings and even real ugliness to the flat, bland, white mainstream corporate commercial mall culture sprawling farther south. Cookie-cutter homes, cookie-cutter shops, cookie-cutter businesses, cookie-cutter cars, and yes, cookie-cutter people. I firmly believed that the suburbanization of the nation was killing the individual soul. I saw that the nation was becoming gated communities with super malls connected by turnpikes. That caused me pain about Los Angeles, so I stayed in my particular middle-class ghettos that pleased me, so I never had to look at the further destruction of my hometown. With everything the same and everyone safe and tame, who would be the fools? The wise men? The artists? The lunatics? The saviors? The eccentrics? Creativity and sensuality needed chaos, mess, and individualism to thrive. But with all the people going from their just-alike homes to their just-alike malls with their just-alike clothes and eating the just-alike food, America was losing its heart. People became more afraid of difference rather than less. The great United States was becoming bland, homogenized, risk-free, and average. What was the difference between Seattle and Chicago? The Starbucks were on different corners.

People need inner cities and windows that open and front porches and secret paths and old women growing herbs in their front yards. People need to hear a rooster in the distance and to have wildlife around them and wild people too. Society needs beautiful bridges and breathtaking parks and unique shops and wildflowers and wonder. Wonder. The mall killed wonder. The mall killed daring. The mall killed window-shopping.

Why don't the cities at least tell the truth about themselves and make postcards of the malls and the snarled traffic around Banana Republic? I didn't understand it. If cities wanted to show themselves as having stunning architecture, why didn't they continue to make it?

"It's everywhere, not just Tulsa," I chided myself, while realizing that if I were to settle in Tulsa for some reason, I would choose to live north.

I returned to Max's. Both Sloane's and Max's cars were gone. I went inside and collapsed into a deep, troubled nap.

I woke to a phone ringing. I stretched and saw I had been asleep for five hours. I had half an hour to get to Lila and Reese's.

I showered, took more allergy pills, dressed, and searched Max's wine rack for a bottle I could give Lila. I consulted the map and plotted my course and left after placing a note to Max on her pillow, telling her where I had gone and when I might be back.

"I'm already whipped," I muttered hatefully, not entirely disliking it.

CHAPTER TWENTY-ONE

At Winthrop Tower, the doorman buzzed the couple to make sure I was expected.

"*No-Ra!*" Lila cried, holding her cigarette holder high and extending her other hand for a kiss. "So glad you could come." Lila embraced me, holding too long. Reese cleared her throat and Lila let go reluctantly. Reese stuck her hand out and I gripped it, winning the macho butch-off. Reese seemed to strain and stretch for tallness and once again, I was fiercely proud of my chiseled body and skyscraper height.

"My pleasure," I purred to Lila as I handed Reese the bottle of wine, dismissing her. Reese just rubbed me the wrong way and I wanted to rankle her. "My, Lila, have you gotten more beautiful since the last time I saw you? What am I saying, of course you have."

"Oh, you darling poppet. You simply must stay in town as long as you can," Lila cried giddily. Reese glared at me. It would be a long evening.

"Let's sit. Nora, you come here close to me." Lila clattered grandly over the parquet floors in her leopard-print mules and settled on the love seat, drawing her billowy, leopard-print dress out of the way and patting the space next to her.

"I believe I will. Tulsa is the welcomest place I've ever

been." Knowing I was flirting with danger as well as with Lila, I grinned big and sat.

"How soon will you be on your way then, Norene?" Reese asked, sitting in an overstuffed chair on Lila's right, touching Lila's knee to bring her attention back.

"Nora," I said. Reese shrugged. "I'm not sure, maybe longer than I planned." I smiled unpleasantly at Reese.

"We'll have to keep her forever. Isn't she just adorable? We'll have to make sure she never leaves, right, Reese Cup?" Lila's eyes smoldered at Reese, who didn't rise to the bait.

"What are you drinking?" Reese rose, shaking the wrinkles from her pressed khakis, and stood before the bar.

"G and T."

"I'll have my usual, Reese darling," Lila said.

"Right. Vodka rocks and gin and tonic. Bombay all right?"

"Sure."

"I had a lover who drank only gin and tonics," Reese said casually, mixing drinks.

"Really?" My chest felt tight. I couldn't ask who it was because I didn't know anyone here and to reveal my Max attraction to this barracuda would be fatal. There was also something going on between Lila and Reese. An undercurrent of rage and passion. They had either fought or fucked recently. Probably both. I knew that Lila's flirtation was just to get to Reese. Well, fine with me. I'd been a part of plenty of ugly lesbian scenes and cruel head trips, one more wouldn't hurt. I knew this territory and was good at it.

"Oh, dear, I'm so sorry, Nora darling, I don't know where my head has been." Lila glared at Reese's back. "I should've invited a nice single woman for you."

"We don't know any nice ones," Reese said, bringing drinks.

"We could call someone now if you have a friend in mind," Lila offered.

"Well, that Max Abbott seemed interesting." I couldn't resist, even though I knew it was a mistake.

Reese came to life. "Yes! Call Max."

Lila tittered. "Call old Max? Maxi-Pad, as she is sometimes known, because she's such a definite rag. Don't be silly. She can barely string sentences together. And if we sing tonight," Lila batted her eyes and tilted her head toward the gleaming grand piano perched in front of the sheet of windows overlooking the city, "she simply wouldn't fit in. She has as much coordination as a quadro in a wheelchair and she can't carry a tune with a handle on it. Besides, she has karate class tonight, I believe. But we can call if you both want to…" Lila shrugged primly, unembarrassed by her tirade.

"I thought that class was tomorrow," Reese said.

"Or watercolor, or church or something." Lila sipped her drink, blinking plaintively at me. "I guess you'll just have to make do with little old me for tonight." She placed her cigarette holder in her mouth and pouted around it.

"You're more than enough woman for a dozen dykes," I said, ever chivalrous in the face of raw need. I was trying to figure out why Reese wanted Max to come over. "I'm afraid I'm a bit like Max, though," I began and hesitated only a little at Lila's sharp, hateful look and Reese's slow stare, "that I can't carry a tune. But your singing makes my sap rise," I added, making sure Lila felt exclusively adored.

"If only we could get Reese to leave, you could have me all to yourself."

"We may be able to arrange that, my pet," Reese said over her cell phone suddenly ringing. She reached into her pocket to get the phone, glanced at the number, and left the room to take the call.

"Reese." Lila rolled her eyes. "Her business keeps her hopping."

"What business is that, exactly?" I sipped my drink. Reese

had given me only tonic water. I debated whether to freshen my drink myself or make Reese do it for me when she returned, but decided that adding alcohol to head games tonight was not a good idea.

"Her painting," Lila answered, staring hungrily at me and licking her lips.

I swallowed this tale and my tonic with difficulty. "Her painting? Her painting keeps her busy?"

"Yes, she's out all hours, meeting models, wining and dining clients, trying to land commissions, attending shows, putting on exhibits, volunteering at galleries."

"Wait a minute. Part-time *portrait* painting keeps Reese busier than you and you own a restaurant/club and have a singing career?"

"I know. It's hard to believe, isn't it? Well, it's true."

"Of course it is," I said, knowing that it wasn't true and also knowing not to push Lila out of this denial. "All the painters I know have beepers and cells." Or maybe they had an open relationship. Maybe they had agreed on primary partnership with polyamory. Maybe that's why Lila was flirting so hard.

"I miss her. She is gone so much. She doesn't seem to realize anymore that I have needs." Lila moved closer to me.

Oh, the old "needs" chestnut. "Of course you have needs," I said without irony. "That's what affairs are for."

"Affairs!" Lila drained her glass and handed it to me with a nod. "Reese and I are monogamous. I would *kill* her and she would kill me twice."

I was troubled but refilled Lila's drink. We sat in silence until Reese returned.

"Behaving yourselves?" Reese asked jovially.

"Nora thought we were nonmonogamous. It might've been a pass," Lila said, pouting at Reese. I cringed, sighing.

"Never, my princess. You are my one and only queen." Reese kissed Lila's wrist. "I never even look at or desire any other women, Nora. I get my deepest pleasure from trust."

Reese stared into Lila's eyes, melting her with sloppy affection. "Complete devotion, total trust, and unconditional love." Reese bent and kissed Lila's nose and forehead. Lila closed her eyes as if receiving a sacrament.

I shifted. "I'm not feeling so well. Perhaps we could postpone dinner."

Lila opened her eyes and glared at me. "Out of the question. We have everything you need here. Ipecac, Pepto, Tums, Alka-Seltzer, milk of magnesia, Maalox, Ex-Lax, Tucks, Preparation H, aspirin, Advil, Tylenol, Benadryl, Visine, booze, sugar, and caffeine. I slaved over this dinner, you simply must stay."

"Okay, sure. Maybe another tonic?" I looked at Reese, who was unruffled and politely rose to refill my glass.

"Well, sadly, I must go," Reese said, rattling ice.

"No!" Lila exclaimed.

"Relax, sweetheart, I can stay thirty minutes or so. Hopefully long enough to show Nora some more of my work and then, regrettably, I have an engagement."

"Reese, I swear. You knew we had this planned with Nora." Lila's chest was starting to pinken.

"Excuse us a moment." Reese handed me the glass, cupped Lila's elbow, and propelled her gracefully into another room, closing the door. I heard Lila's shouts and Reese's calm, measured voice.

I wanted to leave, but felt I was integral to this game, whatever it was, and I was a prisoner of this dinner. Lila had wanted me here, I had come, tried to leave once, it hadn't worked, so I must stay and see this through. It would be over faster if I didn't resist. All would unfold in due time. But I was uneasy and would rather just be at Max's…

The door opened and Reese and Lila emerged. Reese looked sheepish and apologetic; Lila dabbed her eyes with a tissue.

"How's that drink working for you?" Reese asked.

"It leaves me remarkably clearheaded."

"Isn't that nice?" Reese grinned. I got a chill up my spine.

"Listen, if you two have some personal problem—"

"It isn't 'we' who have the problem, it's Lila," Reese answered firmly. Lila sat limply on the couch, blowing her nose.

"Okay, whatever. Please, let's do this another time. This seems too complicated." I felt obliged to try to leave again so they could insist I stay.

Lila's head snapped up. "Absolutely not. I worked all day on dinner and I'm not going to have that ruined because of some"—Lila's voice rose with each epithet—"self-centered, inconsiderate, rude, insensitive, good-for-nothing, freeloading, worthless *jerk*!"

"Simmer down, Lila. You're making a fool of yourself. Have another drink." Reese handed Lila a fresh glass.

"Thank you, darling." Lila switched moods suddenly. Then she curled her body around mine. "Go ahead and go, Reese. Nora promised to take care of me."

"That right, Nora?" Reese looked at me with a steely glint in her eyes.

"I'm not going to be in the middle of this." I extricated myself. "I better just go."

"Well, it's eat dinner here now or never because you're never setting foot in my house again," Reese said coolly.

I stood and stared her down, willing myself to become even bigger and blacker. "Let it be never, then," I whispered.

Reese smiled sweetly, changing tactics. "I'm sorry, Nora. Please accept my apology. It is rare that I get to inflict my pride on someone new, so please stay and let me show you my paintings. Please." Reese held out her hand for a make-up shake.

"Please stay, Nora. Don't leave me alone to have a lonely dinner all by myself while Reese is away. Please," Lila entreated softly.

I looked from one to the other doubtfully. Finally, I shook Reese's outstretched hand and again won the macho butch-off. Reese had remarkably small, soft hands.

"Come, my studio is this way."

"I'll set the table. Don't you two be long," Lila sang, her bubbles and trumpets restored.

Reese unlocked a door and pulled me inside. I was puzzled that Reese would lock a door in her own home.

It was a magnificent studio. Very large with floor-to-ceiling windows to let in all available natural light. There was a panoramic view of both downtown and the river. The room had a deliberate clutter about it, as if Reese had studied magazines about how a true artist's studio should look and copied it. There's linseed oil *just there*, and crumpled rags *just there*, and dollops of paint *there* and a stack of palettes *there* and easels and canvases propped *there* and *there*.

"It's nice," I grudgingly admitted.

"Can't have skylights, obviously." Reese indicated the twenty-foot ceilings with the sumptuous crown moldings done in gold leaf separating theirs from the condo above.

"Here's one I'm working on now." Reese dramatically tore the sheet off a canvas. "Not quite finished, but coming along."

I locked my jaw. It was Max. Max nude. Max naked and sleepy on her stomach, drowsing in a ray of light, her hair tumbled over her back and shoulders, her immense back porch of rosy buttock, and could I be mistaken? Her ass had a *satisfied* look about it. The painting of Max was crackling with eroticism like electricity. Reese's paintings of Lila had not. They had been sweet and sentimental, but a bit dowdy and frumpy compared to this. The portrait of Max was unfinished, yes, but only in the background. Each stroke was loving and sexual, even the pink soles of her feet. In that second it took to register my hurt and outrage, I knew everything about Reese. Reese brought me in here to tell me this.

Reese wasn't just a painter; she was a practiced predator. She fucked everyone she painted and only Lila did not know. She needed Lila for the house and the money and the exposure and the social status, but this room was saturated in sex. Only as I began to contain my pain did I notice the other details in the room: a bathroom and shower, a chaise lounge, a stereo, a basket of toys such as a body brush, feathers, blindfold, body paint and powder, oils, and a *bed*, for Christ's sake.

Out of the corner of my eye, I noticed Reese watching me with a smirk on her face. She wanted me to know this secret, but why? Was she boasting or confessing? And right in Lila's own house? Lord God, that was sick and cruel. My stomach dropped when I considered it. Maybe Reese wanted to claim Max. Or to show me how crazy and reckless she really was?

With purpose born of certainty, I strode to a door in another wall, flung it open, and found it led to the hallway. "Just as I suspected. How perfect for you, Reese, you pro."

For the first time, Reese grinned happily. "Let me show you more of my favorites."

Reese drew the sheet off a stack of a dozen or more paintings leaning against the wall. All of Max.

Max on her back, Max with her legs open, Max brushing her hair, Max curled into a comma, Max draped off the bed, Max washing herself in a metal tub.

"Pretty great, huh? I've had huge offers for these, but I won't sell."

My tongue was a withered root. Apparently I had not won the macho butch-off. "These are okay, but I prefer the ones of Lila," I said after finding my voice. "They are more spatially interesting. They have a wonderful contradiction of language and are leaner. They have more depth and complexity." I congratulated myself on my pompous lies. "They are better. These are simply…boring. Nudes of this lewd style have been done to *death.* But perhaps you could get Hallmark interested in them." I surreptitiously wiped my brow as Reese frowned, studying the paintings. Her face was both sickly and mottled red. "It's a bit stuffy in here; can we go out on the balcony?" I pressed. I couldn't stay in this room another moment without beating Reese senseless and rocketing over to Max's and strangling her too.

"Certainly." Reese recovered her poise, covered the paintings, and opened the balcony door.

Reese and I stood in the breeze in silence, watching the sun set. The multicolored carpet of lawns far below was all different shades of brown. Tan, gold, beige, not a blade of green grass to be seen. Piles of dried yellow leaves from dusty, tired trees followed the wet wind. I thought my skin might boil right off my face, but I felt clearer on the balcony. I ran a hand over my slick bald head. "Naïve women are convenient, aren't they?"

Reese looked at me with another happy wolfish grin. "Women are like a box of chocolates. I want to stick my finger in each one and eat what's inside."

"And Lila?"

"Lila is my rock. Lila is my home base. Lila is my partner. Lila is my *wife*. I need Lila like I need my breath."

"Why tell me all this?"

Reese moved closer. "I thought maybe we had a kinship in kind. I thought perhaps we were alike. And if we were, we could be friends. And friends don't rat on each other. You know what I'd do if any stupid, meddling fuck ever betrayed me to Lila?"

I watched Reese carefully.

"Why, I might just pitch someone like that right off this balcony."

I looked down. It was all dead grass below, but too high to be survivable. "Reese, what you do is your business. You're a shameless dirty dog, but it's not my fight. I'll tell you, though, one kindred spirit to another—you'll be found out. If not sooner, then later."

Reese kept grinning. "No, I won't." Her certainty and bravado were both appalling and disquieting.

"Lila probably has dinner ready," I said.

"Max tells me that you're quite a lover," Reese said.

I was instantly hooked and took a breath to protest when I realized that Reese was fishing. "What else do you know?" I said, staring at the water, watching tiny joggers and cyclists move up and down the river path.

"She says you have a certain…prowess that she's never experienced before."

I decided to play along when I realized what a liar and cunning manipulator Reese was. Reese counted on everyone around her telling her the truth so she had shields of knowledge as power and protection.

"Yeah." I sniffed my two right fingers. "Max is very special herself. It is interesting that she would confide in you. I'm flattered." I turned to Reese and faced her, each of us attempting to make the other blink.

Lila knocked on the locked door of the studio. "It's all ready," she called.

We ate our salads by candlelight. Lila tried to make conversation above the jazz background music by chattering like a caged monkey.

"Well, I told Becky that that was simply unacceptable. Dug 9 cannot be hired without me. We are a package deal. It is Lila James *and* Dug 9. Not Lila James *or* Dug 9. Not Dug 9 with or without Lila James. They need a singer to give the group focus and some zing and pep. Who would want to book a group without a singer anyway? That's simply unheard of. It's silly. I don't do every number." Lila downed another vodka rocks.

I chewed, ignoring Reese and concentrating dreamily on Lila's charming overbite.

"The client will have some instrumentals in between. The clients can even have some input on our play list. But split us up and hire only the pieces you want? No. I told her no, we're a team." Lila waggled her cocktail glass at Reese, who obediently rose, made a refill, and returned it to Lila, who sipped it, frowned, and gave it back. Reese took the drink to the bar a second time, remixed, and gave the glass back to Lila, who tasted, nodded, and smiled. She continued, "Then she asked me if I was the manager and did I speak for everyone. I just about choked. Of course I do, I told her. She said she would have to get back to me. Apparently, her client hates vocalists no matter who they are. Even the mighty Barbra herself. So she will call me back as soon as she can. Huh. Party planners. What horrid creatures. People are crazy; don't you think so, Reese darling? How's the salad, Nora?"

"It's fine, but not the most delicious dish in the room."

Lila shrieked in delight. "I want you to live in my bra. Could she, Reese? Oh, you are so scrumptious you have to be fattening! Reese, did you both enjoy the breadsticks with the salad? I do love playing wifey."

Both Reese and I nodded in response. Reese wiped her mouth with her napkin and stood. "Well, I am so sorry, but I have an important appointment. I do regret having to go. The food is wonderful, as usual, my princess, and the company is marvelous. But a client beckons, or is that a karate class?" Reese met my eyes. I knew Reese wanted to break me. And that she wanted me to believe that she and Max were having a torrid affair. I hated to admit that I believed it. Those paintings! My appetite fell away. Again, I wanted to leave, this time to spy on Reese.

"Let me walk you out, darling." Lila stood. "It's the most I've seen you all week."

"Remember, my pet, leave the kitchen a mess. I'll tend it when I return. It's the least I can do."

"I'll clear the table." I gathered plates.

"Lovely to meet you. Take good care of my Lila, but not too good."

"See you, Reese." I went into the kitchen where I looked for something to subdue my mounting desire for a cigarette. If I could just suck a finger… I stacked the plates in the sink and dropped my half-eaten breadstick in the trash where I saw all the garbage from Lila's hard day of slaving in the kitchen. An empty bag for the prepared salad, an empty bottle of dressing, a sack from the breadsticks, a box each for the frozen lasagna and the frozen chocolate cake and a crumpled paper sack for the garlic bread. I shook my head in disgusted amazement. I found a carrot in the refrigerator and washed it. I planned to gum it into submission unless I could get Lila to find some cigarettes.

CHAPTER TWENTY-TWO

There you are, poppet." Lila sashayed into the kitchen. "You ready for the main course?"

In a split second, I knew what I would do. I took Lila in my arms and growled, "I sure am."

"Oh." Lila was caught off balance trying to arch away just a little. As I held her up, Lila stroked my shoulders. "You are so big and strong. My, my, you make a girl woozy."

"Good." I kissed the hollow of her throat. The same throat that warbled sultry blues to adoring crowds would soon be moaning in surrender and passion for me. "Isn't this what you've been waiting for?" I grinned at the prospect. I knew how to do this so well. Whatever part of me had been affected and altered by Tulsa and Max was gone now; I was my familiar Los Angeles pussy-hound self.

"I've never been with anyone of color before," Lila said, embarrassed and scared. She was blushing, but her eyes sparkled with lust and anger.

"Relax, Blanche, it will be just as you like it." My hands moved from her ribs to her breasts. Lila's nipples were as large as kumquats and just as firm. I listened to her breathing to gauge whether to go quickly, as in ripping off her clothes and taking her here on the floor, or to go slowly, as in carrying her to the bedroom, Reese's bedroom, and kissing her all over and making her wait. Lila's breathing said fast, but I decided on slow. Was

Reese somewhere with Max doing this same thing? That made me bite Lila's neck, making her yelp.

"Don't leave any marks, darling. At least none that Reese can see."

"She knows what you're doing," I said.

Lila pushed me away, her eyes wide. "No, she does not. Honest. I've never cheated on her. I wouldn't. I couldn't. Maybe I can't now—" Lila started crying softly.

Femmes and their tears, good God. I hugged her roughly, patting her back, knowing that this was only stalling. Consciously or unconsciously, Lila had to stall. I had seen it a million times. Oh, we would have sex and a lot of it. Her taking the time to cry merely cemented the deal but only I knew it. Lila had to square her guilt to her desire and rationalize it all in her heart. Then the crying would stop; she would make some transparent femmey seduction move that I would allow so Lila could think she was taking the lead. Then we'd go to the bedroom, where I would bring her down with the force of a ravenous tiger.

"Reese and I have always been faithful to each other. All these years. I don't know why I'm doing this. She has never cheated on me."

"I know, baby, shh."

"She hasn't been around lately. She has been leaving me alone more and more and at all hours. I never know when she will be home. It's always business, she says. I hear noises from the studio from dusk till dawn. What has happened? She makes me so mad. I hate her sometimes, you know?"

"Yes, baby, I know. I'm here for you." I ran a gentle finger across Lila's mouth, wondering idly what it would be like to kiss an overbite. Then I smoothed Lila's glossy black pageboy and let her speak.

"How dare she! If she's not careful, she will lose me. I deserve better." Lila sniffled and her hand slipped into my waistband.

"Yes, baby, you do. I know." I rocked her as Lila's hand cupped my buttocks.

"I have never been treated like this. Reese knows how much I need her. She knows I'm very high-maintenance. What does she think I'll do without all that? She can't just leave me by myself so much and expect me to wait forever."

"That's right."

Lila rested her head on my chest. She had stopped crying. "I want to be safe…to have safe…" Lila whispered, embarrassed.

"Safe sex?" I asked, kissing the top of her head, grateful that this was a one-nighter. I knew the exhaustive work that women like Lila needed.

"Yes." It was almost inaudible. Apparently, the bawdy blues singer was truly a persona for this shy, needy woman.

"Not to worry, I never bareback."

"Reese and I are fluid-bonded, you know."

I bit back the impulse to laugh. "I will keep you safe." I had all my latex in my pocket, just out of habit. I was sure, if we needed it, that Reese would have lube. Maybe we should do it on the studio bed? No, might make Lila too suspicious. Could be all kinds of hairs and smells and stains and panties in that thing. Let her find out in her own time, her own way.

"I really want you…I really do…" Lila's eyes were dark with arousal. "But—"

"Listen, it's okay. I know I'm not the one you really want. It's all right. You're not the one I really want. But we're here now and we can do this for each other."

Lila consented by closing her eyes, wrapping her arms around me, and tilting her chin up for a kiss. I imagined wavy copper-red hair, snapping navy blue eyes, rosebud mouth…oh, Max… I fastened my mouth on Lila's hungrily.

Finally, Lila broke the embrace and took my hand. "I want to show you something," Lila whispered, pulling her leopard-print dress back up over her shoulder. That vulnerable gesture tugged at my heart. I could still leave. I could yet not do this. Max's refusals and Reese's smug grin burned in my chest. I had never left a woman unsatisfied and I wouldn't tonight. Lila led me down the corridor toward the bedroom. "See? I wanted to show you these paintings." Lila pointed. I rolled my eyes. Enough already!

All along the walls were nudes of Lila. Nudes of Lila with something on her arm… I stopped breathing for a second. I stepped closer to the painting. Lights reflected on its shiny oil surface, so I maneuvered right and left until I could get a clear view. Was that an ancient gold coin? On a chain? Under Reese's skilled hands, the coin was rendered in fine detail, its edges rubbed soft over time and the face nearly, but not quite obliterated. And Lila in the painting, smug, oblivious, titillated, hideous.

A fire started at the base of my spine and grew until the flames were in my eyes. Could it really be my grandmother's bracelet? That heifer was wearing my grandmother's bracelet! The bracelet presented to me on my thirtieth birthday. It had been a big surprise party. My team had been there, my friends, my women, and my family. When my mother fastened it on my wrist, I had to wipe my eyes many times. My mother and grama wept outright. With that beloved icon finally mine, I had believed I was invincible. I had smiled and winked at the small nieces staring up at me to whom I would will this bracelet when the time came.

Two years later, on the day I met Michelle, I was playing in a senior league championship and someone snagged my bracelet, snapping the chain. I stopped the game immediately, gathered the bracelet, and tucked it into my sock.

After my team won, Michelle, who was at the game watching friends play on the opposing side, approached to congratulate me and ask about the coin. We had gone for coffee and started dating. That had been on a Saturday and I put the coin in a safe place until Monday when I would go to a jeweler first thing. But Sunday, I had Michelle over for sex and brunch, and the next morning, the coin and chain were gone.

A rage swept through me like a fire. I had pleaded for Michelle to help look for it. We tore my apartment apart. I had gone *crazy*, yelling and cursing and breaking things. In desperation, I had even confronted Michelle and assured her it would be okay if she would just give it back. Michelle had protested so winningly. She had denied everything so earnestly. She had cried over the story of the princess and over my loss. She offered to do everything to help. She even searched the basketball court and called my teammates and asked them about it. Michelle insisted I must have lost it. I had been convinced of Michelle's innocence. I had been grateful for her help. *Grateful!* That lousy rotten evil bitch! Evil. After resigning myself to its loss, I fell into a black depression that had lasted for months. It was a wound that had never healed. I had never told my mother or grandmother. Oh, to have five minutes with Michelle now. Hell, I would even like to beat her corpse to a pulp for good measure. So Michelle had taken the bracelet and given it to Reese. I stared in disbelief at the lifeless paintings.

"Nora, what's wrong? Don't you like them?"

I cleared my throat, tamping down my murderous fury, hoping I could speak. "Sure. They're very sexy. What's that bracelet? It's unusual." Good. Casual and light.

"Oh, that." Lila laughed. "Everyone asks about that. Isn't it hideous? Reese said she picked it up for a song at some tacky flea market in Los Angeles. She thinks it's interesting so she insisted I wear the silly thing. It was an anniversary present. Can you believe that? I read her the riot act over that one, I tell you. I never wear it."

"Do you still have it?"

Lila was puzzled. "Yes, why?"

"I'm a bit of a coin hound. It looks like it might be valuable. Can I see it?"

"Of course you can, darling. Come into my lair."

I followed Lila into the bedroom, which was truly despicable. All clear acrylic and black leather and mirrors. Not a single color or sign of softness anywhere.

I watched Lila remove the bracelet, its chain now repaired, from her jewelry box.

"See? It's not anything anyone would *wear*. It's ugly." Lila dangled it contemptuously from her fingertips.

My eyes burned. I used every ounce of my will to suppress my panther passion against snatching that precious bracelet and running all the way back to Los Angeles. "I'll say. It's awful. Reese is such a jerk. She doesn't know what you need." I took Lila in my arms. "Let's forget about that nasty thing for a while." I used my rage to capture Lila's mouth in a slow, fiery kiss. I felt her dissolve in my arms. I deepened the kiss when I heard with smug satisfaction, the bracelet drop from Lila's fingers and hit the carpet with a tiny, treasured thud.

With the bracelet restored to me, I could focus on the job at hand. I undressed Lila slowly, making her shiver. Her dark, slick pageboy shadowed her face. Her skin was white and lightly freckled. I tossed Lila's dress on top of a lacquered armoire. Little present for Reese. Lila's breasts were heavy with deep brown nipples that looked to me, with my rabid needs, just like pacifiers. I dropped to my knees and embraced Lila, rubbing my face in her pubic hair. It was neat and trimmed, and could it be, combed?

"Your bush certainly is tidy," I said, kissing the crease between hip and thigh. Mmm, they grow them big and beautiful in Oklahoma, ample and tasty, just as I like 'em.

"Reese likes my pubic hair that way. I even use conditioner on it. Sometimes I brush it." Lila gasped.

"That Reese is a piece of work," I muttered to Lila's plump navel.

"Just talk about me, okay? Nobody else but me," Lila whispered, gripping my shoulders. I looked up. Above the rise of her belly, the roundness of her arms and the bulging of her breasts, Lila stared down at me. In all my experience, I had never seen anyone so fragile. Stop; don't do this, an inner voice whispered.

"Sure, just you. Of course, baby. I'm sorry. All you, only you." I ran my hand delicately up the insides of Lila's trembling thighs. "We can stop. We don't have to do this. Are you sure you want to?" I looked up at Lila again.

"Yes!" It was a bellow. A sound of hurt, anger, defiance, and desire.

"All right, baby, let me take you there." I stood and without warning, picked up Lila, carried her to the bed, and laid her down gently.

"No one has ever lifted me before," Lila said, batting her eyes yet sounding like a child.

"I've only begun," I answered, knowing in my soul that what we were going to do wasn't going to elevate anyone. Just the opposite.

I fell on top of Lila, voraciously eating her flesh. She writhed and moaned, her voice not like Max's at all. Her body was not like Max's. Her face was not like Max's. Her hair, her touch, her smile, her stare. Goddammit, they were all different. They weren't even close. How could white chicks be so different? Lila wrapped her legs around me as I kissed and bit her chest and slowly descended to her pendulous breasts. Lila certainly was sexy; her only fault was that she wasn't…someone else. I bit Lila's nipple viciously. She gasped, dragging her nails across my back. I imagined Max's pink pinprick nipple in my mouth, suffocating myself on Max's breasts, Max's body sprawled helplessly under me, ready for consumption. Soon, I would spread Lila's legs and hold her ankles apart as I would regard what waited for me there. I hoped I would see Max's pomegranate cunt, split open to reveal the glistening ruby seeds ripe for me to devour. I would slurp and slather the sweetly tart juice all over my skin. My hands were everywhere, pinching, kneading, massaging, gripping. Lila was a ship rolling gently on the sea. I left Lila's breasts and started sucking her toes. Her shrill shriek of pleasure made me smile smugly. *God, I know how to do this and I do it flawlessly every time*. I moved to bite Lila's heels and suck her arches. I chewed on her calves and spent a long time licking the backs of her knees, that sugary soft spot sensitive and aching to be plundered on every woman.

I was just beginning my smoldering journey up Lila's thighs when she gripped me in a knee lock and whispered, "What's that? Did you hear something?"

I listened, not frightened for Reese to catch us. But would Reese be back so quickly from her assignation? If I knew Reese, then absolutely not. Reese wanted to punish Lila and she would draw it out. Reese also wanted to tempt me with Lila as well as mind-fuck me with Max. It was too soon for Reese to return home.

"It's nothing; relax, baby. Come on." I tried to pry myself from Lila's clenched legs.

"Shh, just listen. Maybe Reese is back."

"You want me to check?"

"Just listen!" Lila barked bitchily.

So we waited. All was still. I watched the clock wearily. If Lila didn't open up soon, I would just leave and return to Max's. Max. Where the hell was she? Was she screaming Reese's name and biting her bloody?

"Come on, Lila, it's nothing," I said roughly, snapping her thighs apart.

"Okay, I guess you're right. Okay." She breathed to relax.

"Now, where were we?" I grinned and sucked the crease between inner thigh and vulva.

Chapter Twenty-three

It was like it usually was, with only two differences.

Usually, my women were wet and starved for me. They thrashed and screamed or whimpered and moaned or laughed and cried. All in my name. I was an all-purpose lover. I was indefatigable and I would do it all. I did whatever it took: licking, sucking, fisting, rimming, spanking, stroking. If they needed toys, I was more than happy to strap one on, put the vibrator on high, snap closed the restraints, use the cane or paddle, or whatever else they might need. I stopped being surprised ten years ago.

So Lila was the same in these ways. She liked it quiet, intense, and gentle. She came many times, each with a grateful gasp and a soft clutch. She smiled radiantly at me, drunk on pure pleasure, another sure sign Reese couldn't miss. I was so aroused by fantasies of Max that I straddled Lila's plump thigh and rubbed until I came. It was a powerful pent-up orgasm, one that astonished me with its depth. I arched into a primal curve. My face closed down and clenched like a fist. I thought of Max's strong, serpentine body and imagined it below me, calling to me. Nora, Nora please, please. I came, shuddering and jerking, panting bitch, bitch, bitch with each breath. That was the first difference.

The second was that afterward, I felt dirty. I normally never felt that way because, while I was promiscuous, I was safe and I had ethics. Never commit adultery was one. I had clean boundaries and discussed them openly with my women before the first date. I was a player, but not a dog. Everyone involved was clear on all the rules, so there were no secrets and no victims. So now, as I lay with Lila, petting and soothing her as she wept, I felt disgusted with myself. Mad at Reese and Max for goading me into this. Heartsick because I had betrayed Max even though we were not involved. Lila sniffled and burrowed into me, as if she could also hide what she had done.

"Do you always react like this?"

"What do you mean?"

"Does having sex with someone other than Reese always make you cry?"

Lila wept afresh. "I've never done it before."

I knew that was a lie. Lila was simply a complicated and difficult affair. She made you pay for every bit of pleasure. But I patted and rocked her anyway. I was tired and ready to go. It seemed as if the full weight of this trip finally overcame me and I wanted nothing better than to stretch out and sleep in a different bed alone. Lila calmed herself at last.

"I'm sorry. I don't know what came over me, I just—" Lila's chin trembled and tears welled again.

"Shh, don't worry. This doesn't mean anything. Reese need never know if you don't want her to know. Relax." I had to get her to sleep quickly so I could get the bracelet and get out.

"I'm going to take a sleeping pill. I'll never be able to calm down if I don't. Do you mind?" Lila stood, waiting for approval.

I shook my head, marveling at little miracles. "Not at all. I'll just get out of your way." I rose and began dressing. I heard Lila in the bathroom blowing her nose, opening a plastic bottle, running the water, flushing the toilet. I extracted the bracelet from the deep carpet and slipped it into my pocket. I grinned hugely at the floor as I slipped on my shoes. My, my, my, how nicely things work out. Lila emerged from the bathroom looking sad and weary and wearing pajamas. I embraced her.

"Thank you for everything," Lila said to my shoulder. "I'm sorry I'm so…"

"Shh, baby, just rest. I'll go. I can let myself out."

Lila nodded, yawned, and flopped on the bed. She seemed to fall asleep immediately. I had one final look around because if I left anything, I knew I would never get it back.

My hand in my pocket, clutching my icon, I caught a glimpse of myself in a mirror. I thought I could see my royalty in my forehead and cheeks. In my imperial lips and broad shoulders. I felt restored again to the connection of my noble foremothers. I even thought I saw my ancestors' faces laid across my own, each smiling, sighing in relief, and disappearing one by one. I saw my mother, my grandmother, and my great grandmother. I saw years ago when my mother, tears running down her face, let me know that my grama was dead only by silently patting the pendant on my arm.

I heard drumming and singing and felt the soil of Africa under my feet, the sun of Africa on my back. It was a strange, split-second time travel, all of these women culminating here and now in the being of a bald lesbian basketball coach and lady-killer whose ex was just murdered by her own family. In this alien place, I felt a longing for my mother's arms, her generous bosom, her big Sunday dinners, and her strong, peaceful hands. Even her clucking disapproval would be a comfort.

I shook my head to dispel the thoughts and tiptoed out of the bedroom. Lila was snoring softly.

As I crept across the parquet floor, I heard rustling and soft groaning coming from behind Reese's studio door. I froze, my blood rushing to my face and feet. It was a woman, all right. If I were in a coma, I would know those sounds of pleasure. I could almost smell the sex wafting from under the door and through the keyhole. That Reese was some kind of superfreak. Right in Lila's home, under her goddamn nose.

"Not my problem," I whispered. Then I headed for the front door. *Oh, no, Max*. Once again, I stopped. My blood began to simmer. That motherfucking psycho Reese brought Max back here. Reese was making love to my Max this second.

"And you're just standing here, taking it," I said to myself. I walked to the door of Reese's studio and listened once more. Quick moans and gasps emanated from the other side. I marshaled my rage and kicked the door with all my might. It was only a lady lock and it broke instantly. The doorjamb splintered and the door slammed open. Reese was kneeling on the floor, her head between the thighs of a curvy blonde. The blonde was flushed and confused and tried to cover herself, but Reese wouldn't let her. I never noticed the woman once I saw it wasn't Max. I focused on Reese, whose slick chin shone in the candlelight.

"Well, well, well, we meet again." I chuckled, relieved.

Reese said nothing, but I could see her suave, cunning mind trying to come up with a retort.

I cupped my crotch and adjusted myself. "We just finished dinner, how about you?" I walked away, laughing.

"Where's Lila?" Reese, suddenly panicked, called after me. There was a scene in the studio, but I paid no mind as I closed the front door behind me. Big night. Big, big night. I clasped the bracelet. All serene, I ambled to the elevator and pushed the button. As the doors opened, there was shouting in the direction of Lila and Reese's and a door slam. The voluptuous blonde came rushing down the hall in tears, wearing only a sheet. We got into the elevator together.

I didn't say a word the entire ride down.

CHAPTER TWENTY-FOUR

I let myself into Max's and quiet as a mouse, I crept to peek in on Max, who was sleeping silently. I returned to the guestroom where I dropped into sleep like a stone into water.

The next morning Max was gone. The maid had come and gone; the house was empty.

I decided to leave today. I had had enough. I needed space and peace. I needed Los Angeles to help get myself together. I needed the traffic and the smog and the ocean roar and the pure sunshine and dry air and my college and my team and my game, my game, my game on my own turf. I needed familiarity to soothe me and give me balance. I needed all that more than I needed the possibility with Max. On my way out of town, I would drop by the McKerrs' to pay my respects and then drive to the airport.

I packed the few things I had, straightened the bed as best I could, and had one last hot shower in that luxurious, decadent bathroom. I looked up florists in the phone book, settled on Miss Dell's, and had a dozen yellow roses sent to Lila—Reese would love that—and two dozen pink, white, and red sent to Max. I thought it was a bargain price as I read my credit card number over the phone. I included no inscriptions. But I did leave Max a note, which read: "Thank you for your generosity. I've enjoyed getting to know Tulsa and especially you. It's been nice during a difficult time. Take care of yourself and say good-bye to Sloane for me."

"Understatement of the year, 'enjoyed getting to know you,'" I snorted, rolling my eyes. Though I was leaving, I knew I was completely sprung. Just the thought of Max was like a finger worming into my underwear and stroking my clit. I felt slick and swollen all the time and half embarrassed by it, like a man with an uncontrollable hard-on. It would take months and lots and lots of one-night ladies to expunge this obsession. "The most powerful cunt is the one not taken," I muttered, shrugging.

CHAPTER TWENTY-FIVE

I hefted my bag onto my shoulder, and feeling fresh and ready to go, yet reluctant, took a huge wet breath at the front door, regarding everything once more. The sun was blinding but bearable because I was leaving. The house, the lake, the swans and ducks. With a gusty exhale, I closed the door and forced myself to walk to the car. I pocketed the house key with a smile.

As I loaded the car, I blew a kiss to the house and immediately felt so foolish that I glanced around with hot eyes to see who might have caught me doing such a soft, sentimental thing.

That's when I saw the car speeding crazily down the street and jerking to a stop directly in back of my car, blocking the driveway. Lila jumped out, wearing the leopard-print dress of last night. Her lip was puffed and bloody, her eye was swollen and black, her hair was in a chaos of black straw.

"Nora! Nora!" Lila screamed. "Come here, I've got to speak to you. Come on. Hurry!" Lila opened the passenger side of her own car and sat inside, waiting for me to sit in the driver's seat. I was wary. Curiosity got the better of me and I locked my car and sat behind the wheel of Lila's.

"Drive! Hurry!" Lila gripped the dashboard and the back of her seat, looking behind us in terror.

"How did you know I was here? What happened?" I stepped on the gas and followed streets randomly.

"I've just got to think. I've got to think." Lila rocked herself. Then, putting her hands on her knees, she finally said, "Reese is after us."

"Us?"

"Yeah. I got a good head start, but not before she smacked me around."

"Reese did all that to you?" I had known without asking. Just wait until the flowers arrive, I thought.

Lila flipped the mirror down to study her face. "Looks like sunglasses and lots of makeup for my gig tonight." Lila slapped the mirror back with anger. "I tell you, Nora, I've had it. *I've had it!* Who does she think she is, taking my money, keeping me in an ivory tower, letting me out only to sing and run the restaurant? While she does whatever and *whomever* she pleases right in my own bed?"

So Lila knew. Good.

"She's hit you before?" I drove, not knowing where I was going, my anger a rising tide. I kept glancing in the rearview, but so far, no other car in pursuit.

"Yeah, but it's no big deal. I love her. I'll always be her girl. Even when she's belting me, she's promising never to hurt me." Lila laughed. "She loves me. It's just how we are. But this time, I don't know, something snapped inside me. This time when we were in the kitchen and she was trying to have sex to make up for this," Lila pointed to her face, "I clocked her with the frying pan to get her off me."

I laughed. "Did it knock her out?"

"Almost. It just made her madder. Damn, I need a drink."

"You want me to take care of that coward for you?"

Lila smiled and winced, touching her lip gingerly. "No, thanks, beefcake. I do all right." The vulnerable girl/woman of last night was gone. In her place was a dame, hard as nails and streetwise.

"Do you?" I wasn't so sure. "Why do you stay, then?" My gaze bored into Lila, who only shrugged and stared out the window.

We rode in silence. I was driving aimlessly with no direction from Lila. How long would Lila want me to do this? I had a plane to catch this afternoon and I meant to be on it, headed home to my silent apartment. Headed to Los Angeles, where the bright heat shimmered off the miles and miles of concrete. Home to the desert mirages. Home to basketball. Home to the open arms of women I hadn't yet met. Home to my winning team and the comfort of my job and great Chinese food. Home to the beach. Home to the city that was lit up and going strong all night. I longed for familiarity. Suddenly, I yearned to be out of this sleepy wet jungle. This subtropical forest where miles of trees hid the sweet evildoings of the preachers and the police. Again, I longed to run and be free of Oklahoma with its innocent face and deep secrets, its heavy humidity that bore down on me like a wet wind shear, its quiet whispered promises in the moonlight, its ease with itself.

"I see her," Lila said tightly, rigid with excitement.

"Where?" I sped up.

"Behind us, nitwit."

At that, I braked and pulled into an empty lot. "Okay, I'm done," I said harshly.

"What the fuck?" Lila was all big, blowsy babe now, her smoke-coarsened voice ordering another round for the sailors she would take home.

"You showed your ass. I'm not your monkey."

"Whatever, Miss Swanson, now drive."

"Fuck that and fuck you, you washed-up wannabe," I snapped. I started to open the door and set off running to purge these people, but I saw Reese jump the curb in an SUV and come barreling toward us. Reese screeched to a halt only after she hit Lila's car in the rear. Lila and I were thrown against the dash. I barely registered what happened when Reese flew out of her vehicle in a rage, waving a gun.

"Oh, my God," I murmured. "The bitch done lost her mind." This was so much worse than I had anticipated. A gun? Who was

Reese kidding? None of this was that big; none of this was that bad. I rolled my eyes as I got a mental overhead glimpse of this sordid triangle. I'm one of those dykes now, I thought acidly, my stomach turning sour. And over a woman I don't want or like. "Oh, I miss LA." I sighed and prepared for war. Reese would have it no other way.

Lila was weeping softly in the passenger seat. "I love you; I love you; I love you," she whimpered and I was startled because I thought Lila was speaking to me. I relaxed when I realized Lila was crooning to Reese, who stood in front of the car, shouting and screaming, mostly inaudibly. I caught the words "shithead" and "big shot" and "slimy piece of shit" and so assumed Reese was challenging me to a duel. Over Lila? She had to be joking.

"I shouldn't've done it. I know she can get this way, I know her. I shouldn't've done it," Lila cried.

"Oh, come off it. Why don't you two just go somewhere alone, talk, and patch it up?"

"No, no, it's irreparable." Lila shook her head, tears streaming down her face.

"Irreparable," I mocked. "It's not irreparable."

"She will kill us," Lila said simply.

"Kill us? Kill you, maybe. But my black ass is gonna be on a plane to LA." I glanced at Reese, who still screamed and beat the hood for emphasis.

I put my hand on the door handle so I could get out and negotiate with Reese. I wanted to calm things down, defuse this situation. Lila put a hand on my arm and stopped me. Reese took aim with the gun and blew a hole in the windshield between Lila and me. I covered my face. Lila, jaw clenched, eyes hard, released the emergency brake and stomped on my foot that rested on the gas pedal. The car lurched forward. Through my fingers, I got a glimpse of Reese's wide-eyed terror before the sickening thump. I was only dimly aware of shouting, "Crazy bitch!" over and over. Lila was silent, grim, and determined. The car stopped almost as soon as it started.

"Get out," Lila barked.

"What?" I was dazed. Glass had peppered my face.

"Pull yourself together," Lila said dryly. "Run. I'll take the heat. Go."

"But…" I looked around. At the edge of this abandoned lot, in the distance, ordinary life was proceeding, ignorant and indifferent of this trauma. Traffic flowed. Lights changed. People walked. The sun shone. The wind blew. And here I was, in hell.

"Oh, man." I sagged against the wheel.

"Are you an idiot?" Lila said harshly. "Get out while you can. The cops are coming."

"How…how do you know?"

"Look, I just know, okay? Come on, get out of this, leave," Lila urged brusquely. "Jesus, what will it take? Do I have to drag your sorry ass out?"

"No." I stood shakily and slammed the car door behind her, Seized by a morbid desire, I walked to the front of the car where Reese lay, her eyes filled with fright and pain. She had blood bubbling from her nose and mouth. "Thank God, Nora, help me. Help," she croaked.

I shook my head and grinned grimly. I leaned close to Reese's face and hissed, "I won, *fool*." Then I sauntered back to the driver's side where Lila was leaning against the car, tearing at her own dress with a nail file.

"Aren't you gone yet?" Lila cried. "And don't you breathe a word of this, hear?" She stuck a finger in my face. "I'll fix this, but don't you tell a soul or else. We know where you live and we've been there *once*."

"You?" I felt shock move deeper into my body like a sweet numbness.

"We trashed your dump. You didn't have anything good anyway." Lila laughed at me.

In the crazy over-wet air, clarity sparkled in my mind. "You killed Michelle." My voice was flat.

Lila laughed. "Don't be silly. Not *me*." She paused

meaningfully. Her eyes rolled toward Reese. "Not *me*," she repeated. "But I didn't mind. And I didn't stop it. Michelle wanted Reese for herself. But I told you, all those nasty femmes better not touch my butch. And Michelle was getting above herself, wasn't she?"

All of a sudden, I knew that Michelle had been having an affair with Reese and that either Michelle threatened to tell Lila, hoping to milk another cash cow with blackmail, or she actually did tell Lila, after which Reese went insane for revenge. No one gets away with destroying the cozy little equilibrium of Lila and Reese's world, right? Michelle and Reese had been having an affair. Reese had to come to Los Angeles a lot, allegedly for shows and gallery openings, so it had been perfect. She and Michelle teamed up while Reese kept the home front with Lila. Maybe things got out of control and that was the desperate phone call from Michelle to me. I smiled bitterly as I thought, maybe it was all just some misunderstanding. Who knew if Reese would even survive this accident? Well, no more than she deserved.

Then Lila nodded at me, as if we had said everything. Then Lila put a finger to her lips for silence and knelt by Reese, smoothing hair from her forehead. Reese's eyes fluttered. "It will be all right, baby, mama's here." Lila spoke coldly to me. "Come on, you don't really care that Michelle is dead, do you?"

"But…but that's no…it's still not—"

"And who the hell cares if it was Reese Cup or me or the two of us? No harm has been done. Justice is served."

"No…you're wrong…it's—"

"Are you going to argue or run? You better run. You don't understand any of this. Last chance." Lila stood and slapped herself in the mouth, causing fresh bleeding. Then, staring straight into my eyes, Lila worked herself into a fever pitch of hysteria. Starting small then building, so by the time I was on the run, I could hear both sirens and Lila's high-pitched wails.

CHAPTER TWENTY-SIX

I ran, totally lost. I ran for miles, burning my muscles and gasping for air. The molasses that was Oklahoma oxygen starved my pumping lungs and incinerated my throat. Max or not, I had begun to regret coming here. Hell, I regretted ever having lived with Michelle. Lived with? I regretted ever having seen her. It was an absurd path of inevitability. That one smile and wink at Michelle three years ago led to me in Tulsa, fleeing a crime scene on foot. God, I am ridiculous, I thought as I ran. Morning traffic was heavy and I dodged cars and looked for landmarks. There were none. I looked for long butts in the gutters. I found none. What now? Follow the game plan, my sane voice said. Follow the game plan. If you do that, everything will be all right. This troubled day will end and sunset will see you on a plane to Los Angeles.

"Yeah," I gasped, bent over with my hands on my knees. "That's right. It's just like a game. I need to stick to my plan. With a plan, I'm invincible. I'm safe. Just do my list and leave. I'll be okay. I'll be fine. I'll be just fine. I'll be all right." I stood, rolled my shoulders and cracked my knuckles. "Just fine."

I went into a convenience store and bought water. I eyed the packs of cigarettes lustfully, my mind justifying and rationalizing in every direction to convince me to buy some. "You haven't bought in a year. That's good. That's commendable. In fact, respectable. But come on. You deserve a good relaxing smoke while you execute your plan. It will help you stick to the list. After all you've been through this morning, hell, the Surgeon General would smoke. Just one pack. No one needs to know. Come on, come on, you'll feel so much better. It's just the thing for your frazzled nerves." I shook my head against that voice. "Max would want you to. She would strip open the pack, pat one out, kiss your mouth, and then place the cigarette in between your lips as her fingers lingered there. Then she would light it for you as you stared into each other's eyes. Come on, do it for Max."

That nasty, sneaky voice.

"And a pack of Marlboros," I said gruffly to the clerk. I looked up taxi services and called for a car. Did I have Max's address? It didn't matter; I could get there. In between huge gulps of frosty cold water, I stared at the cigarettes. I sat on a bench in the shade to wait. I pretended Max was there next to me.

Max took the pack, sliding it from my hand to her own and unwrapped it slowly, like a striptease. Then she smelled the pack with closed eyes. Max cracked the top and slid out a cigarette. She put it in her own mouth and lit it, the fire making a small orange burst on her face. She dragged the smoke deep into her lungs. She held her breath and leaned in to kiss me, smoke pouring out of our joined mouths. Only then did Max place the cigarette to my lips. I spat the cigarette in a graceful arc to the ground. "What took you so long?" Max asked. "Teaching you who is boss," I replied gruffly. "I've always known who was boss." Max laughed. "That's funny, me too," I answered. With smoldering eyes and itchy, hungry hands, I knocked her to her back on the bench. Cars rushed past heedlessly. Max succumbed, letting her head drop off the bench's edge.

I sank onto her soft, yielding body. I filled my hands with her luscious flesh. I popped the snow-white globes that were Max's breasts out of her bra and feasted on them, my head moving quickly from one to the other. I left wet tongue tracks all over her skin. She moaned and writhed, wrapping her legs around me and gripping like a vise. Oh, those thighs! Odes of eternal lust for those strong round thighs. I hated thin thighs; they looked anemic, spindly, unhealthy, and masculine. Women not only held up the world, but also gave birth to it. They needed big, juicy thighs to do that work. They held the earth in their thighs, they walked and worked and fed and loved and fucked with those thighs, and with jobs that important, women must have substantial weight. It was disrespectful to expect women to do their holy work on toothpicks. Thin thighs were a sign of a depleted woman, not fulfilling her role as goddess. Max had grand, wondrous thighs, and I wanted to brand her. Feel her squirm; see her flesh sizzle as the iron burned my mark into her skin. Oh, it drove me crazy not to be able to chew on mouthfuls of Max meat. To lose myself in the sheets of wide muscle, to pinch and stroke and grab abundance by the handful. As I hovered over Max, car horns honked. I drank from her creamy rich tits like a suckling infant. Her nipples swelled from cool pink pinheads to hot sweet berries. Her great hips were undulating under me, urging me on. My hand crept to her navel and she groaned her assent. I slipped my hand down, down, down to the tangle of hair and the slick heat that infused my fingers. Oh, God, yes!

A bus coming to a stop in front of the bench broke my reverie. The bus door flapped open and the driver waited for some sign from me, and I shook my head. I sat alone, smoking and sweating, until the taxi pulled up.

"Swan Lake," I told the cabbie.

"What address?"

"Don't know. I'll know it when I see it, just go." I slammed the door and grimaced at the no smoking sign.

At Max's house, I noticed there was still no sign of her. I sprinted up the stairs to the front door and after extracting one more, I put the new pack of cigarettes in the mailbox.

Chapter Twenty-seven

Finally, I drove away from the house, watching it grow smaller in the rearview. At a stop sign, I closed my eyes and said good-bye to Max. Only someone honking brought me out of the trance. Having forgotten to send flowers to Michelle's mother, I found my way to Miss Dell's and picked up a bunch of lilies. Then I went to Thomas Wynter's grocery and bought an Italian cream cake. Now, I was ready to see the McKerrs.

I dug through my backpack for the tattered paper Sloane had given me. I headed over there, feeling nervous. The homes just got bigger and grander until they passed absurd. The lawns and trees grew and the driveways stretched into squinting. By an educated guess, I turned into one and pulled slowly down the long stone driveway, its curves showing off the landscaping and taking me deeper into privacy. Finally, I saw a black family barbecuing under the trees by the garage. I parked and waved. They all grinned and waved back. Even the weather seemed better here, cooler, drier. The food smelled heavenly, and with sudden grief, I wished I belonged somewhere. I was alone now. Great Grama dead, Grama dead, Ma dead, Michelle dead. Orphaned and single. I wished to be taken under some family's wing, the matriarch cooing and scolding and everybody welcoming and missing me when I was gone. I wanted someone to say, "Where's Nora?" I wanted to be smiled at and cuffed and hugged too long and nagged about churchgoing. Nothing matters but this, I thought, roughly wiping something out of my eyes. I miss you, Grama, I miss you, Ma.

I carried the flowers and cake up to the back door. The family watched silently, the pitmaster waving flies away with his tongs. An old grizzled man snored in a hammock.

"Yes?" A solid matronly woman in a maid's uniform answered the door. I was surprised. It was the woman from Michelle's graveside service. The woman who had arrived and read from the Bible after everyone left.

"I…I brought these for the family," I stammered.

"Are you a friend?" The woman was icy and professional.

"No, ma'am, I am…*was* Michelle's lover," I said.

"Oh." The woman brightened. "Come in, have a cup."

Bewildered, I went in, looking once more at the back lawn that seemingly continued for miles, dotted with trees and graceful hills like an immaculate national park. In the distance, a pristine pool sparkled, crisp and empty and perfect.

"Poor people use every inch of their property. Do rich folks even enjoy all this? You never see anyone around but service people. That pool is going to waste," I dared to say, the glass back door slamming behind me.

The maid ignored my comment and said, "I'm Mabel Harris. Everybody calls me Miss Mazie. Please sit." Miss Mazie took the flowers and put them in a cut crystal vase. "Just beautiful, thank you. I'll put them in the dining room."

I sat, looking at everything. The kitchen was immaculate. It was large and expensive and custom-built featuring every tool and gadget made. There wasn't a crumb or hair or smell to be found.

Miss Mazie returned and poured two coffees. "Slice of cake?"

"No, no, I brought that for the McKerrs."

"Well, we appreciate it, but Charles and Claudia don't eat dessert. Cream or sugar?"

"No, thanks, I take it black. Well, I wanted to give the cake to them just the same."

"And I'll tell them you did, don't worry. In the meantime, why don't you and me enjoy some of this?"

"Sure, I guess."

A boy came running up to the back door. "Miss Mazie, Miss Mazie, Levi told me that Sonny was here."

"No, child, he's not here yet. Go tell old Levi he was mistaken. This girl's a stranger."

I smiled at the boy who stared at me bug-eyed through the door.

"Scat!" Miss Mazie said. The boy ran off. "Pardon him, but you look something like my boy Jefferson."

"How much like?"

Miss Mazie put her hands on my jaw and turned my face this way and that. "Identical," she pronounced.

"Really?" I smiled, embarrassed. I sipped coffee for something to do and burned my tongue.

Miss Mazie sat with two slabs of cake on saucers. Her voice was soft. "Though I think you look more like Felicia."

"Who's Felicia?"

"My daughter. Dead now." Miss Mazie pulled a locket out of her bosom and snapped it open to show me. I was relieved to see no resemblance at all between myself and the teenager in the photo.

"I'm so sorry, how did she die?"

"Cancer. Went at sixteen."

"Oh, I'm so sorry." I felt helpless. "I am so sorry," I repeated, touching Miss Mazie's arm.

"Well, the Good Lord takes us when he wants us," Miss Mazie said with a sigh and snapped closed the locket and returned it to its soft, dark hiding spot. "Where are your people from?"

"Los Angeles. Grew up in Rio Seco, but now I live across the ten near the college where I coach," I answered, thinking about my lonely old apartment and how I suddenly wanted to move. Maybe buy a little house? "Before that, the South. Before that, Uganda."

"What college?"

I was surprised and pleased. Miss Mazie was the first person to ask me this. "Mooreland University."

"Mmm, I've heard of it. Quite distinguished academically and athletically."

I ducked my head. "Go Wildcats."

"What's your name?"

"Nora Delaney."

"Any kin to the Carolina Delaneys?"

"No, not that I know of."

"Oh, if you were, you'd know it. What's it like to coach?"

"Oh..." I was overwhelmed by this woman's matronly kindness. I wanted to hug Miss Mazie and be held by her. If Miss Mazie had asked me to stay for dinner, I would have. If Miss Mazie had asked me to stay the week, I would have. My heart ached with longing for my mother, my grandmother, my father, my siblings. I was tired of hurting and being lonely. I was impatient about emotional pain. I realized that I needed to be near family and I flew through my mental Rolodex. There was one person who stood out: my cousin Ellis, also known as Hambone, who lived in New Orleans. I had not seen him in a while. I swore to visit him immediately. I felt uncomfortable under Miss Mazie's sharp gaze and realized I had not responded to her question. I cleared my throat. "It's the perfect job for me," I answered.

Miss Mazie nodded and smiled. "So you were Michelle's girlfriend?"

"Yes, ma'am, for three years. We split right before she...she was killed."

"She loved my Felicia. Doted on her. They were playmates. Grew up together, closer than sisters. They went to different schools, but they did homework together, went shopping and to the movies together. When Filly took sick, Michelle was there night and day. Wouldn't leave her side until the doctor insisted. Michelle wouldn't eat unless my Filly did. Filly forced herself to eat to keep Michelle alive. Oh, the talks they had. Late into the night. Michelle slept with her too. Michelle lost weight just like Filly. She didn't leave Filly's room for months. Her parents forced her to go to school, and that might've been the start of her break with the family. She and Charles and Claudia would have screaming fights about allowing her to be around Filly so much. When Filly died in her sleep, Michelle went wild. She accused her parents of killing Felicia because Michelle could've saved her if she had been there every minute. She went plumb crazy. I thought we'd lose her too. And now we have." Miss Mazie dabbed her eyes with a linen napkin.

I soaked all this in. Never, never had Michelle mentioned any of this.

"I suppose that's why she became an oncology nurse," Miss Mazie said.

A nurse? Michelle? Good God in heaven, what else was there to know? I reeled. The Michelle I knew couldn't keep a plant alive.

"Of course, we wanted her to become something else like a doctor or a specialist. Maybe a cancer research physician. But she was determined to reject us. She said she needed to be hands on and to do the real work of care. Not be isolated in a laboratory. So she insisted on nursing."

"Reject who?"

"All of us. The McKerrs and the wealth and the life and the traveling and the charities and the luncheons and the business of being rich."

"Are you rich too?"

Miss Mazie laughed. "Law no, honey, not like this. I'm very comfortable, but nothing like this. Hardly anybody lives like *this*."

"Right on," I said, chewing cake. It was moist and rich and reminded me of Max. Everything did.

"Michelle and Felicia latched on to each other, the only girls in the family. I have four sons and the McKerrs have two. Then, when Felicia died, Michelle and I latched on to each other. I was closer to her than Charles and Claudia were. Then she latched on to you. And I can see why."

"We weren't that close, apparently." I was a little hurt, not knowing anything at all about Michelle or her life.

"She was a hard one to love sometimes."

I twirled the coin bracelet around my wrist. "I'll say."

"We all are," Miss Mazie said with pride. "Some more than others."

"What do you mean?"

"I mean I suspect things. Things about this family. They must get right with God."

"I've heard some pretty bad stuff."

"I'm not saying any more. Especially not to an outsider."

"Listen, I know about the race riot thing. I know about their staunch Methodism; their extremely conservative values and that one is governor and another is trying for the Senate. I know that Michelle thought they were ripe for—"

"Stop right there," Miss Mazie sniffed. "Drink your coffee before it gets cold."

Having been brought up with manners, I did as I was told. "Look, just tell me one thing. If you feel they're such bad sinners, why do you stay here?"

"Because I was born here. Because I don't know anything for sure. This is my home. I'm old. And because they love me and I love them. They put all my boys and my grandchildren through college and set them up in business. Because we're family."

"Is Mrs. McKerr at home? I'd like to pay my respects."

"No, child, unless you have an appointment with her, she is never here. But I'll tell her you stopped by. And that you brought the flowers and cake."

"Good. Thank you." I stood to leave and extended my hand. Miss Mazie took it and we smiled at each other.

"Oh, I must read your palm. Sit down, let's see what I can see," Miss Mazie urged.

Wordlessly, I sat and let my hand be unfolded. Miss Mazie's strong old fingers traced lines as she murmured. Finally, she looked into my eyes.

"Girl, you were born for trouble and you didn't even know it, did you?"

"What?"

"Says right there. Born for trouble. That right?"

"No, other than coming to Tulsa, I have no trouble."

"Your trouble is just starting."

"Well, thanks. That's bullsh…that's psychic friend nonsense, but thanks." I tried to pull my hand away and leave. Miss Mazie held it tightly, her eyes deep and sad.

"Tell me about her, just a little," Miss Mazie said.

I relaxed. "Okay." I thought and thought, trying to find some nice story to tell. I wanted to be kind to this woman who had loved Michelle so. And I wanted to be kind to the memory of that Michelle I never knew. "Well, Michelle could make any baby stop crying. I don't know if it was witchcraft or what, but she had a way with babies."

Miss Mazie laughed and nodded.

"She loved hot tea and doing cartwheels in the rain and red tennis shoes and toast with orange marmalade. She loved bright floral sheets and card games and ironing. Did you know that? She actually loved to iron. She hated the cold, she loved hair ribbons and crossword puzzles and math story problems." I said all of these facts from our relationship that I had always trusted were true and now, for Miss Mazie's sake, I hoped were true. Then I realized it didn't matter, so I embellished. "She loved baking cookies. Peanut butter were her favorites, but she could do all of them. She donated blood every month; she volunteered at a women's shelter; she loved poetry and real bubblegum and she hated driving. I don't know why she ended up in Los Angeles if she hated driving, but there you are."

"To meet you," Miss Mazie said simply.

I shrugged, not buying it. I pitied Miss Mazie's mistaken idea that Michelle and I had been soul mates and that we had had a big big love. It just wasn't so. We loved each other, but it wasn't anything special. I continued, "Michelle hated fireworks and she was scared of water. She hated heights and she had claustrophobia. But you know what she said once? That she loved me so much that if I needed her to, she would go into a box full of firecrackers held high above the ocean. Can you believe that?" I was struggling to swallow my lump again, even though at the time, I believed Michelle had said it to escape my wrath in some argument or another. Miss Mazie's eyes were watering. "Michelle didn't like novels or movies, but would watch the news any time and loved documentaries. She used to coach me before a game and get me all fired up. And after the game, she would hold me until I came down again. And if we lost, we'd sleep together. She hoped it would take my mind off it."

Miss Mazie cleared her throat, averting her eyes.

I nodded, unembarrassed. I knew what to say next, so even though it was a lie, it was a lie for love, for virtue. "And Michelle always regretted leaving here. Leaving you. She was always sorry about breaking with the family. And home. She loved you so much. She spoke of you often."

Miss Mazie began weeping. "Thank you. I…thank you. I knew it. I knew it. I told my baby she could come home no matter what, but she was too proud." Miss Mazie seemed lost in her own memories.

"Thanks for the cake and coffee." I closed the back door quietly. I waved to the men in the yard and drove away.

Chapter Twenty-eight

I turned in my rental car and ran for the terminal. Once on board the plane, I reflected on Tulsa. All the bizarre situations and all the comely women, each with her own lies. Pathetic Jhoaeneyie, annoying Darcy with the over-licked lips and ragged cuticles, cold, bitchy Ava-Suzanne, the gruesome twosome Lila and Reese, the flaky Amber, the super smooth Sloane, sad and funny Jack. And Max. I felt my tongue go fat with longing. Max. The airplane began to taxi.

Oh, Jesus, get me home. I twirled and twirled my bracelet. I closed my eyes and leaned my head against the seat, exhaustion overtaking me. Overhead, I turned the air valve on high. I was sick of being funky all the time. Get me home.

I began thinking about Max…Max pink and ripe like a cherub, her russet hair flowing over her breasts, her pelvic bowl bursting with promise, and her ass. Lawd, Lawd, her tribal mother drum ass with food enough for all the world in its curves. The drum I was born to pound. The sacred songs I would compose. The songs it sang to me without me ever having touched it. The whispers that would slide into my ears and nasty little fantasy fingers that would haunt me forever left the ground with me, becoming airborne, clinging to my brow and body like a fever.

The flight attendant smiled at me. “Can I get you something to drink?” She laid down a napkin and a prim package of pretzels.

I nodded, grinning slyly. “G and T.”

Epilogue

I was thirty-five the year I started drinking gin. It's not a pretty story and I don't come off smelling like a rose, but it's time to tell it. With a story like this, gin is the only thing astringent enough to clean the dirt from my mouth. Gin is snappy and crisp and washes away my sins, at least for the night. I love everything about gin, but maybe that's because my love affair with it is new. The smell of it is a cold wintry tang in the nose; the look of it is hard and clear like liquid diamonds, and that's sort of deceptive because the taste of it is smooth and sweet yet sharp too, like a beautiful woman with a knife. Gin slides down my throat like an ice snake. It's bitter and oily, wavering in the glass like a silver mirror, and when it is a mirror is when I drink most. I'll take it any way—neat, a shot, on the rocks, in a martini, in a Tom Collins or a fizz, with stupid fruit draped all over the glass, I don't care. But my favorite way to drink it is with tonic because it reminds me of Her. I got the idea that gin is a disinfectant like hydrogen peroxide and if I drink enough, it will boil out the infection, which is this story…

About the Author

Clara Nipper lives in Oklahoma and enjoys fine dining, bubble baths, long walks, and playing with her dogs, Virginia Woof and Bark Twain. She is drinking and smoking right now while writing Nora's next adventure. Kids, stay in school!

Books Available From Bold Strokes Books

The Seduction of Moxie by Colette Moody. When 1930s Broadway actress Violet London meets speakeasy singer Moxie Valette, she is instantly attracted and her Hollywood trip takes an unexpected turn. (978-1-60282-114-9)

Goldenseal by Gill McKnight. When Amy Fortune returns to her childhood home, she discovers something sinister in the air—but is former lover Leone Garoul stalking her or protecting her? (978-1-60282-115-6)

Romantic Interludes 2: Secrets edited by Radclyffe and Stacia Seaman. An anthology of sensual lesbian love stories: passion, surprises, and secret desires. (978-1-60282-116-3)

Femme Noir by Clara Nipper. Nora Delaney meets her match in Max Abbott, a sex-crazed dame who may or may not have the information Nora needs to solve a murder—but can she contain her lust for Max long enough to find out? (978-1-60282-117-0)

The Reluctant Daughter by Lesléa Newman. Heartwarming, heartbreaking, and ultimately triumphant—the story every daughter recognizes of the lifelong struggle for our mothers to really see us. (978-1-60282-118-7)

Erosistible by Gill McKnight. When Win Martin arrives at a luxurious Greek hotel for a much-anticipated week of sun and sex with her new girlfriend, she is stunned to find her ex-girlfriend, Benny, is the proprietor. Aeros Ebook. (978-1-60282-134-7)

Looking Glass Lives by Felice Picano. Cousins Roger and Alistair become lifelong friends and discover their sexuality amidst the backdrop of twentieth-century gay culture. (978-1-60282-089-0)

Breaking the Ice by Kim Baldwin. Nothing is easy about life above the Arctic Circle—except, perhaps, falling in love. At least that's what pilot Bryson Faulkner hopes when she meets Karla Edwards. (978-1-60282-087-6)

It Should Be a Crime by Carsen Taite. Two women fulfill their mutual desire with a night of passion, neither expecting more until law professor Morgan Bradley and student Parker Casey meet again…in the classroom. (978-1-60282-086-9)

Rough Trade edited by Todd Gregory. Top male erotica writers pen their own hot, sexy versions of the term "rough trade," producing some of the hottest, nastiest, and most dangerous fiction ever published. (978-1-60282-092-0)

The High Priest and the Idol by Jane Fletcher. Jemeryl and Tevi's relationship is put to the test when the Guardian sends Jemeryl on a mission that puts her not only in harm's way, but back into the sights of a previous lover. (978-1-60282-085-2)

Point of Ignition by Erin Dutton. Amid a blaze that threatens to consume them both, firefighter Kate Chambers and property owner Alexi Clark redefine love and trust. (978-1-60282-084-5)

Secrets in the Stone by Radclyffe. Reclusive sculptor Rooke Tyler suddenly finds herself the object of two very different women's affections, and choosing between them will change her life forever. (978-1-60282-083-8)

Dark Garden by Jennifer Fulton. Vienna Blake and Mason Cavender are sworn enemies—who can't resist each other. Something has to give. (978-1-60282-036-4)

Late in the Season by Felice Picano. Set on Fire Island, this is the story of an unlikely pair of friends—a gay composer in his late thirties and an eighteen-year-old schoolgirl. (978-1-60282-082-1)

Punishment with Kisses by Diane Anderson-Minshall. Will Megan find the answers she seeks about her sister Ashley's murder or will her growing relationship with one of Ash's exes blind her to the real truth? (978-1-60282-081-4)

September Canvas by Gun Brooke. When Deanna Moore meets TV personality Faythe she is reluctantly attracted to her, but will Faythe side with the people spreading rumors about Deanna? (978-1-60282-080-7)

Bold Strokes
BOOKS
WEBSTORE
PRINT AND EBOOKS
Romance
Mystery
Intrigue
MATINEE BOOKS
LIBERTY
EDITION
BOLD
STROKES
BOOKS
Adventure
victory
EDITIONS
Erotica
Fantasy
Sci-Fi
AEROS
e
BOOKS
http://www.boldstrokesbooks.com